Memoirs Of The
Sultry Temptress

Memoirs Of The
Sultry Temptress

Wayne Turner

To order additional copies of this book, contact:
Xlibris Corporation
0-800-644-6988
www.xlibrispublishing.co.uk
Orders@xlibrispublishing.co.uk
304843

CHAPTER 1

'OH WHAT A night!' sighed the sultry Lucy Mills, instantly getting the cab driver's attention, who looked into his rear-view mirror to see the smiling face of the stunning brunette.

'Why? What happened?' asked the intrigued cabbie.

On hearing his words, Lucy stared at the rear-view mirror to see his smiling eyes; she smiled as she pondered on her thoughts.

Wondering if she should get into a conversation with a stranger, she couldn't contain herself any longer as she was sexually excited. Her evening had encountered new horizons for her work portfolio, a secretary during the day and a waitress by night.

But tonight had been a night of changes as Sally, the owner, had begged her to dance for her customers. But this was a strip club, where the dancing girls removed their clothes as they danced, teasing and tantalising those staring eyes with their swivelling hips and naked bits and pieces.

Lucy was excited but very nervous by Sally's request. Was she ready to reveal her naked charms to those horny onlookers? Yes, she was and happily agreed to do a solo performance for the sum of one thousand dollars.

Sally stared in disbelief as Lucy demanded one thousand dollars because the customers paid the dancing girls with only a buck here and there as they shed their clothes. The dancing girls made good money, yet Lucy wanted more.

And a thousand bucks was a lot of money. But Sally was stuck because she had only a few dancing girls tonight. She shook her head and said, 'Yes.'

On hearing her reply, the excited Lucy smiled and followed Sally to the changing room and shed her clothes. Standing there naked, she sifted through the lingerie draw, looking for something sheer and elegant to cover her sacred charms. With her ample charms covered, she put on scanty panties to mask her shaven pussy.

With her bits and pieces covered, she turned and walked over to the costume rack and sifted through. She stopped at a white cowgirl suit and tried it on; it hugged her sexy body like a glove.

This was the one she was looking for. She then spun around and walked towards the door; Sally smiled as she watched her new sexual delight walk towards the stage and quickly ran after her. In seconds, she was standing by her side, asking, 'Are you ready, honey?'

Lucy looked at her and smiled; by gum she was shaking. What had she done? She then replied, 'I'm ready, boss.'

Sally then walked out on to the stage and picked up the microphone and began speaking. 'Good evening everybody. Welcome to In Your Vision. We've got a real treat for you all tonight.'

With that, the music began and out walked the stunning Lucy. The wolf whistles of the ogling customers started. Lucy began gyrating, her hips to the music. The customers were captivated by her swaying hips, each one eager to see her naked charms, but the sultry temptress Lucy kept them waiting with her wiggling bottom.

She was driving those sex-crazed men crazy. They wanted to see her naked, not dressed. If they wanted to see dressed women, they would be at home with their wives. It was getting too much for one patron, who shouted, 'Get your tits out, honey, or please get off, as I've got this throbbing cock in my hand and it wants to see some pussy.'

On hearing this, Lucy spun around and stared at Master Bates and then shouted, 'Do you need a hand over there?'

The punter froze. What was he to do? Was she offering to Master Bate his throbbing cock?

He stuttered, 'Yes . . . yes, please . . . please, honey . . . honey, that . . . that . . . would . . . would be nice.'

The cunning Lucy smiled and then replied, 'Come on, everybody. Please give this man a hand.' She then started clapping her hands.

The club was quickly filled with laughter, as the red-faced man ran off to hide himself from those jeering patrons. Lucy smiled as she slowly removed her waist coat; she was Lucy the temptress.

'More, more,' shouted the cheering patrons.

Lucy smiled as she unbuttoned her shirt and suddenly stopped. The men stared at her cleavage. 'Wow, what a cleavage!' one patron shouted. 'Come on, Miss Plentiful, get them out.'

Lucy smiled; she had them captivated by her ample hidden charms. It was time to play the banker; she picked up the microphone and said, 'Well, gentlemen, to see these big tits of mine it's going to cost you.'

The horrified Sally looked on as she watched her horny customers rush up to the stage, waving their money. On seeing their wads of cash, Lucy knelt and said, 'That will be ten dollars, please.'

On hearing this, those horny men held their ten dollars in the air. As Lucy took their money, she leaned forward and tenderly kissed their lips. Those horny men couldn't believe their luck, a kiss and a peak down her cleavage too. It was as if they were in the presence of Wonder Woman. Wow, they couldn't wait to see those magnificent tits released from their entrapment for them all to see.

With the money collected, Lucy rolled it up and tucked it in her panties and then began her striptease. Those horny men stared goggle-eyed as they watched her undo those remaining buttons on her shirt.

Then came the loud cheers as off came the shirt, revealing those ample charms wrapped up in the tiniest bra they had ever seen. Then cheers of. 'Off, off, off.'

As Lucy began undoing that bra, more cheers came, and she showed one strawberry nipple at a time. Wow, what a sight! Sally was delighted at how Lucy was captivating the audience and wondered if she would become a full-time stripper.

Then off came the bra, revealing those delightful ample charms, to the cheers of the captivated audience. They shouted, 'More, more, more.'

Lucy stared at her cheering fans; she was sexually charged, aching to be fucked by one of those horny men. But first she had the striptease to do and more money to be earned. She opened her jeans, then let them fall to her knees, and then turned around and bent over to the cheers of those horny men.

Wow, her ass was voluptuous like her tits, and those horny men began shouting, 'More, more, more.'

The teasing Lucy then quickly pulled her jeans back up and picked up the microphone and turned around and said, 'More? You want to see more? Is there an Oliver in the House?'

Then came the laughter as one man approached the stage; again Lucy knelt and said, 'Do you want to see my pussy, Oliver?'

Oliver nodded his head as Lucy leaned towards him and whispered, 'It's going to cost you, honey.'

Then she tenderly kissed his lips; her lips were soft, and Oliver wanted more, as she had woken his sleeping cock, which was now rigid in his pants, looking for some action.

'How much', he replied, 'for a private lap dance?'

Lucy smiled and quickly replied, 'Ten bucks now, honey, and a thousand later.'

Oliver smiled and handed her ten dollars, then whispered, 'I will give you the thousand later, after you've given me a private lap dance?'

Lucy smiled; she couldn't believe that she was going to earn three thousand dollars for an hour's work. She couldn't contain her excitement and kissed him again; as their lips connected, her hand grabbed his groin.

On feeling his rigid cock in his pants, she pulled away from the kiss and shouted, 'Fuck me. You've got a big one in there.'

As she pointed down at his bulging pants, Oliver smiled, then turned around, and walked back to his seat, leaving the flabbergasted Lucy to collect her ten dollars from all those horny guys. With all the money collected, Lucy waved at Sally; Sally frowned as she slowly walked towards her diamond temptress.

What had she done by asking Lucy to strip? This girl was every man's voluptuous dream date. She had already agreed to pay her a thousand dollars. What did she want now?

Lucy had put all the money in her shirt and then handed it to Sally, saying, 'Could you please look after this for me?'

Sally said, 'Okay,' and then took the shirt from her, then turned around, and walked towards her office, leaving the dancing Lucy to titillate the audience with her sexy moves. Then came the cries as Lucy began undoing her jeans. 'Off, off, off.'

Lucy loved the cheers of those horny guys, as those jeans dropped to her knees, revealing her tiny thong panties. Her mind was in a haze of sexual excitement, with the thought of Oliver's big cock. Would she dare remove her panties to those horny eyes?

She was so horny and off came those jeans, followed by her sexual gyration to the music, and then she turned around and wiggled her bottom as she slowly pulled those panties down.

She was fabulous, and her naked voluptuous body was driving those horny devils crazy. Then came the stage show as she spread her legs, leaned forward, and began caressing her shaven pussy.

The Master Bates society of hand wanker's all had their rigid cocks in their hands, gently stroking them as they watched the erotic show. This woman was driving them crazy with her sexual prowess; suddenly Lucy stood upright and then spun around, revealing her wonderful ample charms and shaven haven too.

Thus the wolf whistles started. Those horny men were applauding with shouts of. 'More, more, more.'

Lucy was electrified by the moment and quickly sat down and began massaging her magical button in front of the cheering men. This was the stage show they would never forget; on seeing this, the Master Bates society had all shot their loads and was on their way home.

The voluptuous Lucy continued massaging her magical button in a way she was pre-heating her oven, for what was yet to come. With her one night spot over she smiled the lights faded and out, came the next dancing girl.

On seeing this, the voluptuous Lucy stood, picked up her things, and ran off the stage and was met by the waiting Sally, who asked, 'Where are you going, honey?'

Lucy smiled and ran into the changing room to dress for the next performance, her solo for that man with the big cock and his thousand bucks. The flabbergasted Sally turned and ran after the sultry Lucy, who was dressing in her sexy lingerie.

'What's going on?' asked the bewildered Sally.

On hearing her voice, the voluptuous Lucy turned around, smiled and then said, 'Oh, hello Sally, I was just dressing for a private lap dance.'

Sally shook her head in disbelief and said, 'Who's paying?'

'He is,' replied the laughing sexy Lucy as she walked on and headed back to the stage, dressed in just a robe and little else underneath. As she walked out on to the stage, she was greeted by a standing ovation; she bowed several times, then jumped down from the stage, and quickly walked towards Oliver, taking him by the hand and leading him to paradise.

Once inside the private dance room, she turned and passionately kissed Oliver's lips, while her hand groped his groin. In seconds, his sleeping cock woke up. She couldn't contain her excitement and curiosity any longer and fell to her knees and stripped his pants.

As his pants fell to his knees, Lucy lifted his shirt and gasped, 'Fuck me. That is one big cock.'

With the words over, she couldn't resist and began sucking on Oliver's big cock. Oliver was in heaven. She had lips of velvet; his eyes suddenly opened wide as she turned the suction on. It felt like he had his big cock in the Hoover. Her suction was unbelievable, and his balls began to churn. Then she took it to another level and began humming while she sucked, sending tingling sensations down his big cock.

Oliver couldn't contain himself any longer and whispered, 'How much, baby, for a fuck?'

On hearing this, Lucy stopped her humming and pondered on her thoughts. She was going to have sex with him for nothing to extinguish her burning loins. But the thought of money was too much. She looked up and whispered, 'Two thousand dollars.'

Oliver said, 'That's fine, honey.'

Then he walked over and sat down on the chair; the excited Lucy quickly stood and removed her robe and danced towards that throbbing big cock, removing her bra and panties along the way.

In seconds, she was gyrating naked in front of him, seconds away from the poking she craved. She suddenly straddled him and gyrated, her hips above his big cock. Oliver couldn't wait any longer and grabbed her hips; they began kissing as his big cock entered her pussy. It was Lucy who took control as she slowly gyrated, her hips on his throbbing big cock.

She was in heaven. *What a man and what a cock!* She thought.

Suddenly, she was brought back to the present by the shouting cabbie, who asked, 'Are you okay, darling?'

Lucy smiled and sighed, 'Oh, what a night!'

She then stared at his badge and said, 'Hi, Sam, my name's Lucy. Do you mind if I sit in the front of the cab with you?'

Sam stared in his rear-view mirror at the voluptuous Lucy; she was beautiful, and the story she had just told him had given him an all-mighty hard-on. *If she was sitting next to him,* he thought, *she might get horny and suck his cock while he drove.*

CHAPTER 2

I T WAS AGAINST company's policy to have a passenger sit in the front, but on this occasion, Sam didn't care. He had a raging hard-on and was wishing for some action, and Lucy certainly couldn't do it sitting in the back.

So he pulled over and said, 'Lucy would you like to join me in the front, darling?'

Lucy smiled and then got out and opened the front door and then quickly got in and closed the door behind her. Sam then drove off as Lucy continued her story; her sexual words were driving him crazy.

Then came contact as she suddenly placed her hand on his thigh. His mind was going crazy as her hand slowly made its way upwards towards his bulging groin.

'Hello, what have you got in there?' whispered the smiling Lucy.

As she began undoing his pants to see what was going on, Sam murmured, 'Oh no!'

As she took out his rigid cock and whispered, 'Is this for me, Sam?'

As she bent and began sucking his cocks, bald head Sam didn't know what to do–laugh, cry, or pull over and enjoy the moment–her lips were of velvet. How could he concentrate? When all he wanted to do was fuck her hard and extinguish his burning lust for this voluptuous woman.

His eyes suddenly opened wide as she turned the suction on. It was like his cock had been sucked by a Hoover. Her suction was phenomenal. This was getting too much. How could he concentrate with what was going on down there in his crotch? His rigid cock was alive and wanted some pussy action.

But that was not on the menu at present, as the sultry temptress Lucy had captured his rigid cock in her mouth and it felt like she was sucking the life out of it. He couldn't handle the excitement any longer, and sensations were getting too much.

He suddenly pulled into a lay-by and turned the engine and lights off, then closed his eyes, and enjoyed the moment. This woman's mouth was electrifying, and he didn't know that this was just an appetiser and there was still more to come.

Suddenly his eyes again opened wide, when Lucy began to hum, sending tingling sensations down his rigid cock. Sam then murmured, 'Oh, oh!'

His milk balls began to churn; it was time for action, or he would be shooting his load in seconds. He wasn't ready to drain his resources yet and whispered, 'Honey, please stop.'

On hearing his whims, Lucy let his rigid cock fall from her mouth and looked up at him and said, 'What's up, Sam?'

As she delicately caressed his balls, her hands were driving him crazy, with one hand gently stroking his rigid cock and the other his balls; disaster was only seconds away. He had no choice but to stop her as his rigid cock was ready to explode with his milky-white fluids.

He quickly took hold of her hand and eased it away from his throbbing cock, then whispered, 'Can I fuck you please, honey?'

Lucy smiled; she too was aching to be fucked. She whispered, 'What? Here?'

Sam looked down at her puzzled-looking face and then quickly started the car, turned the lights on, and sped off down the road, looking for some place quite and secluded to park up and fuck this sultry temptress.

He was slowly losing his mind, as she continued to stroke his rigid cock as he drove; he suddenly gasped, 'Thank fuck.'

As he drove into a parking lay-by and extinguished the lights and turned the ignition off. He couldn't contain his excitement any longer and turned and tenderly began kissing Lucy. As he placed his hand on her naked thigh and slowly made its way upwards towards her shaven haven, Lucy sighed, 'Oh.'

His fingers found her shaven haven and gently began massaging her magical button. She ached for this sexual moment and was craving to be truly fucked by this horny cabbie. She whispered, 'Sam, shouldn't we get in the back, as there's more room back there to play?'

With that, Sam removed his fingers from her honey pot and then removed the keys from the ignition and got into the back with the voluptuous Lucy. She lay there with her legs open and her skirt up exposing her shaven haven, Sam started down on her shaven haven as he didn't know what to do, lick it or fuck it?

His mind was saying, 'Get down on it, and lick it,' while his throbbing cock was saying, 'Get on top, and let me get in there. I want to fuck it.' He smiled as he lowered his head towards her shaven haven. It was time for licking.

His throbbing cock shouted, 'No . . . no, it is my time, not the tongue's time. It was too late.' His weeping cock then deflated back to its normal size. His tongue began probing and flickering at her magical button. Lucy loved his probing of her magical button.

But she truly desired to be fucked, so she excitedly whispered, 'Sam, fuck me. Fuck me now.'

On hearing her cries, there came a stirring in his loins as his sleeping cock shook its sleepy head and began to rise. In seconds, it was standing to attention, ready for pussy action; he was up on to his knees, undoing his pants. In seconds, he released his throbbing cock from its entrapment. Then he guided it towards its Holy Grail that was Lucy's pussy. In seconds, he began to penetrate her and then plunged straight in and gasped, 'Oh no!'

The excitement made his milk balls churn, and disaster lay seconds away; he didn't want this to end so rapidly and quickly, he withdrew his cock.

'What are you doing?' screamed the excited Lucy. 'I want you to fuck me hard.'

Sam looked at her and smiled as he began manoeuvres with his soft kisses, from her neck to her ample charms. His fingers gently massaged her magical button; Lucy loved his gentle touch on her sexual charms but craved for some action too.

So she softly whispered, 'Sam, if you're not going to fuck me, please can we get in the sixty-nine position so that I can play too?'

Sam looked at her with a puzzled look on his face; her mouth was fantastic, and she certainly knew how to suck cock. How long could he prevail in holding back his milky-white fluids if she began sucking his rigid cock with her wonderful sucking mouth?

'You on top,' whispered Sam.

On hearing this, Lucy instantly sat up and let Sam lie down on the back seat, then straddled his face with her pussy just inches from his mouth, and then leaned forward and began sucking on his rigid cock. Sam probed her pussy with his flickering tongue.

While his hands caressed her ample charms, her mouth was driving him crazy. She had the suction power of a deluxe Hoover. Never before had a woman sucked his cock like this.

He suddenly cringed as she began humming while she sucked, sending tingling sensations down his rigid cock, thus causing the churning of his milk balls once again. He had to now take a diversion to stop his rigid cock from shooting his milky-white fluids into her sucking mouth. The thought suddenly came to his mind as he stared at her voluptuously shaped butt, and in an instant, he stuck a finger in his mouth and then stuck it in Lucy's butt.

'Oh!' cried out Lucy, thus instantly stopping her from humming and wonderful sucking.

It was chocolate finger time as he slowly began thrusting his finger in and out of Lucy's tight asshole at the tempo of the tap that wouldn't stop dripping. Lucy's mind lay in turmoil as those wonderful sensations flooded through her body. How could she suck cock when all she wanted to do was shout out, 'Fuck me. Fuck me now'?

Suddenly, her tummy began churning, then came the releasing of her trapped air, as Sam's finger slipped out, and she farted in his face.

'Oh my goodness gracious me,' cried out the choking Sam, now finding it hard to breathe from the stench of her fart.

He quickly lifted her off his face and opened the door, letting the fresh air in, thus extinguishing the shitty smell of her fart. That was it; game over. Sam didn't feel like playing any more.

As the sexual moment had passed them by, he sat up and quickly pulled up his pants and said, 'It's time I got you home, honey.'

'What do you mean?' asked the puzzled-looking Lucy, who was impersonating a Chinese waitress saying,

'I want number one, fucky-fucky before we go.'

Sam stared at her as he opened his pants and released his deflating cock; in seconds, he began stroking it, thus bringing it back to life. He then whispered, 'On your hands and knees please.'

Lucy began to laugh and then replied, 'But there's no room to do it doggy style, Sam?'

'Oh fuck it,' screamed Sam.

'No, fuck me,' replied the smiling Lucy, as she took his rigid cock in hand and began stroking it to death. This was all Sam wanted, to be wanked by this voluptuous woman. There would be no stopping him now.

Suddenly his eyes opened wide, as his milk balls began to churn. Lucy was just seconds away from being shot with his fluids in her face. Then it happened; his balls suddenly tightened, and despatch was on its way. Up through his rigid cock went his milky-white fluids spraying into the air and falling on to Lucy's startled face.

That was it; game over.

With his milky-white fluids dripping from her face, Lucy began to laugh as she watched Sam's cock begin to deflate.

'What's so funny?' asked the bewildered Sam.

'You are,' replied laughing Lucy. 'You give me no warning and cum any way. Look at my face, you messy boy.'

Sam smiled as he handed her his clean handkerchief and said, 'There you go, honey. This may help.'

Lucy smiled at him as she took the handkerchief from his hand and began wiping his milky-white fluids from her face. Sam re-housed his now-sleeping cock and got out and closed the door and then ran round and got into the driver's seat. In seconds, he had started the cab and turned the lights on and then the indicator as he gently caressed the gas pedal and drove off down the road.

As he drove, he turned the meter off and said, 'No charge tonight, honey. You're sure one special lady.'

Lucy smiled; it sure was her night. First she had earned five thousand dollars for her one-hour stripper show and now a free cab ride home too. She wondered what she had done. As she got out of the cab, she tenderly kissed Sam goodbye.

Then she turned and ran towards her front door. In seconds, she was putting the key in the lock and opening the front door. As she entered, she turned the light on and then turned around and waved goodbye to the waiting Sam, who in turn waved back as he slowly drove off. She then shut and locked the door and then turned and ran up the stairs. In minutes, she was naked in the bathroom, standing under a hot spraying shower cleansing her dirty body.

'Oh what a night!' she sighed.

Her mind was disillusioned; she had earned five thousand dollars as a stripper, and that was for only one performance. Sally had paid her a thousand bucks to be a stripper for the night, then came her sultry temptress part, where she teased the horny observers with her swaying hips.

'Get them off,' they cried.

On hearing their whims, she had picked up the microphone and said, 'If you want to see more, it's going to cost you.'

Those horny patrons rushed to the stage, waving their money. She in turn took ten bucks from each customer, and once she had collected all the money, she had folded it and put it in her panties.

Then she began gyrating to the music and slowly began unbuttoning her shirt. The audience were spellbound by her stage presence, each wanting to see her naked charms, but this was just the booby show where she just slowly removed her bra. Giving them a glimpse of each nipple as she danced, she was driving them crazy with her tantalising moves.

Then came the loud cheers when off came her bra, revealing her naked ample charms for all to see. She loved this titillation show, but she kept her business mind on. This was easy money to earn purely for titillation. *Yes, you have to show your naked charms, but who cares?* She thought.

She suddenly came out of her daydream and turned the shower off, then stepped out of the shower, and began drying her body from which water dripped. Then came her hair; she stared in the mirror at her long hair and snarled. She didn't have time to blow dry, so she towel dried it and then curled it up in a bun and pinned it on top of her head.

Naked she ran to her bedroom and turned the light on and walked towards the bed and set the alarm. In minutes, she was in bed and turned the light off. It was an early start in the morning, so she closed her eyes and tried to sleep.

But how could she sleep? She had so much on her mind—why was she working during the day as a secretary when she could earn so much more at night as a stripper?

With her distraught mind in limbo, wondering what to do, her hand drifted towards her pussy. It was time for her to join the Master Bates society. As she began gently massaging her magical button, the sensation felt wonderful. With her mind at ease, she slowly drifted off to sleep.

CHAPTER 3

IT WAS 7 a.m. as the sound of music filled the room; through sleepy eyes, Lucy hit the sleep button, thus extinguishing the sound of the music. She then again drifted back to sleep, but this was short-lived as again the sound of music filled the air.

She threw back the covers and instantly sat up; it was time to get ready to go to her day job.

'Oh yippee,' she murmured as she got off the bed and walked over and opened her wardrobe. She then took out a jacket and short skirt and then closed the door. Then she turned and walked over to her dressing table, dropping the jacket and skirt on the bed as she walked towards it.

As she arrived at the dressing table, she stopped and stared at her shaven pussy in the mirror. She was feeling a naughty lady today and decided to go commando. But she took just a cameo from the draw and put it on to cover up her voluptuous breasts.

Then she ran off to the bathroom to wash her face and floss her teeth and then was back to the bedroom to dress. She walked to the bed and put her short skirt on the jacket and then walked to the dressing table to do her hair and make up.

She just removed the hair clips and let the hair fall, and she brushed it through and then did her make up just a little to enhance her complexion. She looked sensational. Then she went down the stairs and straight out the front door towards the bus stop.

As she walked, she was in flirtatious mood, waving at the sleepy-eyed motorists who beeped their horns at her. She began laughing as she stood waiting for a bus, wondering what joy the day would bring.

It was eight fifteen when her bus pulled up; she frowned and got on. It was standing room only she paid. Then she went and stood next to a young smiling student. He was tall dark and handsome, wearing his sports kit, Bermuda shorts, and sweat shirt.

The bus continually stopped and picked up new fares. On one occasion, the driver stopped abruptly, and Lucy's hand hit the student's crotch. She gasped, 'Fuck me,' when she felt the size of his sleeping cock, then apologised, 'I'm so sorry, young man.'

The smiling student replied, 'Never mind, honey. I sure did enjoy the grope.'

By saying that, he had lit the temptress Lucy's fire and she, slipped her hand inside his Bermuda's and gently began stroking his big cock. The startled student stood there not knowing what to do, as he felt his sleeping cock becoming rigid in her hand.

'Fuck me,' murmured Lucy, as she felt his big cock becoming rigid in her hand. She became very horny and wanted to see it. With her hand firmly wrapped around his big rigid cock, she slowly led him towards the exit door and pushed the bell.

The bus driver frowned and pulled in and stopped; the voluptuous Lucy then stepped off the bus, followed closely by the bemused student, who was getting friskier by the second he put his hand up under her short skirt and caressed her naked bottom.

On feeling no panties, he suddenly stopped Lucy and slipped his hand between her open legs and stuck a finger into her pussy. One finger quickly became two; Lucy was in ore of his openness to fondle her inner child in a public place and whispered, 'Please stop that, honey. I want to feel that big cock of yours in there and not those two fingers.'

The student quickly withdrew his two fingers and slowly followed Lucy; into the bushes they went and soon were camouflaged by the mass of green. Lucy suddenly stopped, then turned and faced him and smiled, then knelt and pulled his Bermuda shorts down, and gasped when she saw the size of his rigid big cock.

She couldn't resist and began gently sucking; the student loved the attention his big cock was getting. But time was of the essence; he had a lecture at 9.30. He whispered, 'Excuse me, lady, but I thought you were looking to be fucked by this big cock of mine.'

On hearing his soft words, Lucy stopped her sucking and stood up and pointed to the fallen tree and said, 'Please go and sit down.'

The student quickly jogged over to the tree and sat down. In a reverse cow girl position, Lucy slowly sat down on his big rigid cock and gasped, 'Fuck me. That feel's so good.'

Then she gently began going up and down on his big cock.

As she slowly bobbed up and down, the student reached around and gently began massaging her magical button. Lucy's mind was suddenly spellbound by the onslaught of sensations coming from her honey pot and she murmured, 'Oh yes, that feel's so good.'

Her bobbing suddenly stopped and she began gyrating, her hips on his wonderful big cock. Those sensations were driving her crazy. But this was just an appetiser, as the student suddenly leaned backwards with his hand caressing her breast. Lucy gasped, 'Oh!'

As his big rigid cock was nestled up against her G spot, more sensations flooded her honey pot as well as the building of her bodily fluids.

This was an amazing way to start the day, sex with a young man with a very big dick. He was experienced for such a young man; he knew how to ignite her sexual charms. She was on her way; next stop Climax City here she comes, but this would be an orgasm of the third kind, a honey pot explosion.

Lucy began murmuring, 'Yes, yes, oh yes.'

As the wonderful sensation rushed through her body up to her exploding mind, her body was shaking and her cries suddenly filled the air, 'Oh my, I'm . . . I'm cumming.'

Then it happened; the student's big rigid cock slipped from her pussy, thus starting her honey pot explosion. She couldn't believe what she was seeing as her built-up fluids sprayed into the air.

Her honey pot was quivering and dripping as the student again pushed his big rigid cock deep inside her. Was she ready for an encore of the third kind? Yes, she was with her heart racing. She again began gyrating, her hips on that big rigid cock.

Those wonderful sensations were driving her crazy; she couldn't stand it any longer and stood and lay down on the ground and said, 'fuck me. Fuck me now, you big-cocked devil.'

The grinning student stood and then got down on top of her, resuming the missionary position with his big cock in hand and guided it towards her weeping pussy. Her eyes opened wide as he penetrated her pussy and even wider as it plunged deep into her quivering honey pot.

Then he was thrusting at the tempo of the clock that wouldn't stop ticking. There was no stopping him now; he was having a good time. Lucy, on the other hand, was pulling faces as his big piston-like cock thrust in and out of her quivering honey pot.

She was on her way to the destination Climax City; she loved this shagging by the student with the big cock. When suddenly the air was filled with a girl's voice, the thrusting student murmured, 'Oh no!'. His milk balls suddenly tightened, and his milky-white fluids were despatched deep into Lucy's pussy. That was it; game over for him.

He then tenderly kissed Lucy's lips as he withdrew his big cock from Lucy's weeping pussy, then stood and re-housed his big cock in his Bermuda shorts. Then he whispered 'Goodbye, honey. Have a nice day.'

With that, he turned and ran towards the girl's voice; as he disappeared, Lucy heard a girl saying, 'There you are. What have you been up to, lover boy?'

Lucy smiled; she had just had the shag of a lifetime. It had been earth shattering with a honey pot explosion. Never before had she experienced one of them; she sat up and took a tissue from her handbag and wiped away those milky-white fluids from her weeping pussy.

Then she stood and made her appearance smart and then walked through the bushes to the bus stop, as the student's milky-white fluids slowly trickled from her pussy. It was soon to be May Day as she had gone commando today, and there was nothing to stop those milky-white fluids.

But she didn't care; she had no inhibitions. She didn't care about the observers. She was a good time girl, a temptress to all who quietly observed her voluptuous curves. As she stood waiting for the bus, those milky-white fluids slowly trickled down her leg.

As she got on the bus, she was aware she was observed by every curios set of eyes, looking for faults in her appearance. Suddenly she heard a woman gasped to the young man sitting next to her, 'What's that running down that trollop's leg?'

The young man's vision was capturing the shape of her voluptuous body, oh how he wanted to see more, as Lucy looked around and frowned at the lady who had passed the comment. She smiled at the young man and then teasingly blew him a kiss, as she bent and scooped a finger full of the milky white fluid and sucked it clean and said 'Lady, that tastes so good.'

The lady frowned at her and then curiously asked 'What is it?'

On hearing this, Lucy smiled and said 'Well, lady, if you must know, it's the milky-white fluids of a young man I had sex with earlier.'

'You trollop,' replied the appalled middle-aged woman, whereas the young man felt a stirring in his pants, and up went his sleeping cock, looking for some action.

Lucy smiled at him when she saw his bulging pants and said 'Is that for me, young man?'

As she pointed down at his bulging crotch, the middle-aged lady looked down at his bulging crotch and shrieked, 'Disgusting!'

Then she stood and moved away; her empty seat was quickly taken by voluptuous Lucy, who instantly put her hand on his thigh and then softly kissed his lips. The young man was shocked by her openness. He too was open to mutual contact and placed his hand on her thigh and slowly moved it upwards towards its Holy Grail, Lucy's pussy.

His eyes opened wide when he found she wasn't wearing panties and instantly began probing her shaven haven with a rigid finger. Lucy's was once again in turmoil. What was she doing? She was so turned on by this moment that she wanted to play too.

So she decided to undo his pants and release his throbbing cock. The young man froze as her hand quickly covered his crotch. He looked at Lucy and whispered, 'What are you doing? We are in a public place.'

Lucy smiled and then replied, 'What do you think I am a glove puppet or something?'

She then stood and walked towards the exit door and then pushed a bell; the driver frowned and pulled in at the next stop and opened the exit door. Lucy then got off and quickly walked towards her office; she was hot flustered and, above all, late.

Red faced, she walked into her office and was told she was needed in the boardroom right away; she then quickly put her purse in her draw and locked it and then picked up a pen and a notepad and quickly walked towards the boardroom. She stopped outside and knocked the door.

'Come in,' shouted a male's voice.

Lucy slowly opened the door and cautiously entered and then with a blushing face ran to take dictation. As she sat down next to young Ned Blogs, she was confronted by the angry chairman John Haskins, the senior partner of the firm.

'Where have you been, girl?' he shouted. 'The meeting was for nine, and where were you?'

The blushing Lucy looked at him and smiled. She wanted to say, 'Getting truly fucked, old man, by a young man with a very big dick'

But she kept those solitude words to herself and pledged, to herself that she would get him later that afternoon when she reviewed the minutes of the meeting alone with him.

Mr Haskins was an old man of seventy-five, recently wed for the third time to his young wife Sandra. Lucy had always wondered how he had got such a wife. He was a white-haired, crinkly-faced old man. Any woman in their right mind would become a stunt woman if they woke up next to such a man and jump out the nearest fucking window with fright.

She too had always wondered how he got it up, as he didn't seem to have any energy around the office and always sat in his big chair, staring at her wonderful big breasts, when she sat next to him taking dictation.

But this afternoon, the temptress would come alive in his presence; suddenly her train of thought was broken by a hand placed on her naked thigh. She froze and wondered what was going on; she was in a meeting, and somebody was getting fresh.

With her heart beating like bongo drums, she turned and stared at Ned who was engrossed in chairman's speech. She wondered what was going on. Suddenly another hand was placed on her left thigh.

She then turned and looked at young Scott, who too was engrossed in chairman's speech. Lucy was in a state of shock when her legs were opened wide and then she gasped, 'Oh.'

As she felt a tongue begin probing her pussy, she wondered who was under the table and then gasped out again, 'Oh my goodness!'

'Is there anything wrong?' asked the puzzled chairman.

Lucy smiled and then replied, 'No . . . no, nothing at all, sir'

Then her eyes opened wide as the probing tongue flickered over her magical button. Her mind was suddenly shaken up by the onslaught of sensations.

'Oh my goodness!' she again cried out. Whoever was under the table was an expert in pussy licking. Lucy didn't know whether to laugh or cry. She was getting so horny; she felt like shouting out, 'Will someone please fuck me, fuck me now?'

Her heart was racing and her mind in a mess. How could she take dictation with all that was going on under the table? Her eyes again opened wide as she felt a finger slip into her pussy while the tongue probed and flickered over her magical button.

Her nipples now stood like bullets; the sexual excitement was driving her crazy and she began murmuring 'Yes, yes, oh yes.'

As the wonderful sensations rushed through her body up to her exploding mind, she was just seconds away from an orgasm. Then John Haskins said, 'Well, that's all, folks. If you have any questions, give them to Lucy, and I will review them this afternoon.'

CHAPTER 4

WITH THE MEETING over, the staff stood and left the room. The only one who remained seated was the voluptuous Lucy, whose pussy was still been licked by that magical tongue. John looked at her exotic smiling face and said, 'What are you waiting for, girl. Get back to work, and see me this afternoon at 3.00.'

Lucy smiled and slowly tried to close her legs; thus, the finger slipped out of her quivering pussy, and the tongue disappeared. Nervously Lucy tried to stand; her legs were shaking and her knees were weak. She couldn't seem to stand on her own feet.

She looked at the frowning John Haskins and asked, 'Please, John, can I run through the minutes with you?'

John smiled at her and replied, 'There's no need. Here's the tape of the meeting.'

As he put it in a case and slid it across the table to Lucy, Lucy smiled and slowly stood, picking up her notepad and tape, and left the room, still wondering who was under the table and whose fingers and magical tongue had given her so much pleasure.

As she opened the door, she turned and looked behind her to see the smiling cleaner Mandy getting out from under the table.

'Wow!' murmured Lucy; she smiled at the blushing Mandy and then whispered, 'Thank you.'

Then she blew her a kiss and left the room. On seeing this, the intrigued Mr Haskins asked, 'What's going on, Mandy, and why were you under the table?'

The red-faced Mandy looked at him with a puzzled look on her face, then smiled, and said, 'I was cleaning, sir.'

Mr Haskins said no more and walked over to the window, while Mandy quietly walked towards the door and quickly left the room. As she walked past Lucy's desk, she smiled and whispered, 'Did you like that, honey?'

Lucy looked up at her and smiled; her heart was racing. Nobody had ever ignited her body like that before. She was so horny and wanted to play too; she stood and walked around the table and took hold of Mandy's hand and led her to the restroom.

Once inside, Lucy quickly walked to a cubicle. It was a tight squeeze, but once inside, Lucy turned around as Mandy closed the door and softly kissed her lips. Mandy responded with her probing tongue, as her fingers softy touched Lucy's shaven haven; this was too much for Lucy. She too wanted to sample Mandy's delights. So she began unzipping Mandy's uniform, revealing her hidden secrets that weren't so hidden.

Mandy's tits were small with protruding nipples that stood erect through her sexual excitement; Lucy couldn't contain her desire any longer and began sucking on those nipples. She slowly pulled Mandy's panties down and delicately massaged her magical button.

Lucy's mouth went on manoeuvres with tender kisses, downward over Mandy's flat stomach towards her sacred haven. This was the first time she tasted another woman's pussy. With her tongue just inches from Mandy's pussy, she then put two fingers either side of the magical button and then, pushed outwards and attacked that magical button with her probing, flickering tongue.

Mandy loved this affection and craved this affection, especially from another woman. She loved to feel the velvety touch of a woman on her naked charms. As Lucy's tongue probed and flickered over her magical button, Mandy began murmuring, 'Yes, yes. Oh that feels so good!'

Just then, the office supervisor entered the restroom; Jane Goody was her name. On hearing Mandy's murmur, she tiptoed towards the closed cubicle and listened. Then again Mandy began murmuring, 'Yes, yes, oh yes, Lucy! That's it, oh that feels so good!'

Curiosity was the name of the game for Jane. So she crept into the next cubicle and quietly closed the door; she then took her shoes off and quietly stood on the toilet and then peeked over the top to see the half-dressed Mandy with her naked tits on display and voluptuous Lucy's head buried in her crotch.

Suddenly, her impulses got the better of her as she watched this erotic show; her own sexual desire was craving this excitement. With her nipples like encased bullets in her bra, she unbuttoned her skirt, and let it fall. In seconds, her hand was inside her panties and gently massaged her magical button, as she watched this erotic show.

It had been a long time since her magical button had endured this kind of action, especially from her own fingers. It felt so good; she wanted to scream but couldn't as she herself became a secret member of the Master Bates society.

What was she doing? 'Enjoying the moment,' she kept telling herself. She was craving to be fucked by a big rigid cock, as she watched this erotic show, and suddenly lost control of her emotions.

'Oh yes,' she murmured, getting the startled Mandy's attention, who was staring up at her, wondering what she was doing. Mandy then smiled at the thought that one day she would have the chance to taste plain Jane's pussy too; now she knew that Jane was captivated by one-on-one womanly action.

She then closed her eyes and enjoyed the moment, as Lucy's velvety tongue was sending an onslaught of sensations through her body. As it probed and flickered at her magical button, those sensations were driving her crazy.

But temptress Lucy hadn't finished; with her other hand, she began finger fucking Mandy's pussy. One finger quickly became two. As she began thrusting at the tempo of the tap that wouldn't stop dripping,

Mandy couldn't contain herself and began murmuring, 'Oh-ha.'

Lucy's fingers slowly thrust in and out of her quivering pussy and her tongue probed and flickered over her magical button. She was on her way to Climax City. With Mandy's constant murmuring, the observing Jane's fingers were taking her on her own journey.

Her magical button was punch drunk from those massaging fingers of hers; it had never experienced a workout like this before, especially at the hands of its owner Jane Goody.

She was biting her lip to silence her murmur, as she arrived at Climax City at breakneck speed. In her excitement, she lost her footing, as her mind exploded from the onslaught of sensations.

'Oh my goodness,' she suddenly murmured.

'Who is that?' asked the startled Lucy, on hearing a voice in the next cubicle. Mandy began to laugh and said, 'Lucy, my darling, I think we will have to stop now and make love on my bed tonight.'

Lucy looked up at her and smiled; she wanted to make love to Mandy, especially on a bed with toys at hand to enhance their sexual pleasure. But she had found a rewarding job that paid well, very well indeed, if the previous night's performance money was a regular occurrence. She knew the thousand dollars from Sally was a one off payment, but she didn't care; she so craved the sexual excitement that stripping brought.

Again Mandy whispered, 'Are you coming over to play tonight?'

Lucy looked up and smiled and then said, 'No, not tonight, Mandy. I'm working, but I would love to spend Saturday with you, the whole day if you like.'

Mandy smiled and said, 'Yes, that would be lovely, Lucy.'

But she wanted to know more about her evening job and whispered, 'Where do you work at night, Lucy? And do you know if there are any more jobs going there?'

Lucy smiled and pondered on her thoughts. Did she really want to tell people she was a stripper at night? She didn't care as she had no reservations, but she wasn't looking for any more confrontations with Mr Haskins.

She still had this afternoons meeting with him, and her only concern was how his heart was, for what she had installed for him was not for the thimble hearted. She said no more on the matter, then stood and softly kissed Mandy's lips, and whispered 'I will tell you on Sunday, Mandy.'

She then turned Mandy around and moved backwards herself, straddling the toilet so to give Mandy more room to open the door. The secretly listening Jane in the next booth pulled up and buttoned her skirt and then slipped her shoes on and waited for the all clear.

It wasn't long in coming as she heard the door open and Mandy say, 'See you Saturday, Lucy. Bye for now.'

With that, Mandy left the rest room, leaving the voluptuous Lucy to re-address her face. As she was re-applying more lipstick on her lips, the blushing Jane Goody walked out of the toilet cubicle and stopped and stared at the voluptuous Lucy's body.

The sultry temptress Lucy smiled and turned around and slowly walked towards her prey; plain Jane stood there mesmerized on the approaching Lucy's swaying hips. What was she to do? By delaying her act of departure, she was at Lucy's mercy.

She stood there stunned as Lucy began kissing her lips; Jane was mesmerized by Lucy's soft lips and responded with her own probing tongue. She was so horny and wanted to play; she put her hand under Lucy's short skirt and began massaging her pussy.

Suddenly her eyes opened wide when she felt Lucy's shaven haven. She wondered where Lucy's panties were, but this was merely a passing thought as her fingers gently began massaging Lucy's magical button.

They were lost in that moment of sexual passion, neither one caring of the open space they were in. It was Jane who stopped the tender kissing and dropped to her knees for her first taste of pussy. It was a desire like no other; she had to taste the voluptuous Lucy's pussy now.

Lucy suddenly made it easier by lifting her short skirt, thus exposing her shaven haven for Jane to see. Jane didn't hesitate and plunged her probing tongue right in, while her two fingers continually massaged Lucy's magical button.

She was a novice at pussy licking but sure was enjoying the moment. She was losing her mind; she loved this sexual experience. It was Lucy, who ruined the moment by saying, 'Jane, don't you think that we should go into a cubicle to finish as we are rather exposed here, dear?'

On hearing this, the panic-stricken Jane instantly stopped her pussy patrol, with her probing tongue, and cautiously looked around and then quickly stood and took Lucy by the hand and ran over to the open cleaner's cupboard and walked right in and closed the door behind them.

With her heart racing, she began unbuttoning Lucy's jacket. In seconds, the jacket was off and thrown to the floor. As Lucy removed her cameo top, revealing her buxom ample charms, Jane stared at her strawberry-sized nipples.

'Wow!' she suddenly murmured as she began unbuttoning her own blouse; she too wanted to be naked and quickly shed her clothes. Lucy stared with bewildered eyes as she watched her supervisor shed her clothes, and she herself stepped out of her short skirt.

Both naked, Lucy stepped towards Jane and began passionately kissing her lips, as her hands began caressing her bottom. Jane was lost in the haze of sexual pleasure; she didn't hear the door open and Mandy creep in.

Mandy stared in disbelief at what she was seeing, two naked ladies in her cupboard. She couldn't believe it and began removing her own clothes so she could join the club too. In a few seconds, she was naked and walked towards the voluptuous Lucy.

As she put her hand on Lucy's boob, Lucy froze.

Who the fuck is that? Wandered Lucy, she slowly opened her eyes. She looked to her right and breathed a sigh of relief when she saw Mandy's smiling face and carried on exploring Jane's mouth with her delicately probing tongue.

The frisky Mandy took it to another level when she began probing Jane's hairy bush with her fluttering fingers. But Jane didn't care. She was lost in the moment and thought it was Lucy's fluttering fingers. Then panic stations for Jane when Mandy began tenderly kissing her bottom.

Who's that? Was it a man with a rather big cock in his pants ready to satisfy her sexual desires? She wondered as she carried on with her passionate kiss with Lucy. Her eyes suddenly opened wide as a finger entered her pussy. One finger quickly became two, and the slow thrusting began. Jane loved this moment; it was sex and mystery all wrapped up in one.

As those two fingers slowly thrust in and out of her pussy at the tempo of the tap that wouldn't stop dripping, Jane got the craving to, once again, taste Lucy's pussy and suddenly stopped her kissing and then whispered, 'Lucy, will you please sit on my face?'

Lucy then replied, 'Of course, I will, darling.'

With that, Jane said, 'Whoever has their fingers in my pussy, please take them out.'

On hearing her command, Mandy stopped her thrusting and then slowly withdrew her two fingers and sucked them, tasting Jane's juices for the first time.

With her pussy now free of the intrusion, Jane lay down on the floor with a startled expression on her face when she saw the third person was Mandy. *What was she doing here?* She wondered, as the voluptuous Lucy slowly lowered her pussy to her face.

With her vision obstructed by Lucy's voluptuous ass, she didn't see Mandy walk over to her cupboard and take out a package. When Lucy saw a rabbit vibrator taken out of the packet, she gasped, 'Where did you get that, Mandy, the magician?'

Then Lucy smiled as she watched the grinning Mandy walk towards her. Mandy then stopped and fell to her knees and was kneeling alongside Jane's hairy pussy. Then she began sucking the eight-inch rabbit vibrator; Jane's eyes suddenly opened wide as Mandy slowly pushed the rabbit vibrator into her pussy and switched it on.

Jane suddenly gasped, 'Oh my goodness.'

As those vibrating ears caressed her magical button, those wonderful sensations flooded her pussy, as they shot through her body up to her exploding mind. This was unbelievable, a three-ladies sex show, with a sex toy too. The only question Lucy was asking herself, where was the paying audience? Many a man would pay good money to see such a show.

Her train of thought was suddenly interrupted by Jane's screams of pleasure as she arrived at Climax City at breakneck speed and her screams. 'Yes, yes, oh yes.' Fillled the room. That was; it game over.

CHAPTER 5

I T WAS 11 a.m. when the blushing Jane reappeared in the office and was immediately confronted by the young Mr Jenks, curious of why she had been so long in the restroom.

'I thought you said you had to spend a penny,' said the smiling Mr Jenks. Then with laughter in his voice, he said, 'Didn't they have any change my love and you went

Wee-wee all over the floor.'

He was impersonating a French man, and as he kissed Jane lightly on the hand, he whispered, 'Mr Haskins wants to see you in his office pronto.'

'Why? What does he want?' replied the curious Jane. With her heart racing, she wondered if she had been rumbled and if there was a camera in the ladies restroom.

She didn't care; she had had a wonderful time. First there had been the self-pleasuring, as she watched Lucy muff diving Mandy in the toilet cubicle.

Then came her naked adventure with the voluptuous Lucy in the cleaner's cupboard and above all her screams of pleasure, as she experienced the rabbit vibrator for the first time. *Oh what an experience that was!*

It seemed Mandy was a magician. In-stead of pulling an actual rabbit out of a top hat, she pulled a sex toy out of a bag and gave her pleasure, which she had never encountered before. *Wow what a woman and what a toy!*

Hot and flustered, she knocked on Mr Haskins door and waited for an answer.

'Come in,' shouted a male voice. Jane cautiously entered, not knowing why she had been summoned.

'Where have you been?' shrieked the agitated Mr Haskins.

'Where . . . where have I been?' replied the stuttering Jane, whose mind was wondering where Lucy worked in the evenings. She had decided that tonight she would follow her and secretly observe her from a hidden place.

She was suddenly brought back to reality when Mr Haskins shouted, 'what is wrong with you now girl.'

Jane stared at him with a blushing face, as her pussy wept in her panties; she didn't know whether to laugh, cry, or wet her panties. What had she done wrong? Why was Mr Haskins so angry with her?

Suddenly, the door opened and in walked the voluptuous Lucy, with a frown on her face as she stared at the agitated Mr Haskins, then said, 'What's wrong with you now, you old fart?'

Mr Haskins stared at the voluptuous Lucy and then looked down at his groin and murmured, 'Why have you forsaken me, oh Willy of mine, when I need you to punish that vixen by fucking her in her asshole this afternoon.'

On hearing this, Lucy smiled and then replied, 'That will be the day, old man. To fuck me in the ass, you need more than a blue pill.'

Mr Haskins frowned at her sarcastic comment and replied, 'I suppose a spanking is out of the question?'

'Me or you, you nasty little man?' shrieked the smiling Lucy, who had switched to her dominatrix mood. She was now in command and whispered, 'Do you really want me, to spank you, little man?'

On hearing this, Mr Haskins smiled and replied, 'Yes please, Mistress Lucy.'

Jane Goody was mystified and quietly crept from the room, leaving her heart's desire Lucy to her own devices. Lucy smiled as she watched Jane leave the room; it was fun time now, and she whispered, 'What are you waiting for, old man. Strip your clothes.'

Haskins couldn't believe his luck; it was a delight to be spanked by the voluptuous Mistress Lucy. He quickly took off his jacket, followed by his tie. Then it was off with his shoes and his pants, he then stared at his approaching mistress Lucy, as he unbuttoned his shirt and whispered, 'you are so beautiful, Mistress.'

Lucy stopped and smiled at him, and then she slowly unbuttoned her jacket. Off came the jacket and she, whispered, 'Do you want to see more?'

Haskins stared in disbelief and replied, 'Yes please, Mistress Lucy.'

Lucy smiled and asked him to loose his Y front under pants and then whispered, 'It's going to cost you.'

She was again playing the role of a stripper. But this time, it was in her work place. And she didn't care, as she held no reservations as she was the sultry temptress.

Haskins nodded and whispered, 'I don't care, Mistress. Show me your boobies.'

'A thousand bucks and the top comes off,' replied the smiling Lucy.

The sexually frustrated Haskins couldn't take any more and said, 'I will give you ten thousand dollars if you take it all off.'

Lucy couldn't believe it and shrieked, 'Ten thousand dollars?'

As she took off her cameo top, followed by her short skirt, Haskins stared in disbelief at the naked goddess that stood before him. His eyes were captivated by her ample charms. Those tits were huge and then, his eyes slowly moved downwards over her luscious curves to her sacred haven. He rubbed his eyes as he couldn't believe that she had a shaven haven.

Temptation was staring him in the face; he couldn't resist temptation. He wanted to taste it, then pointing down at her shaven haven, he whispered, 'Ten thousand bucks, Lucy, if I can sample that delight.'

Dumbfounded Lucy couldn't speak. She was speechless; she was about to earn twenty thousand dollars for ten minutes' work. She began playing charades to show him to lie down on the floor, and she sat on his face, as she couldn't speak.

Haskins smiled and quickly resumed the position. Within seconds, Lucy stood astride his face and slowly lowering her shaven haven towards his awaiting mouth and stopped when she felt his probing tongue begin flickering over her shaven haven.

Lucy wanted to play too. She stared down at his sleeping cock in disbelief; it resembled an acorn that had just fallen from the tree. It was so small, but she had to try and leaned forward and began sucking on its bald head.

Haskins's cock remained small as there was no life in it; unconcerned Lucy started sucking on one of his balls, as though it was a gobstopper from the candy store, and while she sucked she hummed.

That started the churning of Haskins's milk balls. He had never had this pleasure on his genitals in the way Lucy was pleasuring his genitals; his only wish was a rigid cock to fully enjoy this pleasure time with the voluptuous Lucy.

Lucy, on the other hand, was thinking ahead. During her dictation hour that afternoon, she had planned to crush a 100 mg Viagra tablet and put it in Mr Haskins's fruit juice and stand back and titillate him with her swaying hips.

But on seeing that there was no life in his sleeping cock, she decided it should be two; her only concern was, when would she get her money? As to give old Mr Haskins two 100 mg Viagra tablets, might give the old fart a heart attack and that, was not what she wanted a hard dick yes but, a dead man were was the pleasure in that?

Lucy was getting agitated as the old fart Haskins certainly didn't know how to pay homage to her womanly delights. She couldn't stand it any longer and stuck a finger up his ass.

Still there was no action in his sleeping cock that was the final straw for her. With her stomach churning, closure was just seconds away. As she blew an almighty fart out of her ass, which had Haskins choking on the pooh-e smell by gummy that was sure smelly.

While the red-faced Haskins choked on that awful smell, the grinning temptress Lucy stood up and began dressing. First came her short skirt; when she put it on, she was still exposing her hidden secrets to the staring Haskins, then on went her cameo top and finally her jacket.

Fully dressed, she squatted and said, 'Mr Haskins, can I please have my money, sir?'

Haskins smiled as he stared at her shaven haven. Twenty thousand dollars he had just blown for ten minutes of titillation fun. He slowly stood and then slowly walked over to his safe; Lucy smiled as she watched the old man with only one thought on her mind: Viagra.

As Mr Haskins handed her money, she whispered, 'Thank you, Mr Haskins. Do you mind if I have an extra hour for lunch, as I have to get a prescription for my father?'

Haskins stared at her pretty face and then leaned forward and tenderly kissed her lips and whispered,

'mind? I don't mind Lucy. I will see you this afternoon for dictation of the minutes of this morning's meeting.'

On hearing this, Lucy smiled, then tenderly kissed his cheek, then slowly turned around and lifted her short skirt, exposing her naked ass, and slowly walked towards the door. Haskins sat down and watched his horny temptress walk away; his eyes were captivated by her swaying hips, with only one thing on his mind: where could he get a hard-on from?

As he watched Lucy walk out the door, he instantly buzzed for Jane.

'Hello,' said a woman's voice.

'Oh hello, Jane', replied Haskins, 'could you please ask Ned to come in and see me?'

The bewildered Jane said, 'Okay, Mr Haskins. He won't be a minute.'

With that, she switched the intercom off, stood, and went to talk to Ned. As she stood by Ned's desk with her hips swaying to attract his attention, she suddenly whispered, 'Ned, Mr Haskins wants to see you now.'

On hearing this, the bewildered Ned looked up at Jane's smiling face, and then his eyes wandered down her body and stopped at her swaying hips. There was a sudden stirring in his loins, as his sleeping cock began to suddenly rise. He ached to fuck this woman that stood before him; again Jane whispered,

'Mr Haskins wants to see you now, Ned.'

With his imagination imaging her naked body, he suddenly stood revealing a rather large bulge in his pants. On seeing this, Jane gasped, 'Is that for me, big boy,' and reached out and rubbed his bulge. She became so horny that she wanted to be fucked, but Mr Haskins was waiting. She whispered, 'I want you. I want to feel that big cock of yours inside my aching pussy, Ned.'

On hearing this, the rampant Ned kissed her on the lips and then ran to Mr Haskins office and knocked on the door.

'Come in,' shouted the agitated Mr Haskins; on hearing this, the smiling Ned entered and approached the desk.

'What's this?' shouted the angry Haskins with his finger pointing at Ned's crotch. Ned looked down and gawped at his prominent bulge. What was he to say? What could he say? Then with quick thinking, he replied, 'Sorry about that, sir, but I've just seen Lucy bend over a desk. She was smiling at me, as she wasn't wearing any panties.'

The red-faced Haskins knew that as any man seeing her naked hidden delights would have a hard-on.

He stared at Ned and then whispered, 'I want one of them too, Ned.'

The bewildered Ned looked at him and murmured, 'One of what, sir?'

The red-faced and agitated Haskins shouted, 'One of those fucking hard-on things that you got there in your pants, Ned.'

The bewildered Ned shrugged his shoulders, as he didn't know what to say. He just couldn't get one up by magic as he was no magician. He whispered, 'How am I going to do that, Mr Haskins?'

On hearing this, Mr Haskins smiled and handed Ned a folded piece of paper and said, 'Take that to my doctor, Ned, and he will write you a prescription, which I want you to get pronto. See Jane for my doctor's address.'

With that, Haskins handed Ned a hundred-dollar bill and waved him away. Ned smiled, turned, and walked quickly towards the door. In seconds, he was out the door and headed towards Jane's desk to get Mr Haskins's doctor's address.

Jane smiled as she watched her handsome dream lover walking towards her; she stared at his crotch and wondered where the bulge had gone. Ned handed her the folded piece of paper and whispered, 'Jane, please can I have Mr Haskins's doctor's address?'

As he stared down her open blouse at her cleavage he wanted to see more of her hidden delights. There was once again a stirring in his loins; as his imagination took control of his mind, there sat the naked Jane and her nipples stood erect, as did the cock in his pants, once again.

Jane phoned the doctor and requested a prescription for eight Viagra tablets for Mr Haskins and then lost her words as she stared at Ned's bulging pants.

'Fuck me,' she murmured and put the phone down. She then stood and took Ned by the hand and led him towards the ladies' restroom.

CHAPTER 6

ONCE INSIDE, JANE led the panicking Ned to the cleaner's cupboard and opened the door and walked right in; then she turned around and dropped to her knees and then unbuttoned his pants to release his throbbing cock. She then wrapped her mouth around it and began sucking on it, but this was short-lived as her pussy was crying out, 'For heaven's sake, Jane, get your knickers off and let that rigid thing get in here.'

She then let the rigid cock fall from her mouth, then stood and removed her skirt and panties too, then turned and walked over to the boxes, and bent over and opened her legs and then whispered, 'Fuck me, fuck me now, Ned.'

On hearing this, Ned get close to her; in seconds, he was placing his rigid cock up against the entrance to her pussy and then plunged it right in and began thrusting at the tempo of the tap that wouldn't stop dripping.

Jane was in heaven as her dream lover slowly plunged in and out of her quivering pussy; she wanted to scream, 'Fuck me, fuck me harder, Ned,' but she was enjoying the moment and remained quiet with her wishes. But for Ned, he was in a dilemma; he loved the moment fucking the office queen. He was slowly forgetting Haskins's Viagra tablets. Suddenly he upped the pace of his thrusting to the new tempo of the clock that wouldn't stop ticking.

On occasions, he slapped her ass on the withdrawal stroke, shouting, 'you naughty lady Miss Jane.'

Jane loved the feel of his strong slapping hand on her burning ass, secretly craving for it to be harder. Ned was suddenly at panic stations, when he heard the rampant knocking at the door and shot his milky-white fluids deep inside Jane's pussy and whispered, 'Who's that Jane?'

Jane looked around at the closed door and whispered, 'How do I know? I'm no fucking fortune teller.'

The panic-stricken Ned then quickly withdrew his slowly deflating cock. Then he stood and re-housed his deflating cock and pulled up his pants; still the rampant knocking continued.

He looked at the half-naked Jane still bending over the boxes and whispered, 'Please hurry up, Jane. Somebody wants to come in.'

With that, he playfully slapped her ass and then turned around and walked a couple of steps and slowly opened the door, as Jane quickly dressed. With the door slightly ajar, he saw the smiling Mandy standing there and whispered, 'Hello, Mandy, how may I help you?'

Mandy smiled as she tried to push the door open, but the door was held firm by Ned's strong hand.

'Come on, let me in Ned. This is not a knocking shop.'

With that, Ned opened the door, and Mandy saw the smiling Jane standing there.

'Oh, come on,' she sighed as she walked right in. Ned quickly walked out and was on his way to Mr Haskins's Doctor's clinic to get one prescription and then off to the drugstore to collect the prescribed drugs.

Mandy stopped and stared at the blushing Jane; there was a smell of sex in the air. Inquisitively, she dropped to her knees and lifted Jane's skirt. There was a damp spot on her panties. Mandy then leaned forward and sniffed those panties, and the smell resembled a sea food store.

Mandy then pulled those smelly panties down to perform a closer inspection of Jane's hairy pussy, where she saw Ned's milky-white fluids oozing out. She had to taste it; her probing tongue resembled a cat licking its cream, as she licked those fluids up.

Jane stood there enjoying the moment; first she had been truly fucked by handsome Ned, and now she felt like Cleopatra, as Mandy licked away those milky-white fluids from her pussy.

'Oh what a day!' she suddenly sighed; first she had watched the voluptuous temptress Lucy pleasuring Mandy with her probing flickering tongue, while she had pleasured herself by gently massaging her own magical button as she watched.

Then came the encounter with the voluptuous Lucy that blew her mind; never before had she desired a woman's body as she desired the sultry temptress Lucy, the special one with her voluptuous body and shaven haven too.

That had taken her desire to a new level; she was eager to sample the delights of another woman's body more today than yesterday. As yesterday, she was the heterosexual good-time lady, but today she was a bisexual lady eager to sample another woman's delights.

Above all, she wanted to visit a sexual aids store to purchase lots of toys for her new sexual endeavours with the ladies. Mandy had taken her pussy exploration to a new level as she once again inserted that fabulous rabbit vibrator into Jane's juicy pussy and switched it on. Jane's eyes opened wide as the rabbits vibrating ears nestled up against her magical button.

Those sensations were wonderful; Jane was in heaven, never wanting this day to end. She couldn't believe her lucky stars as she approached Climax City at breakneck speed and began screaming, 'Yes, yes, oh yes, I'm cumming, Mandy. Yes I'm cumming.' Her legs began to shake.

Mandy smiled as her conquest Miss Jane experienced that wonderful orgasmic moment, but for her, she didn't feel fulfilled and stood then and walked over to her cupboard. Then she took out a big unopened packet and then turned and walked back to her staring conquest, who curiously asked, 'What's in the packet, Mandy?'

Mandy smiled as she stopped and removed her cleaning uniform; standing there in her panties and bra, she slowly un-wrapped the parcel, as Jane looked on in amazement. Her eyes opened wide when she saw the contents, a ten inch strap-a-dick-to-me. She murmured, 'Well, fuck me gently.'

'I will, I will,' replied the grinning Mandy.

'Give me half a chance to get it out of the package.'

With that, Mandy quickly opened the package and removed the strap-a-dick-to-me and strapped it on. On seeing the size, Jane shrieked, 'Fuck me. Look at the size of that.'

As she pointed at it with a trembling finger, Mandy smiled and said, 'Please turn around and place your hands on those boxes and spread your legs.'

The sexually excited Jane spun around and spread her legs; then she leaned forward and placed her hands on the boxes and waited. In seconds, Mandy was standing behind her with that ten-inch rubber cock in hand, guiding it towards her waiting pussy.

Jane's eyes opened wide as the big rubber cock penetrated her waiting pussy and even wider. As Mandy began to slowly thrust in and out at the tempo of the tap that wouldn't stop dripping.

'God, that feels so big,' screamed Jane.

'Shush!' whispered the panic-stricken Mandy, scared she would get caught and sacked for fucking one of the office staff in her cleaning cupboard. She wasn't ready for unemployment yet, being a young lady of twenty-four. Jane began to laugh.

'It isn't funny,' whispered the on-edge Mandy, so scared she would get caught; she slowly withdrew that big rubber cock and whispered, 'Tonight, Jane, I want to take you on a journey.'

'Where to?' replied the curious Jane.

'Pleasure land,' whispered the smiling Mandy as she un-strapped the strap-a-dick-to-me and sucked it clean of Jane's juices. Jane, on the other hand, turned around and dropped to her knees and pulled Mandy's panties down. It was pussy-licking time. As she probed Mandy's pussy with her flickering tongue, the panic-stricken Mandy froze; Jane's velvety tongue flickered over her magical button. She whispered, 'No no more, please no more, Jane. Save it for later. You come home with me tonight.'

The confused Jane instantly stopped her probing of Mandy's magical button with her flickering tongue and looked up and smiled. Then she stood and softly kissed Mandy's lips and then quickly dressed and then went back to work.

Mandy watched as her groovy chick walked towards the door and whispered, 'See you later, alligator.'

On hearing this, Jane stopped and turned around and snarled, 'Alligator? Am I?'

With that, she snatched the strap-a-dick-to-me from Mandy's clenched hand and whispered, 'Resume the position, honey.'

She opened her skirt and let it fall to the floor and then strapped that fabulous strap-a-dick-to-me around her waist. The petrified Mandy looked at her in astonishment. Jane loved the sexual excitement and was enthralling in her new role as the master with the big rubber cock and Mandy being her slave.

With the wonderful sexual aid around her waist, Jane slowly walked towards her slave with the ten-inch rubber cock in hand. The petrified Mandy quickly turned around and resumed the position as requested; in a few seconds, the dominant Jane was standing behind her and gently rubbing that big rubber cock up against her pussy.

Mandy's eyes suddenly opened wide as she felt that big rubber cock rub up against her butt; her heart began beating faster and she whispered, 'Jane, darling, there's no effing way that's going in there without your first lubricating my butt hole.'

Jane smiled and then playfully slapped her butt and whispered, 'Are you frightened, little one?'

Mandy was scared to speak as she had no words and instead nodded her head; Jane then penetrated her pussy with that big rubber cock. Mandy's eyes opened wider as that big cock plunged deeper into her tight pussy; it was a tight squeeze but Jane didn't care. She was the master and Mandy her slave.

Jane then slowly began to thrust at the tempo of the tap that wouldn't stop dripping. Mandy bit on her lip to silence her cries. That big rubber plunging cock was driving her crazy; she was the slave and Jane her master, and any sound made by her may result in severe punishment.

Jane, on the other hand, was in her element. She was in control of this slowly plunging ten-inch rubber cock and thus became the strict school mistress as she slapped Mandy's bottom on every withdrawal stroke, whispering, 'You've been a naughty girl, young lady.'

Mandy loved the spanking and craved the spanking; she loved the feeling of a hard slap on her ass. She couldn't contain her excitement any longer and whispered, 'Harder, Jane. Let me feel it.'

On hearing this, the confused Jane replied, 'What do you mean by harder, slave?'

Mandy was flabbergasted by her reply as she was the head of the office.

Jane suddenly upped her thrusting speed to the new tempo of the clock that wouldn't stop ticking. Mandy was horrified by this action but said no more. She just enjoyed the moment as her master thrust on.

She was on her way to destination Climax City; here she comes. Jane once again slowed the pace of her thrusting to the tempo of the tap that wouldn't stop dripping and, on occasions, slapped Mandy's butt hard. Mandy was in heaven as the tingling sensations rushed through her body up to her exploding mind.

'Yes, yes, that's it,' cried Mandy.

Teardrops rolled down her face, but these were not teardrops of pain but teardrops of pleasure. She loved this endeavour of sexual pleasure and was eager to explore more by changing positions. She then whispered, 'Jane, Master Jane, can we change positions?'

On hearing this, Jane immediately stopped her slow thrusting and slowly withdrew the big rubber cock and whispered, 'Where do you want me, Mandy?'

'Lie down on the floor,' replied the smiling Mandy.

Jane quickly lay down on the floor, holding the big rubber cock upright for Mandy to sit down on. Mandy resumed the reverse cowgirl position and slowly lowered her pussy towards that big rubber cock. In seconds, it was deep inside her, so she slowly began grinding her hips on that big rubber cock.

Those sensations felt wonderful, yet she yearned for more and slowly leaned backwards. That was it as that big rubber cock was nestled up against her G spot. She slowly began grinding her hips, and those sensations rushed up through her shaking body to her exploding mind. Next stop would be her exploding pussy, as her built-up fluids sprayed into the air.

She was at the point of no return, when the door suddenly opened and in walked the fuming Mr Haskins; he stopped and stared at this wonderful erotic show, and then it happened—the big rubber cock slipped out of Mandy's pussy, releasing Jane's built-up fluids spraying into the air and falling, on Mr Haskins open-mouthed staring face.

CHAPTER 7

I T WAS 12.45 p.m. as Lucy kissed her father goodbye; she had got her stash of ten Viagra tablets, She was the sultry temptress, a voluptuous sex goddess. First port of call was the Bank, to open a savings account to stash her $25,000 away, been the $20,000 she had got from Haskins for her titillation show in his office and her $5,000 earnings from last nights strip tease extravaganza.

Then she was back to work to see if she could resuscitate Mr Haskins's deceased cock; it was a challenge as Mr Haskins hadn't seen life down there for a long time. It seemed he had lost it when he lost his first wife to that dreaded decease cancer.

He had lost that loving feeling, when he had lost her, life had become a choir, a life worth not living without his beloved sweet heart. Lucy smiled as she entered the bank; it was fun time as she was panties free, looking to entice any onlookers to her secret charms. She sat down and waited to speak to an adviser. She smiled at the gawk man, who was sat alongside his wife, staring at her long naked thighs.

His eyes were glued to her naked thighs, eager to see higher what lay beneath that short skirt. Whether she was wearing panties or not was the only thought on his mind? Lucy looked at his stone-faced wife and wondered why she looked so sad. Then the thought passed as she suddenly uncrossed her legs, thus showing a glimpse of her shaven haven.

The horny onlooker was startled by such a sight and slipped a hand in his pants and gently began caressing his sleeping cock. Lucy smiled as she watched him secretly playing with himself and again flashed him as she slowly crossed her legs.

'Oh no,' murmured the horny onlooker as up periscope went his sleeping cock.

'Oh no what?' whispered his inquisitive wife, mystified by his few words. She looked down and saw the big bulge in his pants and whispered, 'You are kidding me. You didn't get any last night, so you sit here portraying Master Bates while you watch that tart flash you her hidden secrets.'

The red-faced horny onlooker looked at his wife and whispered, 'Shush, not so loud.'

On hearing this, the frustrated wife punched him in the nuts and then, looked at the temptress Lucy and snarled, 'Stop that, you tart, or you'll get one too.'

Lucy smiled and slowly uncrossed her legs and whispered, 'Stop what, lady?'

The horny onlooker's hand was now a blur in his pants, as he frantically stroked his rigid cock and stared at her unmasked shaven haven.

The hot and flustered wife stood and whispered, 'If you do that once more, lady, you will need surgery.'

Lucy looked at her and frowned and then replied, 'Why, what are you going to do? Punch me in my pussy?'

That was the final straw for the hot and flustered wife, and she swung her footwear towards Lucy's shaven haven. Lucy smiled and caught the footwear in mid-air and held on tight. The horny onlooker began to laugh, as he watched his red-faced wife hop up and down to stop herself falling over.

On seeing this, the suave good-looking customer service rep. Danny Shaw ran over to calm the situation down and to hopefully stop a full-blown fight between the two ladies. Little did he know Lucy was only playing; she was only having a laugh with the red-faced wife.

Danny instantly took control by saying, 'Ladies, ladies, please.'

Lucy looked up at him and smiled, as she put the frustrated wife's footwear back down on the floor, then stood, and whispered, 'Please, can you help me, young man?'

The red-faced Danny looked at her and smiled, as his eyes wandered over her voluptuous body, and whispered, 'Yes, honey, how I may help you today?'

Lucy smiled as she accompanied him back to his desk to discuss opening up a savings account with high interest. As she sat down, she flashed him a glimpse of her shaven haven; Danny was now goggle-eyed on her long naked thighs.

With his imagination running wild, she now sat there naked in his mind with her big buxom breasts teasing him with their erect nipples. It was like they where saying, 'What are you waiting for, man? Get over here and suck me now.'

His staring at her buxom breasts got Lucy intrigued; she smiled and gently pushed the chair back and then in an instant uncrossed her legs, exposing her shaven haven. On seeing the uncrossing of the legs, Danny's eyes went from her ample charms downwards as he gasped, 'Oh my goodness!'

As he stared down at her exposed shaven haven, he couldn't believe what he had seen. He suddenly rubbed his eyes and tried to compose himself. But he wondered how he was going to talk about opening an interest account, when her hidden treasure would be exposed and enticing his wayward eyes.

His imagination was again running riot with his mind saying, 'What are you waiting for, man? Get down on your hands and knees and lick that pussy.'

His imagination was suddenly brought back to reality when Lucy said, 'Look, Danny, I'm here to invest some money. I can tease you all day long, displaying my sexual charms, but time is of the essence.'

With that, she crossed her legs and smiled and then whispered, 'You want to see more? You can come and watch me dance.'

As she placed a card down in front of him and he read 'In Your Vision', he smiled and picked the card up and put it in his shirt pocket. Then he began discussing the choice of accounts with occasional glances at her naked thighs. Then he asked, 'How much money do you have to invest?'

On hearing this, Lucy opened her purse and took out an envelope and handed it to Danny and said, 'There is twenty-five thousand dollars in there.'

Danny took the envelope from her in disbelief, as he had never encountered such a customer before. He then flickered through the envelope, counting the money, and then suggested to Lucy to open up their gold savings account, which offered 7 per cent interest, which the smiling Lucy readily agreed to and as a thank you flashed her shaven haven one last time, which captured Danny's eagle-eyed vision. The temptress in her suddenly came to life, as she secretly stuck a finger into her shaven haven and smiled; on seeing this, Danny felt a stirring in his loins, as his sleeping cock began to rise. Then devilishly she slowly pulled it out and placed it against Danny's lips.

Danny couldn't resist temptation and gently sucked on her moist wet finger, unaware he had quietly been observed by his supervisor. With the finger sucking over, he asked, 'Do you bank with us, Miss?'

Lucy smiled and handed him her ATM card, which Danny took gracefully and punched her account number into his computer. In seconds, her bank details came up, and he began setting up her new gold savings account while the voluptuous Lucy looked around.

As he printed the documents off to her new savings account, his vision was once again attracted to her exposed shaven haven. His rigid cock was crying out to him, 'Let me out of here. I'm hard and ready for some action. Let me give her one.'

He smiled as he placed the paperwork in front of Lucy for signing and whispered, 'Are you dancing tonight, Miss Beautiful?'

Lucy nodded her head as she began signing the paperwork. That was her main job of the day done; she smiled as she began her encore of sticky licking finger time. As she once again slipped a finger into her shaven haven and then slowly pulled it out and placed it against Danny's lips, Danny was intoxicated and quickly sucked her moist wet finger.

She was turning him on like no other; his throbbing cock was aching to be released from its entrapment. Aching for some pussy action, suddenly Lucy smiled and closed her legs and then stood leaned over the desk and softly kissed Danny's lips.

Danny was in turmoil. Was somebody watching him? The kiss was short but sweet; as their lips parted, Lucy whispered, 'Come and see me dance tonight, Danny boy.'

With that, she picked up her bag and then turned around and slowly walked towards the door; with a scheming temptress mind, she suddenly stopped and looked behind her and smiled. There sat the staring Danny ignoring the next customer, as he stared at her voluptuous body. With a devilish grin on her face she half pace stepped to the side, then keeping her legs straight, she bent over and touched her toes, thus exposing her naked bottom for all to see.

This was too much for the supervisor Miss. Blundell, who rushed over and frantically asked Lucy to stand up, as this was not the kind of place to display her bits and pieces. Lucy smiled and then slowly stood up and faced blushing Miss Blundell and whispered, 'Sorry, is there something wrong, Miss?'

'Yes,' replied flustered Miss. Blundell, 'you are offending our customers.'

On hearing her comments, the sultry temptress Lucy leaned forward and softly kissed her lips; the startled Miss. Blundell then stepped back and watched voluptuous Lucy turn around and walk away.

It was half past one when the puffing Ned returned to work, carrying a pharmaceutical bag with Mr Haskins's prescription in. He ran up to Mr Haskins's room and walked right in and seeing what Mr Haskins was doing he froze. There sat Mr Haskins, muff diving his latest sexual conquest. The naked Jane's eyes opened wide and she waved him over, whispering, 'Let me see it, darling.'

On hearing this, Ned opened the bag and took the Viagra tablets out, as he walked towards his naked conquest. Jane began to laugh as she took them from him and whispered, 'No, silly. Drop your pants I want to see the real thing.'

Ned smiled as he quickly opened his pants and released his throbbing rigid cock and stuck it in her face; her lips instantly wrapped around it and she began to suck as though it was her favourite ice lollipop.

Haskins looked up with envious eyes, wishing he had one of those rigid cocks too to fuck lovely Jane's hairy pussy. As he watched Jane sucking on Ned's rigid cock, he felt as though he was impersonating a man without a cock.

Where was Mandy's tool that wonderful strap-a-dick-to-me thingy? He stood and left the room; he too was looking for some action. He walked quickly to the ladies' restroom, with a handful of money, to entice Mandy on lending him that wonderful tool.

As he entered, he was relieved to see Mandy still there; he walked up to her and whispered, 'Mandy, here's some money. Can I please borrow that strap-a-dick-to-me thing?'

Mandy smiled and took his handful of cash and went and got the tool; on her return, she asked, 'Do you need a hand in putting it on, Mr Haskins?'

The red-faced Haskins replied, 'If you don't mind, girl.'

As he quickly opened his pants and let them fall to his knees, Mandy knelt in front of him and strapped the strap-a-dick-to-me around his waist. Then she pulled his pants up and done them up. Haskins looked down and smiled at his impressive bulge and then said, 'Thank you, Mandy.'

He kissed her on the cheek and then he was off singing, 'Here comes Santa Claus, here comes Santa Claus up down sycamore lane.'

As he entered his office, he shouted, 'Surprise, honey, I'm home.'

As he stood by the door with bulging pants, he looked like he was impersonating a ballet dancer; the mystified Jane looked over at him and smiled and then whispered pointing at his bulging pants, 'Is that for me, Mr Haskins?'

With a happy smiling face, Haskins quickly walked towards his prey who lay in waiting whilst sucking on Ned's rigid cock. Haskins took position instead of muff diving; he opened his pants, letting them fall to his knees. Then took the big strap-a-dick-to-me in hand and guided, it through Jane's hairy bush and placed, it up against the lips of her pussy. Jane's eyes opened wide, as she felt the big rubber cock penetrate her pussy.

'Oh that feels so big, Mr Haskins!' she whispered.

On hearing this, the excited Haskins thrust forward and in plunged the big rubber cock, taking Jane by surprise, which nearly caused an accident. As Jane gently bit down on Ned's rigid cock, that big rubber cock sank deeper into her pussy.

'Ouch, ouch,' cried out the shocked Ned; as Jane's teeth sank deeper into his rigid cock, Ned shouted, 'Take it easy, baby. You've got my crown jewels in your mouth.'

On hearing his concerns, Jane let his rigid cock fall from the mouth and gently began sucking on Ned's balls.

'Oh no,' murmured the anxious Ned; his mind lay in turmoil, wondering what she was going to do next, quietly praying she wouldn't bite on them as they weren't gobstoppers from the candy store. Haskins began slowly pumping Jane's hairy pussy at the tempo of the tap that wouldn't stop dripping.

Oh it felt so good; Jane began humming while she sucked on Ned's balls.

Ned's eyes opened wide, as tingling sensations flooded his marble bag and his milk balls began to churn. She was driving him crazy with her velvety sucking mouth; her sucking was intense with a hint of danger.

Whether she would bite one of his balls or not was his only concern. In the groove, Mr Haskins suddenly upped the speed of his thrusting to the new tempo of the clock that wouldn't stop ticking. The distraught Jane suddenly bit one of Ned's balls.

'Fuck me,' shrieked Ned in pain.

On hearing his whims, Jane let his marble bag fall from her mouth and lay back murmuring, 'Oh-ha.'

As the piston-like rubber cock thrust in and out of her quivering pussy, she was on her way to destination Climax City; here she comes. Suddenly the sound of bells filled the room.

'Fire, fire,' shrieked the panic-stricken Ned, who was pulling up his pants as he ran towards the door. Jane on the other hand loved the moment, as she was fast approaching Climax City and began pleading with Mr Haskins, 'I'm nearly there. Please don't stop, sir.'

Haskins stared at her in disbelief; he didn't want to stop either as he was enjoying the ride too, but what if there was a fire? He had to go; he was an old man, so he instantly stopped his thrusting and quickly withdrew the big rubber cock.

'Oh no,' shouted the disappointed Jane. She had began shouting, 'Yes, yes, I'm nearly there.'

Her cries of joy were no more as the game was over.

CHAPTER 8

IT WAS 2 p.m. as the voluptuous Lucy walked back into the office, ready for her afternoon fun with the decapitated Mr Haskins. She was in for a shock as she quietly entered his office, as there lay the naked Jane sucking on Ned's rigid cock, while old Mr Haskins fucked her hairy pussy. Lucy wondered what was going on. She had no luck in getting his floppy cock to rise.

How on earth did plain Jane succeed? Then on closer inspection, she could see he was wearing that good old sex toy, the wonderful strap-a-dick-to-me, and smiled. Her eyes opened wide when she heard Ned shout out, 'Fuck me.'

As she would sort that request out later, when she had the strap-a-dick-to-me to at hand and wandered what would Ned's reaction be when she told him to bend over and take it like a man? She strapped that big rubber cock around her tiny waist. It was through frustration she quietly left the room and switched the fire alarm on, as she crushed two 100 mg Viagra tablets.

With the tablet crushed, she poured Mr Haskins some juice and carefully scooped the Viagra powder into the juice and stirred. After several minutes of stirring, she switched the fire alarm off, as Ned came screaming from the boardroom shouting, 'Fire, fire, everybody out!'

Then he froze as the sounding fire alarm suddenly ended; he stared at the smiling voluptuous Lucy and smiled. Lucy whispered, 'Hey, Ned, did you really mean what you said in there?'

The baffled Ned stood there rubbing his head, wondering what he had said as he stared at the smiling Lucy and whispered, 'what did I say, Lucy?'

Lucy smiled and whispered, 'you know, Ned, you want somebody to fuck you in the ass.'

'No, I don't,' replied the startled Ned as he walked over to the desk and picked up the juice and took a long sip and said, 'that tastes funny,' and then drained the glass. Lucy couldn't keep a straight face and began to laugh.

'What's so funny?' asked the curious Ned.

'You are,' replied the now–giggling Lucy, who was wondering how long before the Viagra kicked in and up would go Ned's sleeping cock.

Haskins and the flustered Jane next appeared; as Lucy watched Ned walk off to his desk, she was still laughing.

'What's so funny, girl?' asked the furious Mr Haskins, who was still furious at being taking away from his ride of a lifetime. On hearing his voice, Lucy instantly stopped her laughing and then turned and faced him; she couldn't contain herself and burst out laughing again, as she pointed at his bulging groin. It was like she was staring at the reincarnation of that great ballet dancer Boris hard-on.

The frustrated Mr Haskins again shouted, 'What's so funny?'

'You are, Boris.' replied the hysterically laughing Lucy; the curious Jane looked down and began laughing too. Haskins stood there bewildered by their laughter in the stance of a ballet dancer.

'Any one for *Swan Lake*,' said the laughing Lucy.

'*Swan lake*? What are you talking about?' replied the agitated Mr Haskins; with that, he turned and walked back into the boardroom and slammed the door. The laughter carried on, as Jane walked back to her desk and Lucy began crushing up another two 100 mg Viagra tablets to make her new concussion for her sexual fun and games with the placid Mr Haskins or no cock to the ladies. With the tablets crushed, she poured a glass of juice and then scooped the powder substance into the juice and stirred. She then stood and carried the juice to the boardroom door and quietly entered; there sat the frowning Haskins who shouted, 'what do you want now, Missy?'

Lucy smiled and slowly walked towards him, swaying her hips as she walked; Haskins was mesmerized by her voluptuous swaying hips, wishing he could get a hard-on and fuck the ass off this voluptuous temptress.

As Lucy placed the glass on the table, she bent and softly kissed Haskins lips and whispered, 'There is a nice drink to cool you down, sir.'

With that, she sat down next to him and crossed her legs. Haskins eyes were intoxicated by her naked thighs as he drank his juice. His mind was telling him to get down on his hands and knees and worship her shaven haven with his probing flickering tongue. His temptress Lucy was watching his every move, teasing him with her swaying leg. *Will she or won't she uncross it?*

With Lucy in her full temptation mood, she stood and whispered, 'Isn't it hot in here?'

As she slowly began unbuttoning her jacket, Haskins stared in disbelief as he watched her remove her jacket. He was dribbling over her prominent strawberry nipples, on show through her see through cotton cameo top.

'More, more, more,' he whispered as Lucy slowly wiggled her swaying hips.

'More,' whispered Lucy. 'If you want to see more, it's going to cost you.'

Then off came that cameo, revealing her big swaying breasts.

'More, more, more,' shouted the intoxicated Haskins, craving to see more of her naked charms. Lucy smiled at him as she unbuttoned her skirt and let it fall to the floor and then jumped up on to the table and spread her legs. Then it was playtime as she gently began massaging, her magical button in front of staring dumbfounded Mr Haskins.

His eyes suddenly left her massaging fingers, as he stared down in disbelief at his groin, something was going on in there curiously, he opened his pants and stared in disbelief his cock was coming to life.

His eyes left his cock, and he looked up at Lucy's smiling face and whispered, 'By gummy, Lucy, It's alive down there.'

'What's alive?' asked the intrigued Lucy.

'This,' replied Haskins, who was now pointing at his erect cock.

'Oh, is that for me, Mr Haskins?' whispered the kneeling Lucy, who began crawling towards his erect cock; Haskins froze as her velvety lips encased his rigid cock. Just then in burst the furious Ned shouting, 'Look, Lucy, what have you done to me?'

With his finger pointing at his rigid cock pointing up at the ceiling; on seeing the naked Lucy knelt on the table sucking Haskins rigid cock, Ned quickly shed his clothes and ran and jumped up on the table.

In seconds, the horny Ned knelt behind Lucy whispering, 'Hey, Lucy, can I please fuck you doggy style?'

On hearing his request, Lucy got into position, while she continued sucking on Haskins cock, with her on her hands and knees and legs slightly apart. Ned guided his rocket impersonating cock towards her shaven haven; Lucy's eyes suddenly opened wide as his rocket cock plunged into her shaven haven. It felt like she was penetrated by a steel bar; his cock was so hard.

Ned began his thrusting slow at the tempo of the tap that wouldn't stop dripping, and while he slowly thrust in and out, he reached around and began massaging her magical button. Thus Lucy began humming on Haskins rigid cock, as the wonderful sensations rushed through her body, up to her exploding mind,

Haskins murmured, 'Wow!'

The tingling sensations ran down his rigid cock, his mind been stimulated by these wonderful sensations. Never before had a woman sucked his cock like this; it was sensational. He suddenly murmured, 'Oh-oh'

As he felt his milk balls begin to churn, disaster was imminent, he had to stop her; he whispered, 'Lucy darling, I will give you ten thousand dollars if I can fuck you now.'

On hearing this, dumbfounded Lucy let his rigid cock fall from her mouth and then looked around and whispered, 'Hey, Ned, will you please vacate my pussy of your rigid cock, so Mr Haskins can fuck it instead.'

On hearing this, Ned panicked and quickly withdrew his rigid cock and jumped off the table and began walking towards his clothes.

On seeing this, the horny Lucy screamed, 'Where are you going, boy? I haven't finished with your super-powered cock yet.'

On hearing this, Ned stopped where he was and murmured, 'Yippee.'

Before turning around, where he saw Lucy sat in Mr Haskins lap, in a second, he ran and jumped up on the table and then slowly walked towards his temptress Lucy. Gently stroking his rigid cock as he walked, in seconds, he was standing in front of her up on the table; he suddenly dropped to his knees and stuck his rigid cock in her face.

Lucy smiled and then took hold of his cock that was impersonating a rocket and put it in her mouth; it felt so hard, and it was like she was sucking on a rocket-shaped ice lollipop. Ned loved the feeling of her velvety lips on his rigid cock that he never heard Jane quietly enter and begin removing her clothes. Naked she quietly crept towards the table, and then Ned's eyes suddenly opened wide, as a hand cupped his balls and gently squeezed them.

'What the fuck,' he softly murmured; as the hand slowly went from his balls and caressed his butt cheek, he suddenly shouted, 'Fuck me.'

As a finger was pushed up his butt, one finger quickly became two; Ned was suddenly aching to fart, but if he farted would it be wind or something else on despatch? Jane whispered, 'Are you going to fuck me?'

The startled Ned looked around and saw the naked Jane and whispered, 'Hello, sweetie, if you remove those two fingers from my asshole, I'm ready.'

On hearing this, Jane slowly withdrew her two fingers and then ran over to Mr Haskins washroom and quickly washed her hands; on her return she saw Ned sitting with his rigid cock staring up at the ceiling. She softly kissed his lips and then turned around and slowly sat down in Ned's lap; her eyes opened wide as she felt his rock hard cock enter her pussy. She began to bob up and down on that hard cock, so aching to be fucked in the missionary position. Where Ned was in control of his thrusting rigid cock, she wanted to feel the full force of his wonderful rigid cock and quickly stood and lay down on the floor. Ned smiled and got down on top of her and guided his rigid cock through her hairy bush and entered her simmering pussy.

He began his thrusting slow at first at the tempo of the tap that wouldn't stop dripping, but Jane ached for it to harder and faster and whispered, 'Harder, darling. Let me feel it.'

Ned smiled but instead of upping the pace of his thrusting, he began slam dunking her pussy.

'Oh yes. That's it,' whispered the murmuring Jane.

On seeing this, Lucy too was aching to be fucked hard and quickly stood and lay down on the floor, pointing to her shaven haven, saying, 'Fuck me, fuck me hard, old man. I want to feel your rigid cock inside there now.'

Haskins quickly stood and resumed the missionary position on top of Lucy and guided his rigid cock into her shaven haven. This was his time for action; it had been along time but he was eager to perform. He started his thrusting slow at the tempo of the tap that wouldn't stop dripping. His mind was saying, *No not like this, fuck her hard. She wants to feel the full force of your rigid cock. It has been a along time, old boy. You're not out on a Sunday leisurely drive. Fuck her, fuck her hard, silly.*

Haskins was so enjoying his leisurely ride; he didn't want to do what his mind was telling him, so he whispered, 'Mistress Lucy, can I please fuck you doggy style?'

Lucy nodded her head in agreement, as Haskins slowly withdrew his rigid cock and quickly moved to the side to enable Lucy to roll over and get up on her hands and knees ready for doggy style action. Haskins shimmed towards her with his rigid cock in hand, guiding it towards her shaven haven; in seconds, he was penetrating her and he was off, slowly thrusting at first at the tempo of the tap that wouldn't stop dripping, and on every withdrawal stroke, he slapped her ass.

Lucy loved the feel of those tingling sensations in her ass cheek and began encouraging him to slap her harder, by saying, 'Oh, Mr Haskins, are you smacking me for being a naughty girl?'

On hearing this, Haskins smiled and instantly upped the pace of his thrusting to the new tempo of the clock that wouldn't stop ticking, thus extinguishing his slapping hand. Lucy so loved the alternate thrusting change and began crying out, 'Harder, sir, go on. I want to feel it.'

Haskins smiled; it had been along time since his rigid cock had seen pussy action. He didn't want it to ever end and thus slowed his thrusting back to the tempo of the tap that wouldn't stop dripping.

Lucy wanted it harder and faster but yearned for Mr Haskins wishes; he was in control as he was going to pay her, for such a privilege of fucking her voluptuous body. Suddenly Haskins murmured, 'Oh-oh.'

As his milk balls began to churn and in his mind, game over lay only seconds away, there was no stopping his milky-white fluids, as they gushed from his rigid cock into her quivering pussy; *That was it,* he thought as he slowly withdrew his cock. But he couldn't believe his eyes when he looked down and saw his rigid cock staring back at him.

'What's going on?' he murmured. 'Why is my cock still hard?'

'Me too,' shouted the flabbergasted Ned. 'I've just cum and my cock is as hard as a rock.'

CHAPTER 9

'ENCORE ANYBODY?' ASKED the smiling Lucy as she pointed at their rigid cocks and said, 'Well, shall we change partners, or would you rather fuck me in the ass, Mr Haskins?'

'Fuck you in the ass,' replied the intrigued Mr Haskins, who then said, 'But it seems such a tiny hole for this big cock of mine.'

On hearing this, Lucy began to laugh, as she looked around at his six-inch rigid cock, then turned around and began sucking on his rigid cock. Haskins closed his eyes; she had lips of velvet and her sucking was so intense. Then his eyes opened wide when she began to hum, which sent tingling sensations down his rigid cock; he couldn't contain his excitement and shot a second load of cum into her suckling mouth again he thought that would be game over, but it wasn't. He rubbed his eyes in disbelief as his cock was still hard and starring up at him. Lucy smiled and whispered, 'Look, Mr Haskins, It's still hard. Any chance of you fucking me in the asshole or what old man?'

The puzzled Haskins looked at her, not knowing what to do, as he had never had the pleasure of doing a back-door entry before. Did he really want to start now? Being a man of seventy-five, he shrugged his shoulders and whispered, 'I don't know, honey, I have never fucked anybody in the ass before.'

Lucy smiled and whispered, 'Well, there's a first time for everything, even at the tender age of seventy-five.'

Haskins stared at her and then bent and tenderly kissed her lips and then whispered, 'Okay, honey, I will give it a go.'

With that Lucy shouted, 'Yippee.'

Then she turned around still on all fours and whispered, 'Lubrication first spit on my ass before entry.'

As Haskins bent down to spit on her asshole, he got a shock. Lucy farted in his face; the room was filled with laughter at the sound of the loud fart, still blowing in Haskins face.

'I don't believe it,' shouted the red-faced Haskins, who was choking on Lucy's smelly smell, then shouted, 'Pooh e, that really smells.'

With that, he smacked her as hard as he could on her bare ass, which brought tears to Lucy's eyes; she kept calm and waited as the encore was seconds away. As Haskins bent again to begin spitting on her asshole, Lucy let rip for the final time louder than before by golly it smelt like a sewer. Haskins didn't know whether to laugh or cry as he choked on her awful smell.

This time he took his rigid cock in hand and placed it up against her asshole; he was going in dry as he didn't care, as it wasn't his asshole he was about to penetrate. Lucy's eyes opened wide as his rigid cock slowly plunged in, by gummy it was a tight squeeze, but there was no stopping him now. He was a man on a mission, a mission to seriously fuck his voluptuous secretary's ass.

Lucy began pulling faces as his rigid cock plunged into her ass; the revitalised Haskins was off at the tempo of the tap that wouldn't stop dripping. Lucy's ass seemed to be on fire as his rigid cock plunged in and out; she couldn't stand it and screamed, 'Steady on there, you old fart. My ass is on fire.'

Haskins smiled and then whispered, 'What do you want me to do, honey, ring for a fireman to extinguish those burning flames. Ha-ha.'

Hearing this Lucy smiled and whispered 'that's all right, Mr Haskins, It's my turn next, and I hope you're open-minded, old man.'

With that, Haskins froze. What had he done and what did she mean by those words open-minded?

'Oh-oh,' he suddenly murmured as he quickly withdrew his rigid cock, wishing it had never been reborn.

'Ah, that feels better,' whispered the now Mistress Lucy in her dominatrix role, and she suddenly screamed, 'Get up and bend over that table, old man.'

The frightened Haskins quickly resumed the position, still wondering what he had done wrong; his legs began to shake when Mistress Lucy wrapped a scarf around his head, thus extinguishing the light, and then whispered, 'I hope you're ready, sir.'

'Ready for what?' replied the nervously shaking Mr Haskins.

Lucy smiled and then whispered in his ear, 'You've been a naughty boy, and I must punish you, Mr Haskins.'

'Oh no!' murmured Haskins as he let go of the loudest fart you ever did hear; he was quietly praying he wouldn't follow through with the next one. He was literally shitting himself as he was so scared, being a man of seventy-five and any sudden shocks could be fatal to his heart.

He couldn't stand the anxiety any longer and whispered, 'Look, Lucy, I know I have been a naughty boy, but can I be punished with a fine than the punishment you have in mind?'

Lucy smiled and was intrigued at how much he would offer and whispered, 'How much?'

Haskins breathed a sigh of relief as he whispered, 'A hundred thousand dollars if you call it a day.' On hearing this, Lucy's jaw dropped. A hundred thousand dollars was a lot of money and she began saying, 'Yes . . . yes . . . yes.'

The dumbfounded Ned and Jane shook their heads in disbelief at the sum of money Mr Haskins was offering to forfeit his punishment. They stared at the joy of the naked Lucy, dancing around ecstatically, already strapped and ready for action. She sighed, 'A hundred thousand dollars, and we will call it a day.'

Ned stared at that almighty tool around Lucy's waist, that ten inch strap-a-dick-to-me thingy, and yelped, 'Fuck me. I'm next if Haskins is paying instead of taking his punishment like a man.'

On hearing this, the joyous Lucy turned and faced him and said, 'Yes, Ned. I am ready to oblige you.'

The horrified Ned couldn't speak and couldn't run as he was trapped in no man's land. His eyes opened wide as Lucy slowly walked towards him, gently stroking that big ten-inch rubber cock and whispered, 'Are you ready, Ned, to take it like a man?'

The laughing Jane whispered, 'Yes, Ned, you did imply earlier you wanted to be fucked, so please go over and resume the position.'

Ned stared at her in disbelief and whispered, 'You're kidding, right? Have you seen the size of that rubber cock? It's huge and it is not going up my ass.'

On hearing this, the two ladies began to laugh and then dominatrix Lucy came to life shouting, 'Listen, little man, you keep saying fuck me, so bend over that table and spread your legs so that I can fuck you with this big rubber cock.'

Ned couldn't believe it; he was slowly walking towards the table to resume the position and take it like a man. As he bent over the table and spread his legs, Jane was instantly by his side knelt and spread his ass cheeks and began spitting into his asshole. With his asshole lubricated, Lucy moved closer and placed that big rubber cock up against his asshole.

'Oh no!' murmured Ned as she slowly pushed forward and in plunged that big rubber cock.

'Oh my goodness!' cried Ned; his ass had never experienced this sort of action. He began pulling faces and shouting, 'Oh-ha.'

As Lucy began to slowly thrust in and out at the tempo of the tap that wouldn't stop dripping, Ned's eyes began to water and teardrops rolled down his face. These were not tears of pleasure but tears of pain as his ass felt like it was on fire.

Why hadn't he run was what he kept asking himself, as the pain shot through his body from the slow plunging rubber cock. He couldn't restrain himself any longer and shouted, 'Please stop, Mistress Lucy. I can't take it any more.'

On hearing this, the smiling slow plunging Lucy whispered, 'Oh poor boy, am I hurting you?'

'Yes, yes, yes, you are,' screamed Ned.

Lucy smiled and took it to another level by slapping his ass on every withdrawal thrust.

'No more, please no more,' pleaded the anguished Ned.

On hearing this, the kind-hearted Lucy stopped her thrusting and instantly withdrew that big rubber cock.

Then she turned and stared at the observing Mr Haskins and said, 'How are you paying your forfeit money, cash or cheque, sir?'

Mr Haskins stared at the voluptuous Lucy and whispered, 'What money, honey?'

On hearing this, Lucy stood and slowly walked towards him, whispering, 'Money or this up your ass, old man.'

She pointed down at her wonderful sex tool, the ten-inch strap-a-dick-to-me, and whispered,

'your money or your ass?'

The coy Mr Haskins smiled and replied, 'I don't know what you mean, Miss, by those words, money or my ass?'

Lucy stared at him, wishing she had her whip with her to give this grinning fraudster a whipping he deserved. One minute she was thinking of early retirement; and it was taken away by a grinning old prick. In trying to fight her anxiety, she suddenly lost control and took off the strap-a-dick-to-me and held it firmly in her hand and then slowly walked towards now-frowning Mr Haskins, who was frantically wondering, *What was going on?*

Standing in front of him, dominatrix Lucy said, 'For the last time, old man, my money or your asshole?'

Haskins shrugged his shoulders and was about to speak, as Lucy's fist fast approached his face and hit him full on his big noise. That was it game over, job over and day over. She looked down and smiled, when she saw Haskins cock still rigid and looking up at the ceiling and then whispered, 'I want my money.'

On hearing this, Haskins began to laugh, but that struck a match in Lucy's frustration, and she kicked him straight in the nuts. On impact Haskins eyes opened wide, as the full force took his breath away. Then came Lucy's flustered words. 'Goodbye, you old fart, you can stick this job up your ass as I'm off.'

The bewildered Haskins whispered, 'No no, you must stay. I will pay, Mistress Lucy.'

On hearing this, the naked Lucy walked over to the safe and took out a cheque book and wrote a cheque to herself for a hundred thousand dollars and presented it in front of Haskins for signing.

Haskins signed it instantly and handed it to Lucy, who took it gracefully, and to show there was no hard feeling, she softly kissed his cheek and whispered, 'You are a naughty boy.'

With that, she fell to her knees and began sucking on his still rigid cock. Haskins loved the feeling of her velvety lips and closed his eyes to enjoy the moment. As Ned and Jane quickly dressed and returned to their place of work, leaving the voluptuous Lucy sucking on Haskins rigid cock.

Haskins loved the moment that he lost momentum and whispered, 'Marry me, Lucy. I will reward you handsomely.'

CHAPTER 10

O N HEARING THIS, Lucy was dumbfounded and let his rigid cock fall from her mouth and stared up open-mouthed at the smiling Mr Haskins. She was so overwhelmed by his proposal and she murmured, 'what, did you say, Mr Haskins?'

Haskins smiled and whispered, 'Will you marry me, Lucy? Your life will not change. My only request is that you will sleep with me every night so I can hold you and cuddle up to you real tight, till death do us part.'

Then he hit a switch and out blasted Elvis singing, 'Holy smokes and sakes alive. I never thought this could happen to me. I got stung by a sweet honey bee'

On hearing these words, Lucy blushed and got up and straddled Mr Haskins and sat down in his lap and gasped, 'Oh.'

As Mr Haskins guided his erect cock into her shaven haven, she was so happy she wanted to passionately kiss him, but that was never going to happen, as he had a face shrivelled up like a dried prune, and passionate kiss was not for her. Instead she whispered, 'Mr Haskins, I don't know what to say?'

'Yes would be nice,' replied the smiling Mr Haskins.

Lucy thought of succulent strawberries as she leaned forward and tenderly kissed his lips and then cringed when Haskins responded with a probing tongue. She was in hell, but still her mind was switched on like a cash register, thinking up a cast-iron prenuptial agreement to seal the deal.

As their lips parted, she whispered, 'Yes, but there is only one problem.'

'Problem? What problem?' replied the bewildered Mr Haskins.

'The prenuptial agreement,' whispered the smiling Lucy.

'What prenuptial agreement?' asked the intrigued Mr Haskins?

'Well, we will have to have one of those,' replied the straight-faced Lucy, who was portraying a high class business woman.

'You want to marry me, and I have no such desires in marrying you.'

The puzzled Haskins frowned as he had never encountered this before, not even from his young present wife. His eyes suddenly opened wide when he thought of her. 'Oh no!' he murmured.

'What's wrong?' whispered the concerned Lucy, whose mind was engrossed by dollar symbols. She had this desire to swim naked in a pool of dollar bills. Haskins suddenly became a mime and said no more and then bent his head and began sucking on those strawberry nipples. His heart was breaking; he wanted voluptuous Lucy to be his only desire. Her body was of a Greek goddess, with Miss Plentiful tits and slender hips.

She was gorgeous; he couldn't stand it as a teardrop rolled down his face and he began sobbing.

'What is wrong?' asked the concerned Lucy.

With her mind still calculating the many dollars that would be coming her way if she married the old Mr Haskins, her only concern was how much she would put on a prenuptial agreement, as if he died on their wedding night, she might not get anything.

Then the bombshell hit her, bringing her back down from money dream land, when Haskins whispered, 'I can't marry you. My wife won't like that.'

The dumb founded Lucy stared into his eyes, not believing what she was hearing, one minute a proposal the next a bombshell. She smiled and then stood up and slapped Haskins's face hard and shouted, 'Who do you think you are proposing to and then saying you are only kidding?'

With that, she turned and walked away, while Haskins vigorously stroked his rigid cock, while he watched the voluptuous Lucy dress and murmured, 'Oh no!'

As his balls suddenly tightened and his milky-white fluids shot into the air, he couldn't believe what he had seen. It had been a long time since he ejaculated like that. Lucy turned and smiled when she saw his milky-white fluids but didn't pay him know mind and turned and walked towards the door.

'Where are you going?' shrieked the horrified Mr Haskins; again Lucy didn't pay him no mind, as she opened the door and walked on to clear her desk as she would not be returning. On seeing her friends flushed face, the curious Jane asked, 'what's wrong, Lucy?'

Lucy smiled and whispered, 'I am leaving, Jane. I work evenings, so I don't need to be doing this, and Mr Haskins can get stuffed.'

With her bag full, she whispered her goodbyes to Jane and Ned and then picked up her purse and walked out of the office. She walked with a skip in her stride, and she was happy as she was off to deposit more money in the bank. Maybe there would be more titillation for young Danny boy. As she entered the bank, she saw Danny observing her long legs and murmured, 'It's play time.'

The bank was empty, so she walked straight to Danny's desk and whispered, 'Hello, Danny, can you please help me?'

Danny smiled and said, 'Yes of course, Lucy, please do take a seat.'

He was so aching to see her shaven haven once again and get her phone number if he dared to ask.

Lucy smiled and sat down and murmured, 'Let the games begin.'

As her bum hit the seat, she smiled at the observing Danny, whose eyes were glued to her exposed shaven haven, and thus began her play time, as she slowly crossed her legs.

'Oh no!' murmured the observing Danny, who was now staring at a long naked thigh, as something was rising and it certainly wasn't his temperature, no it was his sleeping cock looking for some action. Then came the shaven haven glimpse, as Lucy uncrossed her left leg, thus exposing her shaven haven shimmed on her chair and then slowly crossed her right leg over her left.

On seeing this, Danny's rigid cock was shouting, 'Let me out of here, fuck face. I want to fuck that bald pussy.'

Danny looked at Lucy and asked, 'How may I help you today?'

Lucy smiled and took the hundred thousand dollar cheque out of her purse and placed it in front of Danny and said, 'I would like to invest this.'

Danny picked the cheque up and murmured, 'Fuck me gently, look at that.'

On hearing this, Lucy smiled and whispered, 'Yes, I will fuck you.'

'Fuck . . . fuck me . . . me,' stuttered the bewildered Danny boy.

'Yes,' replied the smiling Lucy.

'You murmured fuck me and yes I will.'

She then took that ten-inch wonder toy from her purse and whispered, 'With this.'

On seeing the big rubber cock in front of him, Danny whispered, 'There's no effing way that's going up my butt. It's huge. It is bigger than mine.'

Lucy began laughing and uncrossed her legs, thus exposing her shaven haven for him to see, and then switched to titillation mood and gently began massaging her magical button. On seeing this, Danny's cock was throbbing in his pants, looking for a way out to fuck that bald pussy.

He whispered, 'Please could you put that big rubber cock away and please give me your number? I will ring you later and please stop that with your fingers.'

With that, he pointed down at her shaven haven, Lucy smiled and put the big rubber cock in her purse, then smiled as she inserted a finger into her moist pussy, and one finger quickly became two. Danny couldn't believe what he was seeing, this young lady was driving him crazy, with her erotic dirty sex show and he so wanted to see more. But that would have to be later, as he had to invest the hundred thousand dollars for her.

And then it was finger-licking time, as Lucy pulled those two fingers from her wet pussy and put them on Danny's lips. Once again she had put temptation in front of him and he couldn't resist. He was like an alcoholic supping the dregs of the glass. Her pussy juices tasted so good that he wanted to explore the real thing himself, with his probing flickering tongue. He was so excited his milk balls began to churn, and in seconds, he came in his pants.

'Oh no!' he murmured.

'Oh no what?' replied the intrigued Lucy.

'I came in my pants,' whispered Danny.

'You came in your pants?' replied the giggling Lucy.

'Shush!' whispered the nervous Danny boy, who smelt like he had just visited a seafood store. The aroma was so strong that he couldn't stand it any longer; he was losing his mind. How could he work, with the sultry temptress Lucy sexually teasing him, with her every move? He whispered, 'Lucy, I will invest your hundred thousand dollars in our platinum savers account, which offers 9 per cent annual interest.'

'Okay,' replied the smiling Lucy and then whispered, 'On one condition. You come and watch me dance and take me home later on tonight.'

On hearing 'the take me home later', Danny's eyes opened wide, as he thought of that ten-inch rubber cock in her purse and her wishes to strap it on and fuck him in the ass. What was he to do? He wanted to watch her dance, but the other thing was out of bounds. He smiled and then whispered, 'Okay, I will be along later to watch you dance.'

With that, he filled the application form and printed it off and then put it in front of Lucy for signing. Before Lucy took the pen from him, she plunged two fingers into her juicy pussy, thrust them in and out a couple of times and then withdrew them and placed them on Danny's lips. Danny instantly opened his mouth and sucked on those pussy-drenched fingers; they tasted so good. Thus began the wakening of his sleeping cock; in seconds, his cock was rigid once again in his pants, looking for some action.

After several minutes of sucking, Danny let those fingers slip from his mouth and handed Lucy the pen to sign said documents. Lucy took the pen from him and smiled and then signed the application form and then handed it back to him. The smiling Danny took it from her and went to stand but couldn't as he had a raging hard-on and a wet patch in his pants. He said, 'Thank you, Miss Lucy; I will see you later on tonight.'

Lucy smiled, stood up, leaned over the table, and softly kissed his lips. Danny was caught hook, line and sinker. He would be her sexual slave tonight; whatever she asked he would do. He would throw his reservations to the side and enjoy the moment with the voluptuous Lucy.

Lucy stood upright and whispered, 'Goodbye.'

Then she turned and walked away. On seeing her departure, Miss. Blundell rushed over and said, 'Danny, we have to talk. Please accompany me to my office.'

Danny was mortified; he couldn't stand because of the raging hard-on in his pants and his wet patch too. He whispered, 'Is it important, Miss. Blundell?'

'Yes it is,' replied the furious blushing Miss. Blundell. Danny smiled and slowly stood holding a file over his crotch and quickly followed Miss. Blundell to her office. Once inside Miss. Blundell closed and locked the door and then turned and faced him and ripped open her popper jacket, thus exposing her naked breasts. Danny stared open-mouthed at her naked breasts and placed the file on the table, thus exposing his bulging pants.

Miss. Blundell gasped, 'Oh,' and quickly walked a couple of paces and then dropped to her knees and opened Danny's pants and released his rigid cock and wrapped her lips around it and began to suck. But her burning desire was to have his rigid cock inside her simmering pussy and not her sucking mouth. She then let his rigid cock fall from her mouth, stood, and lifted her skirt and bent over the table and whispered, 'Fuck me, Danny boy.'

Danny stepped back and stared at her shapely ass. She was panties free and ready for action. He took his rigid cock in hand and guided it towards her simmering pussy; her eyes opened wide as his rigid cock entered her pussy. Danny was off slowly thrusting at the tempo of the tap that wouldn't stop dripping. He was stoking Miss. Blundell's sexual demons; she whispered, 'Harder, Danny boy, fuck me harder.'

On hearing this, Danny boy increased his thrusting to the new tempo of the clock that wouldn't stop ticking.

'Oh yes, yes, that's it, Danny boy,' murmured the sexually electrified Miss. Blundell, who was biting her lip to silence her cries. Her pussy was on fire from Danny's fast-thrusting cock. She began shouting, 'Yes, yes, yes.'

As she approached Climax City at breakneck speed, the nervous Danny put his hand over her mouth and whispered, 'Shush!'

But it was too late she had reached her destination and was experiencing that orgasmic moment. That was a great moment for her, but Danny hadn't finished and carried on thrusting at the tempo of the clock that wouldn't stop ticking. Miss. Blundell was humming M-M-M-M as his rigid cock thrust in and out of her quivering pussy at the speed of the ticking clock. Her heart was racing; her mind in frenzy: Was someone looking for her? Would she be caught with her panties down, being seriously fucked by the amorous Danny boy?

She couldn't stand it any longer and bit Danny's finger and whispered, 'Please stop, Danny boy.'

On hearing this, Danny instantly stopped his thrusting and then withdrew his rigid cock and vigorously began stroking his rigid cock. Then the game was over as his balls tightened and his milky-white fluids shot into the air and landed on Miss. Blundell's open jacket and her butt too.

CHAPTER 11

IT WAS 5 p.m. as the sultry temptress Lucy entered In Your Vision, unaware that she had been secretly followed by the curious Jane. Lucy walked straight to Sally's office to discuss stripping. She was done with being a waitress, and she needed to earn a lot of money, as this would be her only source of income. She knocked on Sally's door and waited; after only a few seconds, the door was opened by the smiling Sally, who said, 'Come in, Lucy. I want to discuss stripping with you.'

Lucy smiled and slowly entered, kissing Sally on the cheek as she walked by, and sat down. Sally closed the door and quickly took her seat and said, 'Lucy, I want you to perform every night, as the In Your Vision star light girl. I will pay you two hundred dollars a night for one tantalising strip. What do you say?'

Lucy was dumbfounded by the offer and shouted.

'Yes, yes, yes.'

Sally smiled; she had got Lucy as the dream girl. She then stood and walked around the table and lightly kissed Lucy on the cheek, then whispered, 'When do you want to start, Lucy?'

'Tonight,' replied the smiling Lucy, who slowly stood and walked towards the door; in seconds, she was outside dancing. She was ecstatic with excitement; she couldn't believe it, two hundred dollars a night plus tips for a one star performer strip. She needed sexual pleasure and ran to the toilet to fulfil her need; she would become a member of the Master Bates society.

As she entered the cubicle, she turned and shut the door and lifted her short skirt and sat down on the toilet and opened her purse and took out that big rubber cock and stared in disbelief. It was covered with pooh.

'Oh-e,' she shrieked, stood, and pushed her short skirt down and opened the door and then got the shock of her life as there stood the smiling Jane asking, 'What you doing?'

Lucy smiled and walked a couple of steps and softly kissed her lips. Jane instantly responded by wrapping her arms around her and delicately probing Lucy's mouth with her tongue. Lucy then slowly began walking backwards into the toilet cubicle. It was pussy-licking time, but who was going to do the licking?

Lucy suddenly stopped where she was and whispered, 'Jane, do you want to give or receive?'

'Give,' replied the anxious Jane who was eager to probe Lucy's shaven haven with her flickering tongue. On hearing this, Lucy twirled her around and Jane backed into the cubicle and sat down on the toilet, while Lucy ran over to the sink and quickly washed the dirty ten-inch rubber cock. With the big rubber cock washed and dry, Lucy turned and ran and joined Jane in the cubicle. Her pussy was aching for sexual play, whether it be a probing tongue or big rubber cock she didn't care. She just wanted sexual satisfaction.

As she closed the door, she felt Jane undo her skirt and let it fall to the floor, and in seconds her tongue began probing her magical button. Lucy was in heaven, but still she wanted more and whispered, 'Hey, Jane, use this.'

As she handed Jane that big rubber cock, Jane smiled as she took it from her and sucked on its bald head. Lubricated she slowly pushed it up inside Lucy's aching pussy and again attacked Lucy's magical button with her probing flickering tongue. Those sensations were wonderful, but more was yet to come, as Jane had purchased a small vibrator while Lucy was in the bank.

While she held that big rubber cock inside Lucy's quivering pussy, she opened up her purse and took out the small vibrator. Then she turned it on and placed it against Lucy's skin, just above her magical button. Feeling the vibrating sensations against her skin, Lucy looked down and smiled when she saw the new sex toy and whispered, 'Where did you get that from, Jane?'

'From the sex shop', whispered Jane, 'whilst you were busy in the bank.'

'Oh,' murmured the voluptuous Lucy, who was on her way to destination Climax City; here she comes. As Jane was about to probe Lucy's magical button with her flickering tongue, she whispered, 'Yippee!'

When she saw an on-off switch on the ten-inch rubber cock, she quickly put the small vibrator in her mouth and turned the big rubber cock on.

'Oh yes,' murmured the ecstatic Lucy as the vibrating sensations flooded her pussy. With that, Jane took the small vibrator out of her mouth and once again placed it against Lucy's skin just above her magical button. Then she probed Lucy's magical button with her flickering tongue. Lucy's mind was all shook up from the onslaught of sensations; she began murmuring, 'Yes, yes, yes, oh, yes.'

She was fast approaching Climax City at breakneck speed. She began screaming, 'Yes, yes, yes.'

The closer she got, there was no stopping her now; with her body shaking and her knees weak, she began screaming, 'Yes, yes, yes, I'm cumming.'

As she arrived at Climax City and was experiencing that magical orgasmic moment, that was a wonderful moment. With her legs shaking, she slowly squatted and tenderly kissed Jane's lips and whispered, 'Oh, that was wonderful, Jane. Please can you help me?'

Jane looked puzzled and curiously asked, 'what do you need my help with, Lucy?'

Lucy smiled and whispered, 'To pick my costume, silly. I'm a stripper.'

Jane stared at her in disbelief and whispered, 'Stripper? You're a stripper?'

'Yes,' replied Lucy as she slowly pulled the vibrating rubber cock from her pussy and then put it on Jane's lips,

'Wow, it's Lollipop time,' whispered Jane as she took the big rubber cock from Lucy and began sucking on its bald head. Lucy's juices tasted divine. Lucy smiled and put her short skirt on and opened the door; she took the sucking Jane by the hand and led her to the costume room.

Jane couldn't believe her eyes when Lucy opened the door, and there were several naked ladies picking out their costumes. Lucy then walked straight in and shed her clothes and walked over to the lingerie and picked her naughty panties and bra.

Jane couldn't believe her eyes in, what Lucy picked a string thong and bra too; Lucy handed them to her and walked over to the clothes rack to pick her costume. She picked a very short dress that barely covered the cheeks of her butt and then came a tasselled waist coat that enhanced her ample charms when done up.

With her costume picked, she walked over to the vanity mirror to dress her face; tonight she was going to be a street call girl, but she wasn't cheap as it would once again be $10 peak a view time. If those horny customers wanted to see her bits and pieces, they each would have to pay, to have the pleasure of seeing those bits and pieces naked.

She sat by the mirror, heavily painting her face with make up; she was going to be the tartest call girl the customers ever did see. With her face dressed, she stood and put on those tiny panties; Jane smiled when Lucy bent over as it looked like she was smiling at her with black teeth.

With her thong on, scarcely covering her shaven haven, Lucy turned around and kissed her stunned friend Jane on the lips and whispered, 'Are you up for any fun later Jane?'

On hearing this, the flabbergasted Jane whispered, 'Yes, I am, but I'm not stripping.'

Lucy smiled as she took the bra from her and quickly put it on; by gummy it barely covered her strawberry-size nipples. She looked sensational in just her bra and panties; she was a horny temptress everyone in the Master Bates society would dream. Then on went the short dress; by gummy it was short. Then on went the waist coat, and she was ready to tease. She was about to go out to wait by the stage, when in walked the smiling Sally, saying, 'You look gorgeous darling.'

Lucy smiled and delicately kissed her on the cheek and whispered, 'I am ready to tease those horny customers of yours, Sally.'

On hearing this, Sally smiled and whispered, 'Give me five minutes and then come to the stage, and your music will be ready.'

Sally then quickly walked back to her office to get an Elvis track; the long-legged girl with the short dress on ran out to the stage and handed it to the DJ and then picked up the microphone and said, 'Gentleman, we've got a treat for you tonight. She drove you crazy last night. Here is the voluptuous Lucy.'

With that the DJ hit the music button and out blasted the singing Elvis.

All right
I've been thumbing rides travelling light
Walked the streets till past midnight
Tramping roads trails and lanes
Scaling cliffs fields and plains
Searching till the early dawn
For that long legged girl with the short dress on,

With that out walked the stunning voluptuous Lucy, waving to the open-mouthed spectators of the club and began swivelling her hips to the music. Up went her short dress, revealing her tiny black thong panties; it was all hands on cocks for the patrons of the Master Bates society of hand wanker's. They quickly unbuttoned their pants and released their sleeping cocks and then gently began stroking it as they watched the voluptuous Lucy dance.

Their cocks were rigid in their hands; they were masturbating. The teasing temptress turned around and wiggled her hips and then teasingly looked around and smiled; the Master Bates society wasn't ready for what was coming. When the horny temptress slowly leaned forward, up went the tiny dress, revealing her smiling ass.

'Oh no!' murmured Charlie, as he prematurely shot his load; game over for him and the loss of a paying customer for Lucy, but was it? As he tucked his deflating cock back in his pants and did them up, the observing Lucy was watching his every move. As Charlie went to stand up, Lucy picked up the microphone and said, 'Where do you think you are going, Charlie?'

The open-mouthed Charlie stared at her in disbelief. *How did she know my name?* he wondered. He then shrugged his shoulders and walked off towards the bathroom; the teasing Lucy stopped him dead in his tracks, when she whispered into the microphone, 'Well, gentleman, there goes premature Charlie, the man who cum's in an instant and that was only on seeing my ass. Oh you must be the master in your bedroom. Hey, Charlie, I bet your wife's never had a headache, hey, Charlie, having sex with the man who cum's in a jiffy.' With that, *laughter* filled the room, and the red-faced Charlie ran off to men's bathroom to hide. On seeing him run, Lucy began to laugh, as she slowly took the waist coat off to the clapping audience. Then came more teasing as she slowly removed the dress and stood there in her tiny panties and bra, which didn't leave much to those horny onlookers imagination. Then came her money request.

'If you want to see more, it's going to cost you.'

'How much?' shouted the returning Charlie.

'Twenty dollars a piece for an all-clothes-off striptease'

'How much for a solo strip tease out back?' whispered Charlie who was standing in front of her.

Lucy then squatted and whispered, 'You couldn't afford it, Charlie.'

With that, she took hold of his hand and placed it under her pussy, then whispered, 'Do you want to sample my hidden delights?'

With that, she pulled her thong to the side, thus exposing her shaven haven for all to see, then took hold of his finger and slipped it inside her bald pussy and whispered, 'Wiggle it around, silly.'

On hearing that, Charlie wiggled his finger and slowly withdrew it and sucked on that finger tasting her juices. He then whispered, 'Oh-Oh!'

As his sleeping cock began to rise, looking for some pussy action, he couldn't stand her teasing any more and put his hand behind her head and pulled her face towards him and tenderly kissed her lips and whispered, 'I do really want to fuck you. How much for a know holds bar private dance?'

Lucy smiled and whispered, 'That sort of pleasure costs one thousand dollars.'

Charlie stared at her open-mouthed; a thousand dollars was a lot of money, but he had to have this horny temptress. He whispered, 'Okay, I want one of your private dances.'

With that, Lucy reached down and cupped his bulging pants and smiled when she felt a rigid cock in his pants. *Oh how she craved for that rigid cock to be fucking her simmering pussy!* She then tenderly kissed his lips and let go of his crotch, as she slowly stood and picked up the microphone and said, 'Gentleman, I am feeling real horny tonight for a no holds sexy striptease, where I will join the Master Bates society, and massage myself here on the stage will cost $50 a piece.'

On hearing this, they all rushed towards the stage waving their fifty dollars; the smiling Lucy willingly took their fifty dollars and waved for Jane to approach the stage. On seeing Lucy's waving hand, Jane rushed up to the stage and took the money from her and put it in her purse.

With all the money collected, Lucy began dancing, as she waited for those horny customers to take to their seats. With all butts on seats, she slowly began the show. She slowly pulled her bra strap down and then unmasked her breast to show an erect nipple and quickly covered it.

On seeing this, all the customers joined the Master Bates society and whipped out their sleeping cocks and gently began to stroke them as they watched. On seeing this, Lucy smiled and slowly pulled the other strap down and then unmasked her left breast again, revealing an erect nipple to the engrossed Master Bates society. Then off came the bra to the cheers of those horny men; Lucy was in the groove as she swivelled her hips and wobbled her massive tits at those horny onlookers.

'More, more, more,' shouted the Master Bates society of hand wanker's.

CHAPTER 12

O N HEARING THIS, the teasing Lucy turned around and leaned forward and then began wiggling her bottom to the cheers of those horny men. Then slowly she pulled those tiny thong panties down.

'There's a full moon shinning,' shouted one horny patron with his finger pointing to her wiggling ass, as the spotlight shone on it; on hearing this, Lucy looked around and smiled, as she picked up the microphone and whispered, 'It was a stormy night as the wind blew.'

With that, she put the microphone to her ass and let go of the loudest fart you ever did hear, as it was in stereo. Those horny men were in fits of laughter; then off came those tiny panties to the roars of the cheering audience.

'More, more, more,' they shouted as the teasing temptress took a step to the side and then leaned forward, thus exposing her asshole and shaven haven too. Sally watched intrigued by her new hot sensation and wondered what Lucy meant by saying she was joining the Master Bates society. The answer came soon enough; when Lucy turned around and asked for a chair, one of the bouncers quickly put the chair on the stage. Lucy smiled as she put it into position at the front of the stage and sat down and then spread her legs and gently began massaging her magical button.

Those horny onlookers were entranced by what they were seeing, so was Sally. She had never seen any of her girls do this before. She too was getting turned on by that sultry temptress Lucy and lifted her skirt and slipped her hand inside her panties and gently began massaging her own magical button as she watched.

Lucy had captured the entire audience with her sexual masturbation show; while she gently massaged her magical button, those horny men were throttling their rigid cocks. Even Jane had taken her knickers off and had her skirt up around her waist, while her fingers frantically massaged her magical button while she watched. She was unaware that she was being watched by the suave bouncer Freddie Good-Enough, who was eager to taste her hairy pussy.

While he watched Jane massage her magical button, he made his way to his boss Sally who too was pleasuring herself, as she watched that sultry temptress Lucy. He whispered in her ear, 'Sally, do you mind if I have a break.'

Sally nodded her head, as she didn't care she was on the verge of an all mighty orgasm. As she watched the temptress Lucy do her fantastic stage show, it happened as Lucy began screaming, 'Yes, yes, yes, I'm coming.'

Then her pussy sprayed her built-up fluids into the air; the audience gazed open-mouthed as they watched her spraying pussy juices. Sally's heart missed a beat as she watched in amazement, wondering what this temptress Lucy wouldn't do; she fast approached the stage, waving her hands in the air, shouting, 'That's enough Lucy; I want to see you in my office.'

Lucy smiled and whispered, 'Won't be a moment.'

Sally then turned around and walked towards her office and then suddenly stopped and stared at a white ass going up and down. Someone was having sex in her club.

'What the fuck?' she cried.

On hearing her shriek, Freddie looked around and smiled and then whispered, 'Anything wrong boss?'

Sally then pointed at him and shouted, 'what the fuck are you doing, Freddie? You are supposed to be working, not fucking somebody. It seems like you're fucking me when you're fucking her.'

Freddie smiled as he watched his angry boss walk away and then continued shagging Jane. Lucy smiled when she walked by and waved at the sexually active Jane being seriously shagged by that beefy bouncer Freddie. Lucy knocked on Sally's door and waited. After several moments, she heard Sally shout, 'Come in.'

She entered cautiously, not knowing what this was all about, and then stopped and stared open-mouthed at the naked Sally and a pile of cash. *What was going on,* she wondered as she walked towards the desk.

'How much', whispered Sally, 'for a one-on-one sexual experience with you, Lucy? I have never before seen anything like your stage show, and I want a piece of the action too.'

On hearing this, Lucy smiled; she hadn't expected a confrontation like this and whispered, 'Can you give me a moment, Sally. I have just got to get something from my purse.'

Lucy quickly left the room, leaving Sally all alone puzzling what she was getting; on her return, the smiling Lucy walked in naked, wearing the strap-a-dick-to-me and whispered, 'Five hundred dollars for a quick shag and much more if you want.'

Sally looked at her with a puzzled face. If she wanted to be shagged, there were plenty of men outside to do that with; but again Lucy intrigued her by wearing that big rubber cock. There weren't too many men out there with a cock that size. She smiled and whispered, 'How do you want me, Miss Lucy?'

'Come round here and bend over your desk and spread your legs,' replied the smiling Lucy. Sally stood showing Lucy her full frontal nudity; she had the body of a fashion girl, slim and so divine. As she approached Lucy, she stopped and that's where the games began; Lucy's lips tenderly kissed hers, as her hands caressed her ass cheeks. Sally was under the influence of her dominant partner and responded with her own roaming hands caressing Lucy's voluptuous ass.

Suddenly Sally's mind was all shook up, when Lucy delicately began massaging her magical button; never before had a woman touched that button. Lucy's massaging fingers were driving her crazy; she loved those massaging fingers on her magical button. But Lucy's fingers were in exploratory mood, and Sally's eyes suddenly opened wide, as Lucy slipped a finger into her simmering pussy. One finger quickly became two as she went in search of the G spot,

'Oh my goodness!' whispered Sally as Lucy's fingers hit that spot.

Sally's body was suddenly engulfed with sensations, rushing up to her exploding mind. Her knees were weak; she couldn't seem to stand on her own feet. She wrapped her arms around Lucy and held on real tight; Lucy smiled and slowly withdrew those thrusting fingers and sucked the juices clean. Then she bent Sally over the table and spread her legs and then took the big rubber cock in hand and put it up against Sally's pussy.

Then with one gentle thrust in plunged that big rubber cock; Sally's eyes opened wide as the big rubber cock plunged deep into her pussy. The temptress Lucy began her thrusting slow at the tempo of the tap that wouldn't stop dripping. Sally's pussy was alive with sensations, but the temptress was only just beginning. As that big rubber cock slowly plunged in and out of Sally's quivering pussy, Lucy reached around and delicately began massaging her magical button.

Those sensations began driving Sally crazy; never before had anybody lit her body up this way. She was on her way to destination Climax City; here she comes. The temptress took her on a journey, a journey full of wonderful sensations that she hoped would never end. The temptress suddenly became the Dominatrix Queen; on every withdrawal stroke, she slapped Sally's ass hard, which sent tingling sensations up through her body to her exploding mind.

'Oh my goodness!' shrieked the sexually charged Sally; oh those sensations were coming from here, there, and every where. But still the Dominatrix temptress hadn't finished and upped her thrusting speed to the new tempo of the clock that wouldn't stop ticking.

'Oh yes, yes!' cried the sexually excited Sally as she got even closer to Climax City. Suddenly temptress Lucy slowed her thrusting and then stopped and slowly withdrew that big rubber cock. Sally's mind was in a haze as she wondered what

Lucy was going to do next; the wait was short-lived as Lucy wrapped her arm around her and eased her backwards to a standing position.

Then slowly she turned Sally around and then sat her down on the desk; it was pussy-licking time as she knelt and stared at Sally's pussy. In seconds, Lucy's tongue was probing her pussy, as her fingers gently massaged Sally's magical button. But this was merely an appetiser for what was still to come; the probing tongue suddenly swapped places with the massaging fingers. Whilst the probing tongue flickered over Sally's magical button, Lucy inserted a finger into Sally's wet pussy; one finger quickly became two as she went in search of the G spot. Sally's eyes opened wide when Lucy's two slow thrusting fingers hit that spot.

'Oh!' murmured Sally as a new onslaught of sensations rushed through her body up to her exploding mind.

'Yes, yes, oh yes,' she cried as she once again began her journey; Lucy's mind was suddenly distracted when she thought of the waiting Charlie and his one thousand dollars for a private striptease. Her fingers quickened up to the tempo of the clock that wouldn't stop ticking, each time caressing Sally's G spot. With her fluids building and her mind in a mess, little did Sally know she was on her way to her first pussy explosion? As the fluids began to dribble from her pussy, Lucy quickly withdrew her fingers and thus released Sally's built-up fluids spraying into the air.

With her body shaking and her screams filling the air, Sally experienced her first earth-shattering orgasmic moment. *Oh what a moment that was!*

Lucy then stood and lightly kissed Sally on the cheek and whispered, 'Later?'

Then she turned and walked towards the door, leaving the ecstatically trembling Sally staring at her behind. This was a sexual encounter that would be embedded in her mind forever. *Who was this sultry temptress?* Wandered Sally; in just two short nights, she had introduced her to a new world in the sexual tease of the striptease and so much more.

'Later, later, later,' murmured the puzzled Sally, as she repeated Lucy's leaving word to herself.

The naked Lucy skipped through the audience, still wearing that wonder toy, the strap-a-dick-to-me. Those horny onlookers rubbed their eyes in disbelief, each and every one of them wondering why Lucy was wearing that big rubber cock. Was she looking for someone's ass to shag?

'Oh no!' shrieked the open-mouthed Billy as the voluptuous Lucy skipped towards him; he frantically stood and ran towards the toilets as the loud laughter from those horny onlookers filled the air. As she approached open-mouthed and staring Charlie, she stopped and took hold of that big rubber cock and whispered, 'Are you ready, Charlie, for your private dance? I have a surprise for you.'

Charlie couldn't speak; his ass was rooted to the seat, as he stared at that big rubber cock in her hand. Then he suddenly whispered those immortal words, 'Fuck me. What are you wearing that for?'

His shaky finger pointed at that big rubber cock; on hearing this, Lucy smiled and whispered, 'As you wish, Master. If you would like to join me out the back, I'm strapped and ready for action.'

'What . . . what . . . action . . . action?' stuttered the nervously looking Charlie, who was panicking that his ass was about to be invaded by that big rubber cock. He couldn't stand this anxiety any longer and shouted, 'There's no effing way that's going up my ass.'

Lucy smiled as she stroked that big rubber cock and whispered, 'Are you quite sure it will be a tight squeeze, but I'm sure it will fit.'

The teasing was over as she leaned towards Charlie and tenderly kissed his lips, as her hand groped his sleeping cock; Charlie s eyes opened wide as his sleeping cock began to rise. Feeling that rigid cock in his pants, Lucy smiled and then whispered, 'Shall we go, Charlie? I'm in desperate need of a good shagging.'

On hearing this, Charlie smiled and then stood and followed the voluptuous Lucy to the quiet room for a good shagging. As they entered, Lucy became an erotic dancer, swivelling her hips as she seated the nervous Charlie. As Lucy continued swivelling her hips, Charlie's vision was not on her luscious curves but on that big rubber cock she was still wearing.

Lucy saw the anguished look on his face and un-strapped that big rubber cock from her swivelling hips and threw it to the side of the room. On seeing this, Charlie breathed a sigh of relief, as he watched the voluptuous Lucy doing her erotic dancing. With a rigid cock of his own throbbing in his pants, Charlie stood and quickly opened his pants and let them fall to his knees and then sat back down and began portraying Master Bates, as he gently stroked his rigid cock and watched the voluptuous Lucy dance. On seeing this, Lucy smiled and moved closer to Charlie and then dropped to her knees and began sucking on one of his balls, while Charlie continued gently stroking his rigid cock. Suddenly Charlie's eyes opened wide, as Lucy began to hum while she sucked on his balls.

'Oh that feels so good!' murmured Charlie, who was lost in the wonderful moment; never before had a woman sucked on his genitals that way. It felt sensational and yet more was still to come, as Lucy suddenly went from sucking his balls to sucking the bald head of his rigid cock. Charlie then moved his hand as Lucy's mouth engulfed his rigid cock; she was a deep throat expert and again hummed while she sucked.

Charlie closed his eyes as tingling sensations shot down his rigid cock and thus began the churning of his milk balls. *Would this be the end to such a sensational blow job?* Charlie had to stop her now before he blew his load, so whispered, 'Please stop, honey. I'm going to blow.'

On hearing this, Lucy instantly stopped her humming and let the rigid cock fall from her mouth and knelt up and tenderly kissed Charlie's lips. Charlie breathed a sigh of relief as his milk balls stopped churning and the disaster had passed and his rigid cock resembled a dormant volcano ready for action.

There would be no sitting on Charlie's lap, as that would once again begin his milk balls churning. She wanted action; she wanted to feel his rigid cock plunging in and out of her simmering pussy. So Lucy stood up and whispered in Charlie's ear, 'Please can you stand up, Charlie? I need the chair to lean on while you fuck me from behind.'

On hearing this, the ecstatically horny Charlie stood up and Lucy then placed her hands on the seat of the chair and spread her legs ready for a poking. Charlie smiled as he looked at her voluptuous ass and took his rigid cock in hand and guided it towards her shaven haven. In seconds, his rigid cock was penetrating her shaven haven, and then with one gentle thrust in plunged his rigid cock.

He then began his thrusting slow at the tempo of the tap that wouldn't stop dripping, and while he slowly thrust in and out, he slapped her ass on every withdrawal thrust.

'Ouch, ouch,' shrieked the teasing smiling Lucy, who was teasing him to spank her harder, but Charlie didn't need encouraging and spanked harder on every thrust. This was sending tingling sensations up through Lucy's voluptuous body to her exploding mind; Lucy loved this stone age type of shagging. She was the naughty girl being rampantly punished by the cave man Charlie. *Oh what a man!*

Suddenly Charlie stopped his slapping and increased his thrusting to the new tempo of the clock that wouldn't stop ticking.

'Oh yes, that's it. Faster, Charlie, let me feel it,' said the enthusiastic Lucy.

On hearing this, Charlie grinned and thrust faster, but this was short-lived when a voice suddenly said, 'Is it my turn yet?'

The nervous Charlie looked around as he shot his load deep inside Lucy and then again murmured those immortal words, 'Fuck me, who the hell is that?'

Lucy looked around too and smiled when she saw the naked Danny standing there and shouted, 'Are you ready, Danny boy?'

'Ready for what?' asked the curious Charlie, who was now wondering why his sexual fun had been extinguished by this handsome naked young intruder.

'A fucking in his asshole,' replied the smiling Lucy.

'But you're first. Twice I have heard you say fuck me. So if you resume the position I have just vacated, I will strap the strap-a-dick-to-me on and let's get it on'

Charlie was horrified by her suggestion and instantly pulled up his pants and quickly ran off; he was that man on the run, running away from his exotic temptress.

CHAPTER 13

L UCY SAT SMILING as she watched the naked Danny boy approaching her, with his rigid cock in hand, gently stroking it as he walked towards his voluptuous temptress Lucy. *Was he ready*, wondered Lucy, *for the fucking he had requested?* But first she would get him in the mood with a little sucking on his rigid cock.

As Danny boy stood in front of her, she whispered, 'Oh Danny boy, let me suck this rigid cock of yours.'

On hearing this, Danny instantly stopped his hand wanking and left his rigid cock alone. In seconds, Lucy wrapped her mouth around it, as she gently caressed his balls and began sucking on his rigid cock's bald head. Danny boy was in heaven as his sultry temptress Lucy sucked with her lips of velvet.

'Oh what a lovely day!' he softly murmured.

Lucy suddenly began deep throat on his rigid cock and began humming while she sucked.

'Oh my, that feels so good!' murmured the delighted Danny boy, but Lucy hadn't finished and suddenly ran her tongue down his rigid cock towards his balls. In seconds, she was humming while she sucked on those balls; his eyes suddenly opened wide as she slowly inserted a finger up his ass, even wider when one finger became two.

'Oh my goodness!' murmured Danny boy; back to sucking delicately on his rigid cocks bald head went Lucy, as her hand gently began caressing his balls. Lucy then began humming on Danny's rigid cock's bald head, which sent tingling sensations down the rigid shaft. Danny loved this sensational blow job, but he wanted to fuck this voluptuous temptress and whispered, 'Miss Lucy, may I fuck you please?'

On hearing this, the smiling Lucy withdrew her two fingers from his ass and whispered, 'Only if I can fuck you first.'

Then in shock Danny boy stared down at his temptress and whispered, 'Fuck me? What do you mean fuck me?'

The smiling Lucy then stood and tenderly kissed his lips, then turned, and walked over and picked up the strap-a-dick-to-me and strapped it on. Then pointing down, she whispered, 'With this.'

She slowly walked back to the horrified Danny boy, whose eyes were wide open as he stared at that big rubber cock. He began pleading with the smiling Lucy, begging for a retraction of his silly words. Lucy loved the uneasiness Danny boy was showing. But she was dying to fuck him in the ass with that big rubber cock; she wanted to hear his screams, as that big rubber cock entered his asshole.

Danny boy couldn't stand his built-up anxiety any longer, as he stared down at that approaching big rubber cock; he began shouting, 'Okay, Lucy, you win. I will pay you one thousand dollars if I can have sex with you and forget the other thing.'

Lucy stopped and stared at the shaking Danny boy and then smiled at him as she removed the strap-a-dick-to-me and threw it across the floor and then ran and jumped into Danny boy's outstretched arms and wrapped her legs around him and whispered, 'Fuck me hard, Danny boy. I want to feel your rigid cock inside me now.'

With that, Danny boy lowered her to the ground and then quickly resumed the missionary position as he then guided his rigid cock into her shaven haven. Then with one gentle thrust in plunged his rigid cock; he began his thrusting slow at the tempo of the tap that wouldn't stop dripping. Lucy loved his slow thrusting but ached for it to be harder; then a dirty thought crossed her mind, and she stuck a finger in the slow thrusting Danny boy's ass.

On feeling this, Danny boy's eyes opened wide, as he quietly prayed it wouldn't become two, maybe three, or even four. He shuddered as he tenderly kissed her lips, at the same time increasing his thrusting speed to the new tempo of the clock that wouldn't stop ticking. Reluctantly Lucy removed her finger from his asshole and smiled; there was nothing for her to do but enjoy the shag.

Lucy's mind was in a haze, counting all the money she had earned that night, approximately two and a half thousand dollars from her stage show earlier plus the five hundred from her delightful boss Sally, and then there was the thousand dollars from Charlie and a thousand more from the fast-thrusting Danny boy.

She shook her head in disbelief—five thousand bucks in less then two hours. She kept asking herself why she hadn't got into stripping years ago.

It was all over for Danny boy as he felt his balls suddenly tighten and his milky-white fluids flooded Lucy's shaven haven. He then began tenderly kissing

Lucy's succulent lips as he slowly withdrew his deflating cock, but Lucy wasn't finished and stuck a finger up his ass. One finger quickly became two; Danny boy began making faces as Lucy's fingers slowly began to thrust in and out of his asshole at the tempo of the tap that wouldn't stop dripping. Danny boy was lost in the moment and didn't seem to have a care in the world. When suddenly Lucy's slow thrusting fingers hit his prostate gland, he murmured those immortal words, 'Fuck me.'

As his sleeping cock hit hard-on status in the blink of an eyelid, he shouted, 'Here we go.'

As he inserted his rigid cock into Lucy's shaven haven, he again started his thrusting slowly but suddenly stopped and whispered, 'Doggy style.'

He then instantly withdrew his rigid cock and moved, letting the voluptuous Lucy get on to her hands and knees and slightly spread her legs ready for action. Danny boy then took his rigid cock in hand and then guided it towards her shaven haven; as he was about to enter, he stopped and stared at her tiny asshole and thought, *let's try in there.*

He spat on his hand and then lubricated Lucy's asshole; Lucy smiled as his rigid cock slowly entered. She whispered, 'It's all right to fuck me in the ass, but yours is out of bounds?'

Danny boy smiled, and on his withdrawal stroke, he slapped her ass and whispered, 'Cheeky.'

Lucy loved the feeling of his hard slap; it was sending tingling sensations through her body, and the temptress was aching for her revenge as she stared at the strap-a-dick-to-me. She was aching to fuck a butch man in the ass tonight.

She shouted, 'No more, Danny boy. I want to fuck you in the ass, or I am off.'

On hearing this, the stunned Danny boy withdrew his rigid cock from her ass, stood and ran out of the room, leaving the giggling Lucy to her sexual fantasies as he went in search of his clothes to cover his naked body.

Still giggling, Lucy stood and walked over and picked up the strap-a-dick-to-me and strapped it on. Then she went skipping from the room in search of a man's ass to fuck; those horny onlookers began cheering as she skipped around.

Then the prey she was in search of suddenly stood and dropped his pants and then bent over the table, smiling at her. On seeing this, Lucy took the big rubber cock in hand and ran up behind him and rubbed that big rubber cock over his ass.

The prey's eyes opened wide as that big rubber cock penetrated his asshole, and he shouted, 'Fuck me rigid. That's a big one you have there, honey.'

Lucy smiled as she slowly thrust forward, 'Oh-ha,' shouted the silly man; his asshole was on fire from that big rubber cock slowly plunging in and out of his cindering ass.

With tears in his eyes, he wondered why he had participated in such a silly game with his so-called mates; he began shouting, 'No no, please no more, you voluptuous temptress.'

On hearing his whims, Lucy withdrew the big rubber cock and moved on, still looking for her ultimate prey, the open-minded man. Then cheers filled the house as a young man stood up and pulled his pants down and shouted, 'Over here, honey. I take it up the ass regularly.'

Lucy smiled and ran over to her awaiting prey and stuck that big rubber cock up against his asshole, then with one gentle push in plunged that big rubber cock. She began her thrusting slow at the tempo of the tap that wouldn't stop dripping, and as she slowly thrust, she reached around and began stroking on his rigid cock.

Wow it felt wonderful! The young man felt like he was in heaven as he was being fucked by the voluptuous Lucy, and whilst she fucked his ass, she stroked his cock too. *Oh what a girl!* Lucy was now getting in the swing of this thrusting lark and upped the pace of her thrusting to the new tempo of the clock that wouldn't stop ticking.

It was like the young man was mimicking a mime, as that big rubber cock pulsated in and out of his asshole; one second he had an open mouth, the next a screwed-up face, but he never made a sound. His eyes opened wide as Lucy suddenly stopped her thrusting with that big rubber cock embedded in his ass. She then began furiously stroking his rigid cock, and the young man knew his time was up as his milk balls began churning.

It was all over in a couple of minutes as his rigid cock exploded, spraying his milky-white fluids into the air, which landed on the face of his open-mouthed friend. That was it; game over. Lucy then slowly withdrew that big rubber cock; the young man then instantly turned around and kissed her hard on the lips and whispered, 'Thank you, honey. That was lovely.'

With that, he pulled out a huge bundle of dollars and gave her five one-hundred-dollar bills and then pulled up his pants and went and sat next to his staring friend, who was still wiping away his milky-white fluids from his face.

The startled young man asked, 'what you doing, Ollie?'

Ollie looked at him and frowned and then shrieked, 'Well, there's another fine mess you've gotten me into.'

The young man shrugged his shoulders and then picked up his glass and took a long drink of his beer.

The sultry temptress had wandered off in search of her friend Jane; it was time to go as she wanted to take Jane home and attend to her hairy pussy. It was only seconds when she saw her lonesome friend sitting all alone and drinking from a wine glass. She ran up to her and whispered, 'Are you ready to go, Jane?'

Jane looked at her and then her eyes travel downwards over Lucy's voluptuous body and stopped as she stared at that big rubber cock still strapped around her waist and whispered, 'Why are you wearing that?'

As she pointed a finger at that big rubber cock, Lucy looked down and smiled and then whispered, 'You will see later, honey bun.'

With that, she took hold of Jane's hand; Jane instantly stood and followed the voluptuous naked Lucy by the hand to the changing room, where Lucy hit the shower to cleanse that big rubber cock and her body too. She was quickly joined by the naked Jane, who began washing away at her spunk-filled hairy pussy.

Lucy smiled when she saw the naked Jane standing by her side and turned to kiss her, and then her hands cupped her ass cheeks. Jane responded with a probing tongue as her hands too cupped Lucy's ass cheeks. But this was short-lived as that big rubber cock was pressed up against her hairy pussy; on feeling this, Jane stepped back and then turned around and then bent over and spread her legs as she looked at Lucy and whispered, 'Fuck me, fuck me hard, darling.'

On hearing this, Lucy smiled as she slapped Jane hard on the ass and whispered, 'Not here, not now. Let's cleanse our dirty bodies, and then dry ourselves, dress, and go.'

'Where to?' whispered the excited Jane.

'Back to my place,' whispered the voluptuous Lucy.

'I have some grooming to do on your hairy pussy.'

As she pointed down at Jane's thick bush of pubic hair, Jane frowned and whispered back, 'Okay, as long as it's not like yours, Kojack style.'

Those words tickled both of them, and they began to laugh, as they once again cuddled one another, then it was off with the strap-a-dick-to-me, as they stepped from the shower and began drying their dripping bodies. In minutes, they were dry and began dressing; it was the bare necessity for Lucy: her short skirt and jacket too. Then it was on with the shoes, and she was ready to go.

She looked at Jane and frowned, as Jane was a slow coach and was still putting on her bra. Lucy then whispered in her ear, 'Wait here, honey.'

As she softly kissed her lips and then picked up her purse as she left the changing room. It was time to collect her money; first she went in search of Charlie, who was still watching the dancing girls strip their clothes. She walked right up to him with her hand held out and whispered in his ear, 'Money please, Charlie.'

Charlie frowned as he took his wallet from his pocket and then took ten one-hundred-dollar bills from it and handed it to the smiling Lucy and whispered, 'Any time, any place I will do you again for the same money.'

'Do me!' shrieked the flabbergasted Lucy, stunned in what she had just heard and thought, *Fuck this,*

And then slapped him hard across his face and then turned and walked away and stopped; it was sexual teasing time. As she bent over, up went the short skirt, thus exposing her naked charms for all too see. With the teasing over, she stood and turned around and stared at the gawping Charlie and smiled as she lifted her short skirt, thus exposing her shaven haven. She stood there shaking her head as if to say, 'Never again.' Then she turned and walked away; her only concern was to get Jane home and groom her hairy pussy.

CHAPTER 14

I T WAS MIDNIGHT, as the light fingered Lucy began cutting the hairy forest that camouflaged plain Jane's hidden delights. She was going for the short back and sides look, bald around the pussy lips with a little hair on top. With the forest groomed to a lawn finish, she whispered, 'Would you like it shaved or waxed, Madame?'

On hearing this, Jane looked down and smiled; her pussy looked great. She shook her head and then whispered, 'that will be fine, Lucy.'

Lucy smiled and then led Jane by the hand to the bathroom and turned the shower on, as Jane washed her neatly groomed pussy. Lucy picked up her razor and began shaving her own pussy as she stood under the shower with Jane. Jane looked with curiosity as she watched Lucy shave her bald pussy and wondered what it would feel like if she was bald too. She couldn't resist temptation and whispered, 'Lucy, will you shave mine too?'

On hearing this, Lucy dropped to her knees and delicately began shaving Jane's pussy; in no time at all, they both had shaven havens, and it was time to play. Jane's heart was racing as she dried herself, as she wondered what Lucy had in store for her. Once they entered her pleasure dome with their bodies dry, Lucy took the naive Jane by the hand and led her to her playroom.

The excited Jane could barely breathe as they stood outside the room; she then gasped, 'Oh.'

As Lucy placed a blind fold over her head and tied it tight, with her vision gone Lucy opened the door and led her prey by the hand into her pleasure dome that revealed her four poster bed, covered with sex toys and bondage gear. In just minutes, Jane lay spread eagled across the bed, with her hands and ankles tied; she was going nowhere. Thus the games began with tender kisses from the temptress Lucy, as she fingered Jane's shaven haven.

Jane was in heaven; never before had she tasted sexual erotica this way. Then Lucy went on manoeuvres with her tender kisses, from her lips to her neck; she went with those tender kisses. Then onwards to Jane's erect nipples, where she sucked and teased those nipples, before she moved on to the Holy Grail that was Jane's shaven haven.

In seconds, she began probing Jane's magical button with her flickering tongue, as her two fingers slowly thrust in and out of Jane's shaven haven at the tempo of the tap that wouldn't stop dripping.

Jane's pussy was alive with sensations from Lucy's flickering tongue on her magical button; those two slow thrusting fingers inside her shaven haven too. Little did she know Lucy was already planning, her next stage in her sexual mystery tour on her naked body. As her imagination pictured the insertion of the egg shape {Angel} sex toy being inserted into Jane's shaven haven, a smile crossed her face as she withdrew her thrusting fingers and then sat up and clapped her hands saying, 'Well that's the appetiser, now on to the main course, honey.'

'Main course?' whispered the excited yet panicking Jane, as she wondered what Lucy meant by main course? The answer quickly came as the insertion of the angel sex toy was pushed deep into her shaven haven.

'What is that?' enquired the sexually inquisitive Jane, whose mind was going crazy. *What was she going to do next,* she wondered. The answer came quickly as Lucy began lubricating her asshole with that K Y jelly stuff.

'Oh,' murmured the excited Jane.

'What are you doing back there, Lucy?'

The answer came abruptly as Lucy inserted the butt plug into her ass.

'Ooh-e,' shouted Jane. 'What is that?'

Then came, 'oh my goodness!'

As simultaneously Lucy switched them on, there were vibrations in her pussy and asshole too; this was the beginning of Jane's sexually mysterious tour and then came those vibrating nipple clamps. Jane's mind was all shook up from the onslaught of sensations, as she began her journey destination Climax City. The temptress Lucy then began probing her magical button with her flickering tongue as she held the small vibrator against the skin just above the magical button. This was the final instalment of Jane's sexually mysterious tour. Jane's mind was going into orbit, as the onslaught of sensations was coming from here, there, and everywhere. With her body shaking, she had arrived at Climax City in record time and was experiencing that orgasmic moment of the third kind, which she had never encountered before. She began shouting, 'No more please, no more, Lucy. That was sensational.'

Lucy smiled and began removing all the sex toys and untied the ropes, then off came the blindfold to reveal Jane's smiling eyes. In seconds, they were locked in an embrace, as they shared a tender continuous kiss.

Jane was falling in love with her sultry temptress Lucy; just yesterday she was a heterosexual young lady eager for the feel of that rigid cock. But now she was a bisexual nymphomaniac, eager to sexually satisfy a man or a woman; she had no preferences. From a kiss, Jane went on manoeuvres, with tender kisses on Lucy's neck, as her fingers gently massaged her magical button. From Lucy's neck went Jane to her plentiful breasts, where she began sucking on those strawberry-size nipples. In seconds, those nipples resembled bullets, and Jane went lower to her heart's desire, Lucy's shaven haven. Her tongue probed and flickered at Lucy's magical button while she slipped a finger into Lucy's shaven haven; one finger quickly became two, as she gently began to thrust them at the tempo of tap that wouldn't stop dripping.

Lucy loved her novice girl friend's attempts to pleasure her womanly charms, but she was getting bored and whispered, 'Jane, I know you're doing your best, but I am aching to fuck you in the ass with that ten-inch strap-a-dick-to-me thingy.'

Jane looked up and smiled; she new she was just an amateur in pussy licking, but she had made a promise to herself that she would get better from now on, learning from her girl friend, the temptress Lucy if only she would teach her.

But that would remain a daydream as she quickly got on all fours on seeing this Lucy smiled and picked up the strap-a-dick-to-me and strapped it on. Then she picked up the K Y jelly and began lubricating Jane's asshole. In seconds she was placing that big rubber cock up against Jane's ass and then with a gentle thrust in plunged the rubber cock, taking Jane's breath away. Then slowly Lucy began to thrust at the tempo of the tap that wouldn't stop dripping.

'Ouch, ouch,' screamed the flabbergasted Jane; at first the pain was unbearable, but after a couple of thrusts, Jane kind a liked it. Lucy on the other hand was in exploratory mood as she reached around and began massaging her magical button.

'Oh my goodness!' murmured the distraught Jane, as new sensations flooded through her body up to her exploding mind; thus Jane began her journey destination Climax City; here she comes. Lucy was driving her crazy with her magical fingers and the slow thrusting.

Jane was losing her mind and began screaming, 'No more, please no more, my temptress lover.'

Lucy smiled and instantly stopped her thrusting with the ten-inch rubber cock fully embedded in Jane's ass; she frantically began massaging Jane's magical button. This was the final, as Jane screamed, 'Yes, yes, oh yes, I'm coming.'

She arrived at Climax City and was experiencing that wonderful orgasmic moment. *Oh what a moment that was!*

With Jane trembling by that wonderful orgasmic moment, Lucy slowly withdrew that big rubber cock and fell on to her pillow. With the fun over, she unfastened the strap-a-dick-to-me and let it fall to the floor and then whispered, 'Hey Jane, it's none night time'

On hearing this, the relieved Jane smiled and lay down beside her lover Lucy and stared into her smiling eyes and whispered, 'Lucy darling, before I go to work in the morning, I will have to go to Church to see Father Brian to confess my sins, for I have been a naughty girl.'

On hearing this, Lucy softly kissed her lips and whispered, 'I will join you, Jane.'

Jane's eye's opened wide, as she wondered what her sultry temptress Lucy was thinking of; she smiled and tenderly kissed her lips as she placed her hand on her ass and closed her eyes too.

The night passed quickly, as the sound of Lucy's alarm filled the air; on hearing this, Jane's eyes opened wide, wondering where she was. On hearing the alarm extinguished she slowly turned and saw Lucy's smiling face coming towards her. In seconds, they were locked in a smouldering kiss, with Lucy's fingers gently massaging her magical button. Jane's mind was lost in wonder, as Lucy went on dawn patrol with her tender kisses.

From her lips to her neck went Lucy with tender kisses and then quickly on to her tits; in seconds Jane's nipples were erect, and then Lucy moved downwards towards the Holy Grail that was Jane's shaven haven. As her massaging fingers went on finger fucking patrol, her probing tongue flickered over Jane's magical button. Jane couldn't stand this sexual wake up call any longer and sat up and lifted Lucy's head away from her shaven haven and whispered, 'Can we please play later, honey, as I have work, but first church to confess my sins to Father Brian.'

Lucy smiled and whispered, 'Okay.'

She then got off the bed and ran to spend a penny; in just seconds, she was joined by her hovering friend, as she sat peeing on the toilet and the sound of hissing water filled the air.

The frantically hovering Jane couldn't restrain herself and said, 'Come on, Lucy, I want to pee too.'

But Lucy didn't pay her know mind and carried on peeing; Jane was now at bursting point and stepped into the shower and turned it on. As the spraying water hit her body, she let go of her inhibitions and began peeing; then started Lucy's chorus.

> Golden rain, Golden rain,
> When, you were peeing in the shower.
> golden rain.

Jane turned and looked at the pointing singing Lucy and began to laugh, in turn so did Lucy as she joined her latest flame under the spraying water. As they stood there laughing at one another under the spraying water, Lucy delicately began massaging her magical button.

But there was no time for any hanky panky; she had to ring Father Brian to see if he would see her for confession early this morning. She whispered, 'Not now, darling.'

She gently removed Lucy's massaging fingers from her magical button and brought them up to her mouth and tenderly kissed them, from her fingers to her lips went Jane and then stepped from shower and began drying her dripping body. In just minutes, she was dry and went in search of her mobile phone. Lucy looked on bewildered by her girl friends reluctance to play, so she began washing her body while she planned for this morning's adventure.

It had been a long time since she'd been to church and confessed her sins, as to do that would have educated the secret Master Bates Preacher, as he gently stroked his rigid cock as he listened to her erotic tales in the confession booth.

'Oh', she murmured, 'I'll have to investigate that while Jane's confessing her sins to Father Brian.' With that, she turned the shower off and then stepped out of the shower on to the bath mat and began drying her dripping body; she then went to investigate what Jane was doing.

As she approached the bedroom, she heard Jane speaking. She stopped and peeked through the open door and smiled as she watched her latest flame sat massaging her magical button while talking too Father Brian. *Who was this Father Brian, was he hot, big cock?* wandered the intrigued Lucy.

She knelt down on the floor and slowly approached the bed like a lion that cautiously hunted its prey. In seconds she was by the bedside watching her closed-eyed self-pleasuring latest flame. Then like a Hawk, she was on her, sinking her two fingers into her wet honey pot.

'Oh,' murmured Jane.

'What was that?' asked the curious Father Brian.

'Oh nothing, nothing at all, Father,' replied the erotic smiling Jane as she closed her eyes and enjoyed the moment. She was lost in a haze of sensations and began murmuring, 'Oh.'

As the sensations travelled through her body up to her exploding mind, the bewildered Father Brian asked, 'Are you there?'

'Yes, yes, oh yes, I am here,' replied the ecstatically happy Jane. 'Will you see me for confession, Father, as I have been a naughty lady?'

'Why? What has happened, my child?' asked the concerned Father Brian.

Then it happened that magical orgasmic moment as Jane's honey pot exploded, spraying her built-up fluids into the air and then her cries of 'Oh my god!' filled the air.

Her body shook from that wonderful orgasmic moment. *Oh what a moment that was!* The stunned Jane was brought back to reality by the concerned Father Brian, who was literally shouting down the phone to get her attention.

'Are you all right Jane? What's going on my, child?'

Jane was lost for words as Lucy continued probing her magical button with her flickering tongue, as her two slow thrusting fingers caressed her G spot with every thrust; Jane was on her way next stop Climax City; here she comes.

'Are you there?' asked Father Brian as he listened to her murmuring of Oh-ha, as Lucy continually hit that special spot; again Father Brian asked, 'Is everything Okay, Jane?'

There was no answer, so Father Brian decided to hang up and continue eating his breakfast; for Jane she was fast approaching Climax City at breakneck speed and began screaming, 'Yes, yes, oh yes, I'm cumming!'

With that, Lucy withdrew her two fingers, thus releasing Jane's built-up fluids spraying into the air; with her body shaking and her fluids, a mere trickle Jane whispered, 'What was that, Father Brian?'

Then disappointment spread across her face when she heard just a constant tone; disappointment quickly turned to shock as she felt that big rubber cock penetrate her sacred haven and whispered, 'For heaven's sake, Lucy, two orgasms is more than enough for breakfast.'

Lucy looked up and smiled as she slowly withdrew that big rubber cock and then put it in her mouth and sucked Jane's fluids, which tasted divine, so Lucy impersonated Winnie-the-Pooh and began muff diving once more on Jane's honey pot.

'Oh come on,' whispered Jane, 'we've got to go to church.'

On hearing this, Lucy sighed as she reluctantly withdrew her probing tongue from Jane's weeping honey pot and looked up and smiled, and then, she got off the bed and began dressing whilst Jane headed off to the bathroom to shower once more.

CHAPTER 15

IT WAS 8.45 a.m. as the panicking Jane entered the church; she was going to be late for work, but she didn't care. She had to confess her sins to Father Brian to gain his forgiveness, so she could start the day with a clear conscience. She entered the confessions booth and sat down and was startled when a voice said, 'Good morning, my child.'

'Good morning, Father,' replied the smiling Jane and then began her confession.

'Father, please forgive me, for I have sinned. I have been a naughty lady, Father. It all started yesterday at work, Father, when I went to spend a penny, Father, I heard a murmuring and curiously investigated.'

'What was the noise?' asked the intrigued Father Brian.

That's when Jane hesitated to go any further, as she was going to tell her dirty sexual secrets to a priest; she shook her head in disbelief as she wondered what she was doing there. She just couldn't do it; she so wanted to run but couldn't move as her conscience was telling her to off load her sins.

'No . . . no,' she murmured.

'What was that, my child?' asked the curious Father Brian.

'I . . . I can't tell you, Father,' sobbed Jane.

That's when the sultry temptress Lucy entered to comfort her sobbing lover; she wrapped her arms around her and softly kissed her lips and then took centre stage as she began telling Jane's story. Jane was horrified and didn't know what to do as she quietly listened to Lucy's tales.

'I stood on the toilet on tip toe and looked over, Father, where I saw my work colleague Lucy munching on the cleaner's pussy. The more I watched, Father, and

I was getting turned on myself. My nipples were like bullets in my bra, Father, so I opened my skirt and let it fall and then slipped my hand inside my panties and began massaging my magical button, Father'

'Oh no!' murmured Father Brian.

As he felt a stirring in his loins and his sleeping cock began to rise, he looked up and murmured, 'Oh my goodness, it's alive, my holy one.'

On hearing this, Lucy instantly became the temptress and began saying shocking things, which shocked the blushing Jane and Father Brian too.

'That's not all, Father,' she whispered. 'We three ladies went into the cleaning cupboard and stripped naked, Father.'

On hearing this, Father Brian looked up and murmured 'Why?'

Lucy continued her story on the speechless Jane's part.

'Yes, Father, while Lucy and I were locked in a passionate embrace, Mandy, the cleaner, went over to her cleaning cupboard, Father, and got a sex toy out. It was a rabbit vibrator, Father. I got a shock whilst I lay on the floor, Father.'

'Why? What happened?' asked the curios Father Brian.

'Well, Father', replied Lucy (still talking for her red-faced friend Jane), 'whilst I was busy probing Lucy's pussy with my flickering tongue as she squatted just above my face, Mandy inserted that sex toy into my pussy and turned it on. Oh my god, it felt wonderful, Father, with the body vibrating inside my pussy and the ears massaging my magical button (clitoris), Father.'

That was the final straw for Father Brian, he unbuttoned his pants and released his throbbing cock; he smiled then frowned as he looked down to see his rigid cock smiling back at him as he took it in hand and gently began to stroke it.

'Oh that feels so good!' murmured Father Brian as he joined the Master Bates hand wanking society; on hearing his soft words, the inquisitive Lucy was on the move, as she continually talked about her sexual escapades. Outside the cubicle she got down on her hands and knees and crawled towards Father Brian's cubicle to take a peeking view of his actions.

In seconds, she was peaking through the drawn curtain, staring open-mouthed at the Masturbating preacher. She smiled and then turned around and quickly crawled back to Jane's booth; in turn she stared open-mouthed at Jane who herself was portraying Miss Bates, the sister of Master Bates, as she sat there half-naked massaging her magical button.

Lucy smiled and again turned around and headed back to Father Brian's booth; with her tales getting more erotic by the second she whispered, 'Father, I got shagged by my friend come lover Lucy.'

The bewildered Father Brian whispered 'I'm sorry, my child. I don't know what you mean?'

On hearing his words, Lucy smiled and whispered, 'You know, Father, you have a hard cock, she had a rubber cock, Father, strapped around her waist.'

Father Brian smiled and looked down and saw his rigid cock staring back at him and wondered how she knew he had a hard cock. Was there a window he didn't know about what? His thoughts were instantly brought back to reality when he felt a hand on his hand that he was gently stroking his rigid cock with.

He opened his eyes and looked down and saw Lucy's smiling face.

'Oh no,' he murmured as Lucy unwrapped his fingers that were hugging his rigid cock and then began sucking on his rigid cock's bald head. He looked up and whispered, 'Why me, Lord?'

On hearing this, the startled Jane asked, 'What was that, Father? Why me Lord what?'

'Oh nothing, my child', replied Father Brian, 'I was just meditating on your dilemma.'

That's when the velvety mouth of Lucy took it to another level and began humming while she sucked; the startled Father Brian whispered, 'Oh that feels so nice.'

'What's so nice, Father?' asked the curious Jane.

'Oh, oh, oh, be careful down there,' whispered Father Brian.

As Lucy began sucking on one of his balls, they were not gobstoppers; they were his testicles. They were tender and so not uses to this sort of action, as they were normally confined to his underpants with his cock too.

The curious half-naked Jane stood up and went to investigate what was going on. She stepped outside her booth and quickly tiptoed a couple steps and got down on her knees, unaware she was being watched by a new nun Sister Susan, who was smiling as she watched plain Jane's actions.

When she saw Jane peek into the priest's booth, she curiously moved closer to see what was going on. She was a young nun, just turned twenty-one, escaping the sins of the big wide world, especially the sex world, where she had been a stripper, teasing the customers with her naked charms, and now those demons were haunting her again.

As she stared at Jane's naked shapely bottom through lust-filled eyes; as she was bisexual, it was a temptation too great to be ignored; she then picked up a candle and slowly walked towards her prey. Quietly she crept up behind Jane and slowly dropped to her knees and then slowly inserted the candle into Jane's pussy.

As the candle entered her pussy, Jane gasped, 'What the fuck is that?'

'Shush!' whispered Sister Susan, who was panicking at being caught in the act of ungodliness in the church; with that she tenderly kissed Jane's ear and whispered, 'Come with me, you naughty lady.'

Jane froze when she looked around to see the nun's smiling face and murmured, 'What have I done?'

She was half-naked in the church, feeling horny as she stared at the nun's smiling face and whispered, 'Sister, please can you remove that object from my pussy.'

Sister Susan smiled and then slowly withdrew the candle from Jane's pussy and slowly stood; Jane stood up in an instant and followed the slowly moving nun, wondering what delights lay under that black gown. She stopped and shook her head. What was she doing, thinking of a nun naked in a church? She wanted to run but couldn't move as her eyes remained fixed on the nun's tiny waist still fantasizing her naked. She whispered, 'Sister, where are we going?'

On hearing this, Sister Susan stopped and then slowly turned around and smiled, as her eyes captured her half-naked prey; then like an eagle, she glided back to Jane and whispered, 'To have some fun, silly.'

With that said she tenderly kissed Jane's lips and then took her hand and led her to her secret place. Jane pinched herself to see if this was reality or merely a dream; on feeling her pinch, she murmured, 'Ouch, this is really happening.'

The sultry temptress Lucy had gone from sucking Father Brian's rigid cock to bobbing up and down on his lap. She was in heaven; he was heading for hell and, he could hear Johnny Cash singing

I went down-down-down and the flames went higher
That burning ring of fire

He couldn't stand it any longer and pleaded with the bobbing Lucy, 'Please . . . please stop that, young lady.'

'Stop what, Father?' asked the smiling, bobbing Lucy.

On hearing her reply, Father Brian put his hands on the cheeks of her ass and lifted her upwards. Out slipped his throbbing cock, and then he stood up and re-housed his rigid cock and he was off, leaving the sultry temptress bewildered and laughing in her seat. After several minutes, she composed herself and then stood and began dressing her naked charms.

Dressed, she stepped out of the booth, turned, and walked a couple of steps and then turned and looked into an empty booth and wondered where Jane was as the sound of a ringing phone took her concentration to her purse. She opened the purse and took out the phone and frowned when she saw Haskins's name on the screen and murmured, 'Oh no, here we go.'

She composed herself and then became Dominatrix Lucy, when she answered the phone saying, 'Good morning, Mr Haskins, could you hold on for a moment?'

Then came her screams of

'Harder, Father Brian, oh that's it, oh that feels so good, Father. God has certainly blessed you with a rigid cock, Father, unlike my former boss Mr Floppy.'

'Oh sorry, Mr Haskins, I can't really talk as the preacher is giving me a good poking with his stiff cock. Goodbye.'

With that, she hung up and went and sat down in the booth and pulled the curtain and waited; in seconds, her phone began to ring. She looked at the face and smiled when she saw Haskins's name; then in her strictest voice, she answered 'Hello. Oh, Father, where did you learn how to shag a woman. This is wanderful shag, Father. You're so masterful.'

Haskins frowned and then hung up and shouted, 'who the fuck does she think she is.'

Then he sat back and closed his eyes as the frustration Blues set in as his mind began picturing the naked Lucy there, sat massaging her magical button; suddenly his eyes opened wide as he felt a stirring down below. He instantly stood up and opened his pants and let them fall to his knees followed by his shorts. He shook his head in disbelief when he saw his rigid cock staring back at him and shouted, 'What the fuck is going on?'

As he took it in hand and gently began to stroke it and shook his head in disbelief, why it was so hard when just earlier it was floppy, then he smiled as he recalled those words of his temptress Lucy. Was she really having sex with a preacher and was he really a sensational lover? He couldn't stand it and he picked up his mobile and dialled Lucy's number; after several rings, Lucy answered, 'Hello. Oh, Father, you're so naughty. I thought that was an exit door for no. 2. Oh it's such a tiny hole and your cock feels so big. Hello, who's there?'

'Hello, Lucy, It's me, Mr Haskins, with a very hard cock in my hand. I must see you, as you are the one.'

On hearing this, Lucy smiled and pondered on her thoughts before replying, but the anxious Mr Haskins couldn't wait and shouted, 'A million dollars if you would be my Mistress Lucy.'

On hearing this, the stunned Lucy pinched herself to see if she was awake and began stamping her feet. She couldn't believe it, a million dollars to be someone's fuck buddy, especially someone who couldn't even get it up. Her lips were mimicking a mime saying one million dollars; the impatient Mr Haskins said, 'Are you there?'

'Yes I'm here.' murmured the speechless Lucy still in shock from the million-dollar offer, Haskins took it to another level saying, 'This offer comes with your own apartment and clothes too. You may also have a maid to be at your beck and call.'

On hearing this, the stunned Lucy's mind instantly came to life, saying, 'What's the catch, you old fart?'

On hearing her last comment, Mr Haskins frowned and composed himself before saying, 'There's no catch, Lucy. You ignite my fire, and I want you and only you, Lucy.'

Lucy sat there pondering on her thoughts and counting all the money and then thought about her evening job; she didn't want to give that up. It was sexually stimulating and fun too. She loved being a stripper. She composed herself and said, 'Thank you, Mr Haskins, that's a very nice offer. What is your wife going to say sir?'

Haskins frowned and shouted, 'Wife, fuck my wife. Lucy, I want you.'

Lucy smiled and then the temptress in her replied, 'Fuck your wife? I would like to fuck your wife, sir.'

On hearing this, Haskins smiled as he pictured his young wife sleeping and the shock on her face when she felt something hard entering her pussy. This was merely a fantasy he wanted to see and shouted, 'Yes, Lucy, I would like to see you fuck my wife. How about coming round late on Saturday evening? I will pay you fifty thousand dollars for the privilege of seeing such a sight, and if you come into work today, I can pay you and discuss the million-dollar offer.'

Lucy smiled and then said, 'See you later, alligator.'

And then she hung up, stood up, and went in search of her lover plain Jane.

CHAPTER 16

THE NAKED JANE lay lost in a haze of wonderful sensations from the half-dressed sister munching on her shaven haven, and she didn't hear her lover Lucy enter and gasp, 'Fuck me, look at that.'

As she quickly removed her clothes and opened her purse and took out the strap-a-dick-to-me and strapped it on, it was time to fulfil her wildest dream to fuck a nun. She approached Sister Susan with a smiling face, as Susan was in position to be taking doggy style as she munched away on Jane's shaven haven. In seconds she was on her knees behind Sister Susan, guiding the big rubber cock towards its Holy Grail that was Susan's naked pussy.

Sister Susan froze as she felt something big penetrate her pussy and slowly go deeper into her forbidden delight. Was this the devil fucking her for being a naughty girl? But he would be rewarding her for her sins not punishing her. Then came the slow thrusting that took her breath away, she wandered what was going on. Was it Father Brian punishing her for being a naughty nun? No, his genitals were forbidden as well.

The unknown intruder suddenly took the sexual dilemma to another level, when they reached around and began massaging Sister Susan's magical button, Sister Susan didn't know whether to laugh, cry, or shout to the Lord for his forgiveness. *Oh how her world was changing!* She had run from this sexual excitement and sought sanctuary in the house of our Lord, but oh how she was missing the sexual fun, as those wonderful sensations flooded her body and she began screaming, 'Oh yes harder, whoever you are?'

On hearing this Jane's eyes opened wide; she couldn't believe her eyes when she saw the smiling Lucy shagging Sister Susan, did her temptress have no reservations. She shook her head as she knew that was a silly question. As her fingers began massaging her magical button, Lucy smiled as she listened to the eccentrically screaming nun.

'Oh yes, that's it, you lovely person.'

Lucy then upped the speed of her thrusting to the new tempo of the clock that wouldn't stop ticking. Sister Susan was in heaven as her soul headed for hell; she so loved the feeling of a hard thrusting cock inside of her quivering pussy and wondered why she had ever sought sanctuary in the house of our Lord.

As a teardrop escaped her watering eyes and rolled over her puffing cheeks, she arrived at Climax City at breakneck speed and shouted, 'Yes, yes, oh yes, that was wonderful.'

But the smiling temptress hadn't finished and carried on thrusting at the tempo of the tap that wouldn't stop dripping. Sister Susan's eyes opened wide as she again started her journey destination Climax City; here she comes. Her mind kept wondering when she last enjoyed such a wonderful journey; there hadn't been many as most of her lovers were the come-and-go merchants. Who was this fantastic lover and did they have balls of steel and not milk? who was fucking her a robot? All good questions lost in the moment; she closed her eyes and enjoyed the moment as she arrived at Climax City for her second orgasm of the day. She started murmuring, 'No more, please no more, as I'm late for chapel.'

On hearing this, Jane opened her eyes and shouted, 'Fuck me, It's ten o'clock. Oh I'm late too.'

On hearing this, Lucy began giggling as she slowly withdrew that big rubber cock from Sister Susan's wet pussy; as she felt the rigid cock slip from her pussy, Sister Susan looked around and gasped, 'Oh my god, it's a woman.'

Then she stood up and straightened her dress wear and then bent down and tenderly kissed Lucy's lips and whispered 'Thank you, honey that was wonderful.'

Then she turned and blew a kiss at the rising Jane then turned and went on her way to chapel; on seeing her lover Jane rising, Lucy whispered 'Where you going, missy? We have some unfinished business here.'

'Un-finished business what un-finished business?' replied the bewildered Jane?

Lucy smiled as she moved closer to her prey Jane, in seconds her lips were on hers and her fingers began massaging Jane's magical button. The stunned Jane tried to pull away this wasn't time play it was time to go, she was late for work and she wasn't looking for unemployment.

'What's wrong?' asked the puzzled Lucy

'I'm late for work,' replied the panic-stricken Jane.

'Don't worry', said the smiling Lucy, 'I'm coming with you.'

On hearing this, Jane relaxed and responded passionately and began caressing Lucy's bottom, in seconds they locked lips in a smouldering kiss, as Jane slowly laid back down on the floor with her legs open. Lucy wasted no time and penetrated her instantly with that big rubber cock strapped around her waist and began pulsating, her hips up and down at the tempo of the tap that wouldn't stop dripping. Jane was instantly lost in the moment and forgot all about her worries of being late for work. Lucy on the other hand had fifty thousand dollars on her mind and began slam dunking Jane's simmering pussy.

'Oh-ha,' murmured Jane on Lucy's slam dunking hips; she was on her way next stop Climax City; here she comes, then came the sound of clapping hands, the startled Jane's eyes opened wide and she gasped, 'Father Brian.'

For the slow thrusting temptress Lucy carried on without a care in the world, she had given Father Brian pleasure earlier with her velvety sucking mouth and bobbing up and down on his rigid cock. She held no religious morals to stop her sexual fun; again the sound of clapping hands filled the air and then Dominatrix Lucy stopped her thrusting and looked around and said, 'Oh hello, Father Brian, do you fancy continuing our fuck from earlier?'

Father Brian looked up for forgiveness; on seeing this the temptress Lucy withdrew the big rubber cock from Jane's shaven haven and then turned and like a praying mantis, she was at Father Brian's feet and opened his pants.

'Oh no,' murmured Father Brian as he looked down to see his floppy cock being coaxed to life by the smiling face of the temptress Lucy, as she began sucking on his floppy cock; again Father Brian looked up as he felt a stirring in his loins and his cock became rigid in Lucy's mouth.

'Oh no,' he murmured. What was he to do? He felt like he was in heaven, but his soul was heading for hell; the devil in him was saying, 'What are you waiting for, man fucker. You know she wants it, get in there and give your rigid cock the work out it deserves.' The smiling angel was saying, do not be a fool; be on your way, you are a preacher and not an evil fucker. 'Get out of here.' But the sultry temptress Lucy had taken it to another level when she began humming while she sucked on his rigid cock, thus sending tingling sensations down his rigid cock and starting the churning of his milk balls.

He just couldn't stand it; the temptation was driving him crazy. He, just had to have her and whispered, 'Please stop, honey. I want to sample your heavenly delights.'

On hearing this, Jane murmured 'Well, fuck me gently.'

On hearing this, Lucy replied, 'Okay, one at a time, lover girl. I will sort you out after Father Brian gives me a good fucking with that stiff cock of his.'

'Shush!' whispered the nervous Father Brian, who was frantically removing his clothes to get ready for action, in seconds he was naked and approaching his waiting temptress, who was bent over a table with her legs apart. His waiting temptress looked around and said, 'Oh is that for me, Father?'

She looked down and saw his rigid cock staring up at the ceiling.

'Oh yes it is, oh forbidden fruit of mine,' replied the smiling Father Brian.

Then the Garden of Eden came to mind, where Adam told Eve not to eat that forbidden fruit and yet here he was approaching his forbidden fruit; he suddenly stopped and murmured, 'Oh no, what am I doing?' as he stared at his forbidden fruit that was Lucy's naked charms. Wow they were wonderful! Just like Eve he had to sample it. No, he had to taste it. So he quick stepped over to Lucy and then dropped to his knees and sank his tongue into her shaven haven. As he licked and sampled her womanly delights, Lucy murmured 'Let us try the sixty-nine, Father, so I can play too.'

On hearing this, Father Brian quickly laid down on the floor and waited for his forbidden desire, and in seconds Lucy's honey pot hovered above his face and then she leaned forward and begun sucking on his erect cock. Father Brian lifted his head and began tasting his forbidden delight and the frowning man up stairs {God} sent a message down; Lucy then murmured, 'Oh-oh,' as she felt her tummy rumble and then blew a kiss out of her bottom at Father Brian, but this was no ordinary kiss no; it was the smelliest fart you ever did smell. On smelling this, Father Brian withdrew his tongue from Lucy's honey pot and looked up. Was the man upstairs {God} saying, 'Run, you fool, run before No 2 is despatched'? Too late Lucy farted again but this was no ordinary fart. It was wet and windy, spraying his face with muddy colour water {diarrhoea}, the stunned Father Brian looked over at Jane and said, 'I have heard of that saying I washed my face in muddy water. I know it didn't say shitty water. I'm out of here. Thank you for opening my eyes to the dark side of humanity, madam.'

With the shit dripping off his face, he stood turned and picked up his clothes and became that man on the run in search of water to wash his dirty face; it was unbearable trying to hold his breath from the stench that was on his face, and he began choking. The choking quickly turned to vomiting when he took a breath, wow the smell was unbearable he couldn't stand it no longer and ran into the ladies, to wash his dirty face and froze there stood the shouting Mildred.

'Oh my goodness, Father, put that thing away.'

As she pointed down at his sleeping cock, Father Brian looked down and said, 'Never mind that, Mildred, let me by, I have to wash my face.'

On hearing this, Mildred stepped aside and let the Father by; as Father Brian rushed by her, Mildred shouted, 'Wow what that smells? Pooh e, it smells like . . .'

Father Brian stopped her there and said, 'I'll stop you there, as I know what you're going to say and yes it is that awful stuff, a little boy had an accident and I had to clean it up with my trousers.'

On hearing this Mildred smiled, as she slowly approached Father Brian who was washing his face and dropped to her knees and began caressing his sleeping cock.

'Oh-oh,' murmured Father Brian, as he felt a sudden stirring in his loins and his sleeping cock began to rise and Mildred began sucking on its bald head.

'Here we go again,' murmured Father Brian; with his face washed Father Brian looked down and said, 'Mildred, please, I have to get ready for play group.'

On hearing this, the frowning Mildred let his rigid cock fall from her mouth and began sucking on one of his balls,

'Oh my goodness,' murmured the panicking Father Brian who was at panic stations as they were not boiled candy she was sucking on; no they were his tender balls; any biting would bring tears to his eyes, and he wasn't ready to be crying in the chapel.

'Please stop that, Mildred,' he cried.

With her sexual endeavours terminated by the sound of the ecstatic Father Brian, Mildred let the marble bag fall from her mouth stood and tenderly kissed Father Brian's lips and then turned and slowly walked away to the relief of the smiling Father Brian. As he watched Mildred leave the toilets, he began dressing, as he was adjusting his dog collar, in walked the naked Lucy, Jane, and Mildred too and stopped side by side in the stance of Charlie's Angels, but these weren't Charlie's Angels. No they were Father Brian's Angels.

Then came the titillation show, when all three angels turned around with their backs to him and spread their legs and leaned forward.

'Oh-oh,' murmured Father Brian as he felt a stirring in his loins and up periscope, went his sleeping cock. How could he resist temptation like this when all three of his angels bent over, smiling at him with their naked bottoms? His rigid cock said, 'Let me out of here look at those naked butts over there. Let my sample paradise one last time, man.'

Father Brian couldn't stand it as he watched Jane and Lucy caressing each other bodies and then came the kissing. This was too much for him and he began shedding his clothes; naked he ran over to his angels and got in on the sexual action with Mildred. As his hands gently caressed her ass their, lips were locked together in a smouldering kiss that took Mildred's breath away; it was like Father Brian was a man possessed.

In seconds Mildred was lying on the floor with Father Brian on top of her guiding his rigid cock into her aching pussy, a pussy that hadn't seen any action for such a long time and gagging for it. Mildred sighed, 'Oh.'

As Father Brian penetrated her pussy, there was no stopping him now, and he began thrusting slow at the tempo of the tap that wouldn't stop dripping, with his only concern if he would blow his load before he had time to enjoy the ride. Mildred was in heaven; she had been missing the action between the sheets and loved, the slow thrusting of Father Brian, but shock was about to take this sexual moment to another level.

When the sultry temptress Lucy began sucking on Mildred's erect nipples while Jane went down stairs and gently began massaging Mildred's magical button; the stunned Mildred's body was flooded with sensations coming from here, there, and everywhere. This was sex of the third kind for the sophisticated Mildred, whose usual sexual encounters were of the heterosexual kind with a man.

But this was wonderful she never new the touch of another woman on, her sexual charms was so tender, suddenly Lucy was on the move from her nipples to her lips she went with her velvety lips, as Lucy's velvety lips kissed hers Mildred hungrily responded with her probing tongue. She was thrilled at been slowly fucked by the handsome Father Brian while plain Jane massaged her magical button and now, locked in a passionate kiss with Lucy.

She was sexually intoxicated by the moment and reached out and began massaging Lucy's magical button, but oh how she wanted more. She so wanted to taste Lucy's shaven haven and unlocked lips with Lucy and whispered, 'Please sit on my face, you sexual goddess.'

On hearing this, Lucy smiled and quickly got into position and knelt just above Mildred's face and then like a hungry wolf Mildred lapped away at her shaven haven with her probing flickering tongue. This was getting erotica of the third kind, and Father Brian decided it was time to shag another pussy and whispered, 'Hey, Jane, could you please move around and then get up on you're knees so I can shag you doggy style?'

Jane looked up at him and smiled as he slowly withdrew his rigid cock from Mildred's quivering pussy and then moved back, allowing plain Jane to get into position; in seconds Jane was in position, and he was staring down on her smiling ass. Then he looked up when he heard Saint Peter say, 'don't bother climbing those golden stairs when you die, Brian, as the door is closed and you're not coming in, you naughty preacher.'

'Where am I going to go?' he whispered.

'Downstairs.' replied Peter. 'The Devil's got a warm bed waiting for you, which lasts an eternity. I just hope he doesn't ask you to stoke the fire as it's very hot down there.'

'Oh no', whispered Father Brian, 'I don't want to go down there. I've been a good guy. I want to come up there please, Saint Peter.'

With that he switched his imaginary friend off and took hold of his rigid cock and placed it up against Jane's shaven haven, and then with one thrust in plunged his rigid cock and he was off thrusting at the tempo of the tap that wouldn't stop dripping. Jane felt like she was in heaven, being fucked by a randy priest with a very stiff cock, as she began muff diving on Mildred's pussy while her fingers gently massaged Mildred's magical button. Her mind was telling her to swap her massaging fingers for her probing flickering tongue.

Taking the muff diving Mildred by surprise when she felt a finger plunge into her pussy; one finger quickly became two, and Jane began slowly thrusting them in and out at the tempo of the tap that wouldn't stop dripping. While her tongue probed and flickered over Mildred's magical button, which began Mildred's moaning of m-m-m as sensations rushed through her body up to her exploding mind.

This wonderful erotic show came to an abrupt end when in walked mother superior, shouting, 'Goodness, gracious me! Father, what are you doing?'

On hearing her voice, the caught-in-the-act Father Brian shot his load deep inside Jane's pussy and boyishly looked at mother superior and whispered, 'I don't know.'

He then slowly withdrew his rigid cock and then stood; on seeing his rigid cock, mother superior gasped, 'Oh.'

It had been a long time since she had seen a man's genitals in that state of arousal and quickly looked away; on seeing this, Father Brian smiled, then turned around, and walked over to his clothes and began dressing his naked body. The blushing mother superior shyly looked back and was relieved to see Father Brian dressed and then clapped her hands to stop the three naked ladies continuing with their very erotic show.

On seeing mother superior standing there, the frantic Mildred pushed Jane's face away from her pussy and then sat up and tried to cover her naked charms, as the giggling Lucy and Jane walked away. Then came those words of authority from Mother Superior.

'Come on, let's be having you, please get back to work, Mildred, as there is a lot of work to be done.'

With that said she turned around and left room, followed by the flabbergasted Mildred in search of her clothes; for the giggling temptress Lucy and the red-faced Jane, it was time to dress and go to work. But work was the last thing on Lucy's mind, as she had finished yesterday, and the only reason she was going in was to have this confrontation with Haskins about fucking his wife Saturday night and to collect her fifty thousand dollars and nothing else.

CHAPTER 17

IT WAS TEN fifty five as the sultry temptress Lucy and the red-faced Jane entered the office, for Lucy she went straight to Haskins's office and knocked on the door, while the blushing Jane went and sat down at her desk. There was no response to Lucy's knock, so she opened the door and stormed right in and stopped as she stared open-mouthed at the counting Mr Haskins and asked, 'What are you doing, Mr Haskins?'

On hearing her voice, Haskins looked up and smiled and said, 'Oh there you are, darling. I have something for you.'

'Oh yes', replied Lucy, 'what would that be?' as she slowly walked towards the desk.

'Here you go, honey.' replied Haskins.

As he picked up five bundles of cash and said, 'Here's your fifty thousand dollars, your reward for Saturday night's pleasure.'

Lucy smiled and replied, 'Reward, Mr Haskins, I will get my reward Saturday night when I'm fucking your wife in her asshole.'

'Oh my goodness,' replied Haskins, 'here is another fifty thousand dollars. I would pay you good money to see the look on her face when you plunge that big rubber cock in and out of her asshole.'

Lucy stared open-mouthed at the ten bundles of dollar bills and opened her purse and Haskins dropped the money in and said, 'Oh there's so much more. Here's another ten thousand if you would tantalise me with an erotic strip.'

Lucy smiled and said, 'Make it twenty, Mr Haskins, and there will be so much more.'

On hearing this, Haskins picked up three bundles and put them in her purse and Lucy instantly closed it and turned around and walked over to the table and put the bag on a chair and then walked over and switched the music on and out blasted Elvis singing

A little less conversation a little more action

On hearing this, Lucy turned and instantly went into titillation mood, swaying her hips whilst she slowly began undoing her jacket. Haskins looked enthralled in the beauty that was dancing before him. Then off came the jacket, thus exposing her naked breasts.

'Oh-oh,' murmured Haskins as he felt a sudden stirring in his loins and up periscope went his sleeping cock.

'It's alive,' he shouted as he quickly opened his pants to release his throbbing cock.

'What's alive?' asked the nearly naked Lucy. 'This,' replied the standing Haskins who was pointing down at his rigid cock.

On seeing it, Lucy began to laugh and jokingly said, 'How many Viagra tablets did you take?'

'No Viagra,' replied Haskins. 'It is all me, on seeing your naked charms I get the horn.'

'Oh really,' replied Lucy.

As she quickly walked towards him and dropped to her knees and then began sucking his rigid cock as she tenderly caressed his marble bag, Haskins looked up and whispered, 'Oh thank you, Lord.'

He so enjoyed Lucy's velvety lips on his rigid cock and began murmuring, 'Oh that feels so good! Your mouth is so divine, honey.'

But Lucy hadn't finished and began humming while she sucked.

'Oh-oh,' murmured Haskins as tingling sensations ran down his rigid cock and began his milk balls churning; he had to stop her before his milk balls exploded and flooded her mouth.

'Stop that please; stop the humming, honey, before I blow my load.'

On hearing his whims, Lucy instantly stopped her humming and let his rigid cock fall from her mouth and began sucking on one of his balls. Haskins didn't know what to do as he quietly prayed she wouldn't bite them. His eyes suddenly opened wide when Lucy began humming while she sucked on his balls. This was too much; he had to stop her and whispered, 'Ten . . . ten thousand dollars if I can fuck you, Lucy.'

'What was that?' asked the confused Lucy, who was trying to figure out what he said—was it ten thousand dollars or did he mean a hundred thousand dollars as ten x ten equals one hundred?—and then whispered, 'How much did you say, big boy?'

As she gently began caressing his marble bag containing his two balls, the confused Haskins looked down at the smiling Lucy and wondered what he said. As the wrong answer may upset her and result in a squeeze of his marble bag, cautiously he whispered, 'How much do you think I said, honey bun?'

Lucy smiled up at him as she gently caressed his two balls that were encased in his marble bag and whispered, 'I'm very confused by what you said, you old fart.'

She was now in her Dominatrix role and gently began squeezing Haskins marble bag; Haskins eyes opened wide and he quickly said, 'A hundred thousand dollars, Lucy?'

Lucy smiled and slowly released her clenched fist that held his balls and whispered, 'Yes, that will do very nicely. You may fuck me, But can I ask, did you really not take any Viagra tablets? I'm up for a fuck but not an all day one, as we still have to discuss Saturday night and your darling wife.'

With that, she stood up and walked over to the table and stopped and slowly turned around and said, 'How do you want me, old man?'

On hearing this, Haskins frowned as he asked himself why she was so nasty when he kept giving her all this money for meaningless tasks; yes he loved her but how much more could he take as he slowly walked towards her stroking his rigid cock and whispered, 'Turn around, honey, and bend over that table.'

Lucy smiled at him and quickly turned around and resumed the position as requested by him and spread her legs; on seeing her naked voluptuous ass smiling at him, Haskins rushed over and penetrated her shaven haven with his rigid cock, and he was off. Starting his thrusting slow at the tempo of the tap that wouldn't stop dripping, and while he slowly thrust, he began slapping her ass.

Oh those stinging sensations had Lucy shouting, 'Ouch.'

With every slap, she quickly entered her enticement mood and began shouting, 'Ouch, ouch, oh ouch. Mr Haskins, are you punishing me for being a naughty girl?'

On hearing this, Haskins smiled and began slapping her harder; the shouting Lucy was in her element on feeling those hard slaps on her bare ass, she had got what she wanted, so it was time to tame the monkey, as she stared at the pot of pens on the table and one in particular, a fountain pen that would be inserted into Haskins ass. While he was fucking her on the table, she couldn't wait to see the expression on his face and shouted, 'Change, let's change positions, Mr Haskins.'

'What do you have in mind, darling?' replied the intrigued Mr Haskin whose only interest was to give his absentee cock the work out it deserved; now it stood proud without the help of Viagra, only his desire to fuck Lucy's shaven haven as he loved her so. As he then slowly withdrew his rigid cock, he whispered 'What next, my love?'

Free, Lucy got up on the table and quickly crawled towards the pot of pens and got the fountain pen and smiled, and then it was time for action as she then sat up on the table and looked at the smiling Mr Haskins, who was gently stroking his rigid cock and whispered, 'Can you get up on here, old man, or do you need a hand?'

Haskins frowned and released his cock, and then the adrenaline kicked in and he jumped up on to the table. Then he began swaying; the swaying turned into staggering, as he tried desperately to steady himself before falling off the table, which had Lucy in stitches as she thought of Charlie Chaplin and his comical ways and shouted, 'Stunt man in the house, steady on there, old man. Do you need a hand?'

Haskins frowned and pulled out a chair and stepped up on it and then the table and slowly crawled towards his laughing temptress Lucy and whispered, 'What's so funny?'

'You are,' replied the giggling Lucy, who still couldn't get over the falling-off-the-table part and the shock on his face as she watched the staggering seventy-five-year-old fart fall off the table as though he was a stunt man looking for his next part. With that she lay back on the table and whispered, 'Fuck me, fuck me now, old man.'

As she pointed down at her shaven haven, in seconds Haskins was on top of her in the missionary position, penetrating her pussy with his rigid cock, and he was off, starting his thrusting slow at the tempo of the tap that wouldn't stop dripping. Haskins was in heaven as Lucy stared up at him, but her eyes were not on him but on the fountain pen she was holding, as she wondered how she was going to insert it in his ass, when she couldn't see the hole it was going in. She then whispered, 'Oh your cock feels so good, Mr Haskins. Oh that's it, keeps it fully penetrated and grinds your hips. Oh that's it.'

With that she slowly moved the fountain pen into position and whispered, 'Oh, Mr Haskins, kiss me. Mr Haskins, kiss me now.'

On hearing his angel's request, Haskins smiled and began hungrily kissing her; as his lips connected with hers, Lucy took pot luck and ran the fountain pen between the cheeks of his ass and suddenly stopped. On feeling this, Haskins pulled away from his heavenly kiss and murmured, 'Oh-oh, what is that?'

As the fountain pen slowly entered his asshole, his eyes opened wide as the pen went deeper and suddenly stopped, and then Lucy started wiggling it around and stopped when Haskins shouted, 'Oh my god, what is that?'

As it felt like his cock had become a rocket and his milk balls were churning but in liquidation mode, that was it; his milk balls exploded and flooded his temptress pussy and that was game over or was it not. As Lucy held that fountain pen firm up against his prostate gland and smiled, as it felt like Haskins cock was reenergised; it remained hard as though it had been supported by Viagra.

'What are you doing?' asked the very concerned Mr Haskins with the intruder still in his ass; Lucy smiled and began caressing his prostate gland with the slow thrusting fountain pen. Haskins murmured, 'Oh-oh.'

As he felt his milk balls begin to churn, Haskins shouted, 'For heaven's sake, Lucy, will you stop that?'

'Stop what?' replied the smiling Lucy, who was also caressing his balls, while she slowly thrust that fountain pen in and out of his asshole. Haskins knew his time was up as he felt his balls suddenly tightening, thus starting his second coming of his milky-white fluids, shooting deep into Lucy's pussy, and he shouted, 'Get it out, get that thing out of my ass, Lucy. I can't stand it any more.'

With that, Lucy reluctantly, slowly withdrew the fountain pen from his ass and whispered, 'That wasn't so bad, old man, was it?'

Haskins frowned; he had never experienced a back-door entry before and wondered if he ever would again as he slowly stood and then slowly hobbled to his chair. Lucy began to laugh as she watched old Haskins walk and shouted, 'Is there something wrong, old man?'

'Something wrong?' shrieked Haskins in pain.

'It feels like I've been shot in the ass and not by a bullet either.'

The intrigued hysterically laughing Lucy replied, 'What hit you then?'

Haskins couldn't stand it; her amusement was driving him crazy. How dare she stick something in his ass and think it was funny?

'No more, no more with the laughing,' he shouted. 'Let us get down to business. What time should I expect you Saturday night?'

'I don't know,' replied Lucy.

'I'm not a psychic. I don't know what time your wife goes to bed, do I?'

'No no, I will tell you,' replied the smiling Haskins.

'Well, what time does your wife go to bed?' asked the smiling Lucy, who was slowly crawling towards him.

'Oh-oh,' murmured the curious but smiling Haskins, who was wondering what his voluptuous temptress was up to now. There would be no more intruders up his ass today, as his ass was so sore from the first time. As his temptress came closer, Haskins came to his senses and shouted, 'Ten o'clock, she goes to bed at ten o'clock, Lucy. What time can I expect you, my darling sexy goddess?'

On hearing this, Lucy stopped and pondered on her thoughts before replying, 'Why don't you invite me to dinner at seven thirty, and before ten, we can be all in bed together.'

'Together?' shrieked Haskins. 'What do you mean, my wife's not into threesomes; or sex, of any kind with me.'

Lucy smiled and whispered, 'Trust me, old man; changes are a coming, especially for your frigid, frosty wife and her untouched vagina.'

Haskins smiled; he couldn't believe what he was hearing and began wondering how Lucy was going to break the combination of his wife's panties and her frigid ways in the sexual department. He shook his head as those dirty thoughts flooded his mind, of his sultry temptress Lucy sampling his wife's untouched vagina with her probing, flickering tongue on her magical button, while her two fingers slowly thrust in and out of her vagina.

'Oh no,' he murmured as those dirty thoughts began a stirring in his loins and up periscope went his sleeping cock. What was he to do? The answer to the question was already in action as he looked down to see Lucy's head bobbing up and down on his rigid cock. His temptress was intoxicating and he loved her so; with her velvety sucking mouth driving him crazy, he shouted, 'About Saturday night, Lucy. Seven thirty will be fine, and if you manage to seduce my wife and get her in the bedroom with your sexual prowess powers, I will reward you well.'

On hearing this, Lucy stopped her sucking and looked up and smiled and said, 'Well, Mr Haskins, that's very kind of you. How about one last fuck before I go?'

'Why? Where you going?' asked the confused Haskins.

'Why don't you remember, sir? I don't work here any more,' replied the smiling Lucy.

'Oh yes, you do,' shrieked the enraged Haskins.

'Oh no, I don't,' replied the laughing Lucy.

'Don't you remember I quit yesterday over the stewards enquiry of payment for your deferral of an ass fucking by me and a promise of a hundred thousand dollars as a forfeit?'

'Oh,' murmured the confused Haskins.

'Oh, but I paid you the money in full,' replied the smiling Mr Haskins.

The fully dressed Lucy smiled at him, picked up her purse, turned, and walked towards the door.

'Where are you going?' shrieked the red-faced Haskins as he watched the voluptuous Lucy leave the room. He sat there in a bemused state of mind, not knowing what to do; as the door slowly closed, he hit the intercom button.

'Hello,' said a woman's voice.

'How may I help you, Mr Haskins?'

'Is that you, Jane?'

'Yes, it is me, Mr Haskins,' replied the smiling Jane as she watched her temptress Lucy's swivelling hips leave the office and said, 'How may I help you, sir?'

'Can you please come in and bring your notepad?'

'Coming, Mr Haskins.'

On hearing this, Haskins smiled and murmured, 'Don't worry, you will be.'

As the smiling plain Jane entered his office, he shouted, 'Stop where you are Jane. I will give you Five thousand dollars, for a sexy strip.'

'Who? Me, sir?' replied the bewildered Jane; she couldn't believe Mr Haskins was asking her to strip and he was going to pay her five thousand dollars. She closed the door and quickly walked over to the music centre and switched it on and began dancing to the music. Haskins smiled; she wasn't sexy but he was aching for more pussy action and she would have to do as he sat there gently stroking his floppy cock as he watched her slowly remove her clothes, down to her bra and panties. Haskins smiled as he felt his floppy cock come to life; and his eyes opened wide when she pulled her panties down to reveal her shaven haven.

'Wow!' whispered Haskins.

'Hairy muff yesterday, shaven haven today. What's going on?'

On hearing this, the naked Jane smiled as she slowly walked towards him and whispered, 'Have you got something hard in your hand for me, Mr Haskins?'

Haskins smiled and stood up, still gently stroking his rigid cock and replied, 'What? This?'

He let go of his rigid cock and whispered, 'Another five thousand dollars, Jane, if the mouse goes in the house.'

He pointed down at his rigid cock and her shaven haven too.

'Yippee!' shouted Jane as she ran around and dropped to her knees and began sucking on his rigid cock.

'Oh no,' murmured Haskins; her lips were not of velvet as his sultry temptress Lucy's were. This was an amateur blow job at its best, and Jane just wasn't doing it for him; he had the best blow job earlier from Lucy and whispered, 'Jane, can you please stand up and bend over the table as I want to fuck you?'

On hearing this, the bewildered Jane looked up and smiled and then quickly stood up and turned around and put her hands on the table; whilst spreading her legs she leaned forward and was in position ready for action. She looked around and whispered, 'What? Like this, Mr Haskins?'

Haskins smiled as he then stood behind her with his rigid cock in hand guiding it towards its Holy Grail that was her shaven haven; penetration was a formality as Jane's pussy was dripping wet as she thought of the ten thousand dollars.

'Ah,' she murmured as Haskins's rigid cock plunged into her shaven haven {pussy} and he was off, but unfortunately for Jane or on the other hand fortunately for her, this was a two stroke wonder fuck over in the blink of an eyelid. That was ten thousand dollars for a fuck that wasn't really a fuck, but a premature ejaculation on Mr Haskins's part. Haskins smiled as he slowly withdrew his cock and slapped her on her bare ass and said, 'Thank you, Jane. I'll just get you your money.'

CHAPTER 18

IT WAS LATE Friday night as Lucy finished her final private lap dance; it had been a good night, as she had amassed another four thousand dollars to go to her growing fortune and decided to make it an early night as she watched her customer leave the room. It was eleven thirty and she quickly dressed and then quickly followed her last customer out into the cheering crowd. On seeing her star performer girl walking towards her, Sally jumped up on to the stage and picked up the microphone and said, 'Gentleman, I've got a special treat for you tonight.'

The audience erupted in cheers and whistles; on hearing their cheers, Lucy stopped where she was and listened to Sally saying, 'Gentlemen,'–the cheers and whistles continued–'please for one night only, the starlight girl Lucy and I will do a striptease together here on the stage to stimulate your intoxicating eyes.'

On hearing this, the place erupted as they watched the dumbfounded Lucy make her way towards the stage and her smiling boss Sally, as Lucy looked up at the smiling Sally, she whispered, 'What are you doing?'

On seeing this, Sally said 'Here she is, boys. Give her a hand.'

The place erupted with cheers and clapping, as the shell-shocked Lucy got up on to the stage and slowly walked towards her voluptuous lady boss and started the show by locking lips with Sally in a smouldering kiss. It was hands on cocks for everybody as they whipped out their floppy cocks and gently began to stroke them, as they watched their erotic dream show of two luscious ladies kissing each other on the stage. But that was not all that was happening as Lucy slowly peeled off her bosses outer layers; the startled lost in the kiss Sally was wondering what she had done, down to her panties and bra.

While the fully clothed sultry temptress Lucy carried on with the sexy striptease of removing all of her clothes as she unclasped her bra; Lucy began her manoeuvres from her lips to her neck she went with tender kisses, then onwards slowly downwards with tender kisses towards her unmasked breasts, while her fingers gently massaged her magical button. This was the ultimate stage show for the Master Bates society of hand wanker's.

As Lucy began sucking on her nipples, Sally couldn't contain her excitement and shouted, 'Oh my god, Lucy, you're sensational.'

On hearing this, Lucy instantly stopped her nipple sucking and shouted to one of those horny hand wanker's for a chair; on seeing the chair approaching the stage, Sally murmured, 'Oh-oh what is she up to now?'

Her smiling face suddenly was in a state of shock when Lucy pulled her panties down and sat her down on the chair and spread her legs; on seeing this, the society of hand wanker's cheered 'More, more, more.'

Lucy didn't disappoint as she inserted a finger into her lady boss's pussy; one finger quickly became two as she went in search of her G spot. As she located it, Sally screamed, 'Oh my god, what are you doing?'

On hearing her boss's whims, Lucy looked up at her and smiled as she then slowly began to thrust those two fingers in and out of Sally's pussy at the tempo of the tap that wouldn't stop dripping and on the inward thrust caressing her G spot.

'Oh my goodness!' cried out Sally; as unbelievable sensations rushed through her body up to her exploding mind, she was fast approaching Climax City at breakneck speed. There was no stopping her now as she began screaming, 'Yes, yes, oh yes.'

That was all the encouragement Lucy needed and increased her thrusting fingers to the new tempo of the clock that wouldn't stop ticking. This was the final onslaught for Sally as her body began to shake, and she experienced that orgasm of the third kind. With her body shaking and her screams filling the air, Lucy withdrew her two fingers and watched Sally's pussy explode, spraying her built-up fluids into the air.

Sally stared in disbelief as she watched her watery fluids spray into the air; this was a simultaneous explosion, as each of the hand wanker's of Master Bates society shot their loads into the air too, and the place instantly smelt like a seafood store.

It was all too much for Sally when Lucy began her encore moment and inserted a finger back into her pussy; one finger quickly became two. Sally shook her head and screamed, 'No more, please no more, Lucy that was sensational. Now it's your turn.'

Lucy smiled before replying, 'Oh but I haven't finished, Boss.'

With that, she stood up and disrobed and Sally gasped, 'Fuck me,' as she stared open-mouthed at the big rubber cock.

Lucy was wearing the ten-inch strap-a-dick-to-me, and she was ready for action, asking the horrified Sally to stand up and turn around and holds on to the chair and spread her legs to the cheers of those horny patrons. Sally did what Lucy asked and then gasped, 'Oh no.'

When one horny patron shouted out, 'Fuck her in the ass, Starlight Girl.'

Lucy turned and looked at the audience as she picked up the microphone and asked, 'Who said that?'

'I did,' replied a six-foot-six smiling man. Lucy stared at him and then instantly turned into Dominatrix Lucy, as she jumped from the stage and walked towards the smiling giant with only one thing on her mind: to fuck him in the ass. But first she had to get his pants down. She stopped in front of him and said, 'Hello, hello, tall man, big cock I wonder?'

The tall man gasped, 'Oh.'

Her hand went inside his pants and grasped his sleeping cock. Oh what a handful! She wanted to see more and opened his pants with the other hand; as his pants dropped, she saw a snake that was his cock. Oh what a size it was! As she dropped to her knees, the giant looked up and murmured 'Oh why me, Lord?'

As her lips engulfed his rising cock, Chris, the giant man, looked down and smiled; she had lips of velvet that gently sucked on his big rigid cock. From her sucking to humming she went whilst trying to deep throat his big rigid cock.

'Oh my god, you have lips of velvet and humming too . . .'

His sentence was cut short, as her humming was sending tingling sensations down his big rigid cock, thus making his milk balls churn, and disaster was eminent; he had to stop her before he blew his load and shouted, 'Honey, please stop that.'

But it was too late; his milky-white fluids were on despatch from his churning balls, up through his long rigid cock into her humming mouth; game over or was it, as Lucy gulped down his milky-white fluids, her mind was planning the next move. Then as Lucy let his cock from her mouth, she instantly stood up and ran around behind the giant and waited; the unconcerned giant didn't look behind him and bent to pull up his pants.

With a full moon shining at her, Lucy murmured, 'Jackpot.'

As she ran up behind the giant with the big rubber cock in hand and placed it up against the giants smiling asshole, and then penetration followed, as she thrust her hips forward and in plunged the big rubber cock, taking the giants breath away. As it sank deep into his ass, he shouted 'What the fuck are you doing, lady?'

On hearing this, Lucy smiled before replying 'Well, tall man, I am doing to you what you wanted me to do to the lady up on the stage.'

The in pain giant looked up on the stage and saw the naked smiling Sally waving at him and then clasped her hands together as though she was praying and whispered, 'Few wee.'

As she then shook her head whilst patting her behind, implying thank heavens it was his ass and not hers, as Lucy then slowly began to thrust at the tempo of the tap that wouldn't stop dripping. This was the final straw for the giant when he began screaming, 'Get it out, get it out of my ass, you horny thing.'

On hearing this, Lucy began slapping his ass on every withdrawal thrust, as she thought he was encouraging her not to stop as he was enjoying it so much. But the giant wasn't enjoying; it he was in so much pain from the big slow thrusting rubber cock and shouted, 'No more, please no more. I will give you two thousand dollars if you stop now.'

His laughing buddies shouted, 'No, don't stop, honey. We will give you three thousand dollars if you carry on.'

'No no', shouted the giant, 'I will give you five thousand dollars if you stop.'

'No no', shouted a laughing buddy, 'make it ten thousand if you increase the speed of your thrusting.'

That was like waving a red flag at a bull with the sum of ten thousand dollars ringing in her ears; there was no stopping her as Lucy then grabbed hold of his hips and simultaneously increased her thrusting speed to the new tempo of the clock that wouldn't stop ticking. Giant Chris had teardrops rolling down his face, but these were not happy tears. No, these were tears of pain as it felt like he was being poked in the ass with a red hot poker.

'No more, please no more, honey. Twenty thousand dollars if you stop right now.'

On hearing this, Lucy immediately stopped; then with big the rubber cock embedded in his ass she reached around and grabbed hold of his big rigid cock and whispered, 'How much?' as she furiously began to stroke it.

'Twenty thousand dollars for fuck sake. Get that thing out of my ass.'

'Twenty thousand dollars?' whispered Lucy in his ear. 'How are you going to pay?'

Giant Chris couldn't believe it, a steward's enquiry on how he was going to pay, when all he wanted was that big rubber cock out of his ass so he could run to the toilet and extinguish that burning pain with cold water as it felt like his ass was on fire. He murmured, 'Oh, oh.'

As he suddenly felt his milk balls churning, he looked down to see Lucy's hand vigorously stroking his big rigid cock and whispered, 'Oh my god, I'm cumming.'

As his milky-white fluids shot into the air and hit one of his laughing buddies full in the face, laughter turned to shock for the laughing buddy as the milky-white fluids dripped from his face and he shrieked, 'Oh come on, Chris, we were only having a laugh.'

On hearing this, Chris smiled and replied, 'You've only got something on your face, where as I have got a sore red ass back there and it feels like it's on fire, and if this young lady would kindly remove that big rubber cock from there, I will be on my way to the toilet to extinguish those burning sensations.'

'What about my money?' asked the laughing Lucy.

'Money, money is all that you're interested in. My ass is on fire,' screamed the frustrated Chris.

'I need to get out of here to extinguish those burning sensations. What are you waiting for? Get that thing out of my ass.'

On hearing his whims, Lucy slowly withdrew her big rubber cock from his ass, as it slipped from his ass, giant Chris breathed a sigh of relief and then pulled up his pants and turned around and became that man on the run with the cindering asshole, as he then sprinted off towards the toilets to wash and extinguish those burning sensations. On seeing him run off like a mad man, Lucy turned around and made her way back to the stage and her laughing naked boss Sally.

As she walked towards her lady boss Sally, Sally looked horrified as she pointed at the big rubber cock strapped to Lucy's waist and shouted, 'Pooh e, there is no way that's going in there.'

As she pointed down to her pussy, Lucy stopped and looked down and murmured, 'Oh.'

When she saw the big rubber cock covered in brown muck and murmured, 'Oh yuck.'

She then turned and run off stage to wash that mucky rubber cock; before returning she went and got something from her purse: a small vibrator, to enhance the sexual pleasure she was about to perform on the naked Sally. But Sally had gone; Lucy stood centre stage not knowing what to do. As she looked around for her lady boss, she was still strapped and ready for action; suddenly one patron stood up and shouted, 'Hey, honey, over here.'

He then turned around and dropped his pants and bent over a table waiting to be taken.

'Shine on Harvest moon,' shouted another laughing patron and then there was laughter all around him, as they stared at his white ass glowing under the spot lights, Lucy smiled and jumped down off the stage and ran up to her waiting prey. The place erupted in shouts of

'Fuck him-fuck him'

Lucy took hold of the big rubber cock and placed it up against her prey's asshole; her prey's leg began to shake, as she then grabbed hold of his hips and thrust forward, in plunged the big rubber cock, bringing tears to her prey's eyes he shouted, 'Fuck me.'

On hearing this, Lucy smiled and whispered in his ear, 'I am fucking you, you tantalising little prick.'

With that, she reached around and gently began to stroke his rigid cock. Her prey was in heaven as her light fingers gently stroked his rigid cock, while she slowly thrust in and out of his asshole at the tempo of the tap that wouldn't stop dripping. Lucy on the other hand had diamonds on her mind. She was going shopping in the morning to buy herself a lovely diamond necklace, as this would be appropriate attire for her evening meal with her former boss Mr Haskins and his young wife.

She was going to portray a high class business woman for the meal. Oh she needed clothes too, which would be all paid for by the old fart that was soon to be her fuck buddy Mr Haskins, when she gave him the final bill for her sexual service. She suddenly came to her senses, when she looked at the head in front and then looked down and smiled and murmured, 'Fuck this. I've got to get out of here. I need my beauty sleep.'

With that she let go of his rigid cock and then placed her hand on his hip and increased her thrusting speed to the new tempo of the clock that wouldn't stop ticking. Her prey's face was a picture one second shocks the next normal, as that big rubber cock pulsated in and out of his asshole at the tempo of the clicking clock. This was the final moment for her prey as he shouted, 'I'm cumming.'

On hearing this, Lucy instantly stopped her thrusting, leaving the big rubber cock fully imbedded in his ass and quickly turned him around to face his laughing mates and vigorously began to stroke his rigid cock. With his milk balls churning, he murmured, 'Oh, oh.'

He watched his milky-white fluids fly through the air and went into one of his laughing buddies' mouth, and he repeatedly tried to spit it out; on seeing this, Lucy shouted, 'Jackpot.'

As she then slowly withdrew that big rubber cock, turned, and went on her way, as her watching audience gave her a standing ovation, she walked on by and headed for the changing rooms to shower. As she showered, she was joined by the smiling naked Sally who embraced her, as they shared a tender kiss.

This ignited Lucy's sexual prowess, and she gently began massaging Sally's magical button.

'Oh,' murmured Sally as wonderful sensations flooded her body, meanwhile Lucy's other hand was on the move, from caressing her ass to the insertion of a finger into her tingling pussy.

'Oh-oh,' murmured Sally as one finger quickly became two and Lucy was off with her slow thrusting fingers at the tempo of the tap that wouldn't stop dripping. Sally's mind was all shook up as she tried to wonder, as sensations flooded her body, where this horny sultry temptress had been all her life, as the sex with her was exhilarating and she never knew what was coming next, as Lucy was like an alcoholic she never knew how to stop.

Sally was losing her mind, as the wonderful sensations rushed through her body and couldn't restrain her desire any longer and shouted, 'Lucy, I love you.'

But those words didn't stop the sex crazed Lucy who carried on massaging Sally's magical button, whilst her two fingers slowly thrust in and out of her pussy at the tempo of the tap that wouldn't stop dripping. Sally couldn't stand it and shouted, 'Didn't you hear me, Lucy? I love you.'

Still Lucy didn't pay her know mind and carried on with her multi-finger attack on Sally's pussy. Sally was travelling at breakneck speed towards her destination, which was Climax City, and began shouting, 'Yes, yes, oh yes, my god, Lucy, marry me.'

On hearing this, Lucy increased the speed of her two thrusting fingers to the new tempo of the clock that wouldn't stop ticking; this was the final as Sally screamed, 'Yes, yes, yes.'

She arrived at Climax City and was experiencing that wonderful orgasmic moment, but Lucy refused to finish and carried on with her fast-thrusting fingers; thus Sally's multiple orgasmic moments began. This was a moment Sally would never forget; with her body shaking and her mind in a mess, she impersonated a stuttering person saying, 'Please . . . please . . . stop . . . stop, Lucy.'

But again Lucy was oblivious to her words and carried on with her fast-thrusting fingers, and Sally's mind exploded; this was an unbelievable moment that would never end as end was not in Lucy's portfolio and she didn't know how to stop if she was having a good time. With her body shaking as though she was on a fairground ride, Sally couldn't speak and instead slapped Lucy hard across the face and ended the game.

On feeling the slap, the stunned Lucy's fingers stopped as she looked up at Sally and whispered, 'What's wrong, boss?'

'What's wrong?' replied Sally. 'My god Lucy that was sensational. I can't take any more. I've experienced the multiple orgasm roller coaster rides that just wouldn't end. My mind is in a mess. Don't you ever stop, Lucy? I'm sorry I slapped you, but I just can't take any more.'

On hearing this, Lucy smiled as she slowly withdrew her two fingers from Sally's quivering pussy and then slowly stood and tenderly kissed Sally's lips and whispered, 'It's been fun, boss. Have a nice weekend. See you Monday, bye.'

On hearing this, the stunned Sally whispered, 'Bye.'

As she watched the naked Lucy walk away and wondered what she meant by see you Monday; her curiosity got the better of her so she turned the shower off and ran after her diamond asset shouting, 'Lucy, what do you mean by see you Monday? Aren't you working tomorrow?'

Lucy stopped, turned around, and looked at her puzzled looking boss and replied, 'Sorry, Sally I won't be here tomorrow or Sunday night as I'm having dinner with my former boss Mr Haskins and his young wife tomorrow evening, and I will be taking things down, in particular his young wife's panties.'

'Oh,' murmured the excited but very curious Sally, who was eager to know more and asked, 'Why is she into threesome, darling, or something?'

'I don't know,' replied the smiling Lucy.

'But after tomorrow night who knows, but one way or another I'm going to fuck her with my big rubber cock and more.'

'Really?' replied the smiling come laughing Sally who couldn't keep a straight face as she said, 'you're not going to do to her what you've just done to me, are you?'

'Maybe.' replied the smiling Lucy, knowing damn well she was sure going to try on the young frigid Mrs Haskins; her only wish was that they had a four poster bed to tie her to; all she had to remember was to take the rope. On seeing her smiling face Sally, shrieked, 'Oh no, you're going to do it.'

'Yes I am.' replied the excited Lucy as she walked towards the bewildered Sally, as she watched her diamond performer coming, Sally murmured, 'Oh.'

As Lucy began finger fucking her pussy again, first one finger quickly followed by a second the game was fully on as Lucy's lips locked with hers, as they passionately kissed Sally's mind lay in disarray, as she wondered if her temptress would ever tire. As she again began her journey destination Climax City; here she comes, a sudden thought came to mind as they tenderly kissed, Lucy's pussy was free from obstruction and Sally was eager to return the compliment and began finger fucking her diamond performer.

But Sally's fingers were not on the same par as her diamond lover Lucy's, as she was lost in wonderland, as the wonderful sensations flooded her body and her two fingers slipped from Lucy's pussy, as she fast approached Climax City for the umpteenth time tonight.

'Oh what a night!' she sighed; with her body shaking and her mind in a mess, she began screaming, 'Oh my god, yes, yes, yes.'

She arrived at Climax City and was experiencing that wonderful orgasmic moment; with her mission complete, Lucy smiled and slowly withdrew her two fingers from Sally's pussy and sucked them, tasting Sally's fragrant juices that tasted divine. It was time for her to go now, so she tenderly kissed Sally's lips and whispered, 'Goodbye, Sally, I will see you Monday evening.'

With that she turned and walked away, leaving the stunned Sally watching her voluptuous swaying hips, wishing she would stay. But time was of the essence, as Lucy quickly dressed and then left the locker room and in turn the club, she then went in search of a cab to take her home.

CHAPTER 19

A S SHE WALKED along the sidewalk in search of a cab, the sound of screeching brakes suddenly filled the air; it was Sam, the cabbie man, beeping his horn to attract her attention. Lucy stopped, turned around, and smiled when she saw it was Sam shouting, 'Hey, darling, can I take you home?'

As he ached for more sexual fun with the voluptuous Lucy, she ran to his cab and got in front with him and tenderly kissed his lips; her hand opened his pants to release his rising cock; Sam looked up and whispered, 'Thank you.'

As her velvety lips then encased his rigid cock, Sam quickly pulled over and parked the cab and turned off the ignition and lights too and enjoyed the moment; her sucking was so intense on his rigid cock. Sam murmured, 'Oh-oh.'

As he felt his milk balls begin to churn, he had to stop her and whispered, 'Honey, can we get in the back? I want to play too.'

On hearing this Lucy instantly stopped her intense sucking and then looked up and smiled then whispered, 'Okay, Sam that will be nice.'

As she sat up in the seat, she opened the door and got out and then closed the door as she loosened the buttons on her jacket; she then opened the back door and waited for Sam to get in and lay down on the back seat. Before stepping out of her miniskirt and getting in herself with her pussy just inches from his mouth, she again encased his rigid cock in her mouth. Sam murmured, 'Let the games begin.'

With that he began probing her pussy with his flickering tongue, but this was short–lived, as the expert cock sucker got into the groove; from her intense sucking, she began humming, sending tingling sensations down his rigid cock. This was like heaven to the smiling Sam as her tried in desperation to stop his milk balls churning, but it was no good; disaster was eminent, so in desperation he sucked a finger and stuck it in her ass.

Taking the sucking Lucy by surprise, thus releasing his rigid cock from its entrapment as his finger sank deeper into her ass, Sam breathed a sigh of relief as his milk balls stopped a churning and disaster had been avoided. It was time to change positions, but there was no room to enact the joys of sex, so Sam whispered, 'Let me take you home, honey, and maybe as a thank you a cup of coffee.'

Lucy smiled and whispered back, 'Fuck coffee. I want you to fuck me hard, big boy.'

With that she again engulfed his rigid cock and instantly began humming while she sucked on his big cock.

'Oh-oh,' murmured Sam as tingling sensations ran down his rigid cock and began those milk balls a churning; there was no stopping her now as Sam was lost in the heavenly moment; never before had a woman sucked his cock like this. He began murmuring, 'Oh yes, oh that feels so good, honey.'

On hearing this Lucy thought of another compliment to her sucking expedition and ran a finger slowly from his balls to his asshole; on feeling her finger pressed up against his asshole, Sam murmured, 'Fuck me, what are you doing back there?'

Too late was the answer to that question as her finger sank deep into his ass; his eyes suddenly opened wide as she hit his prostate gland. His cock went like a rigid bar in her mouth, and his milky-white fluids were on dispatch and that was game over as his fluids flooded her mouth.

He shook his head in disbelief and wondered who this voluptuous woman was and where she learnt how to suck cock; and the finger thing was out of this world mind blowing.

'Oh my god, where did you learn how to do that?' he shrieked. 'That was unbelievable.'

Lucy smiled and decided to change the subject and whispered, 'Did you mean it?'

'Mean what?' asked the puzzled looking Sam.

'Fuck you,' whispered Lucy as she tenderly kissed his lips.

'Do what?' shrieked the panicking Sam who shouted, 'You want to fuck me? Fuck me with what?'

With that Lucy opened her purse and took out the big strap-a-dick-to-me and whispered, 'With this, silly.'

As she waved it in front of his face, again speaking before engaging his brain, Sam said

'Fuck me, look at the size of that. There's no way that's going up my butt. No effing way, it's such a tiny hole.'

'Oh come on', replied Lucy, 'you didn't have any objections to a finger going up your ass.'

'Oh I know,' replied the smiling Sam.

'But that was a finger. Look at the size of that. No way?'

'Oh but it will fit,' whispered the smiling Lucy; as she again tenderly kissed him on the lips, the intrigued Sam asked, 'What do you mean it will fit how?'

'Lubrication,' whispered the smiling Lucy, as she began coaxing his floppy cock to life.

'Lubrication?' shrieked Sam. 'What lubrication?'

'K Y jelly, silly,' replied the laughing Lucy, who was now gently stroking his rigid cock in her hand. Next on her agenda was sucking time as she bent and engulfed his rigid cock; as her velvety mouth encased his rigid cock, Sam looked up and whispered, 'Thank you.'

Her sucking was so intense; it was like he was being sucked by a deluxe Hoover. This was so real, but it hadn't finished yet; he suddenly held his breath, when Lucy began to deep throat his big rigid cock. But it still hadn't finished and Lucy began to hum whilst she sucked, taking Sam's breath away; this was a blow job of the third kind.

His milk balls were churning like a whippy ice cream machine; he was getting ready to blow his load, when suddenly he heard a tapping on the window and looked to his left and froze when he saw the face of Officer Hardcock looking in. What was he to do? What could he do? He had a woman's head in his lap and murmured, 'Oh-oh.'

Without letting his rigid cock slip from her mouth, Lucy tried to say, 'What's wrong?'

But that sent unbelievable sensations charging down his rigid cock, and his milk balls erupted, sending his milky-white fluids on despatch up through his rigid cock into Lucy's sucking mouth, again Officer Hardcock tapped the window. Sam looked and whispered, 'What?'

That frustrated Officer Hardcock, and he said, 'Lower you window please, sir.'

Reluctantly Sam lowered the window; with the window fully down, Officer Hardcock said, 'Do you have a problem, sir, and why, is that young lady's head in your lap?'

On hearing a man's voice, Lucy looked up and smiled at the in looking officer Hardcock and said, 'Oh hello, Officer.'

On seeing her pretty face Officer Hardcock smiled back at her and whispered, 'What have you been up to, Young Lady?'

Lucy smiled at him as the sultry temptress in her came to life and whispered, 'I was just giving him a blow job, Officer, but that's over with now. Do you fancy one too?'

Officer Hardcock smiled at her and then whispered, 'Wow!'

She sat up, revealing her naked ample charms, and he said, 'Not half, Young Lady.'

On hearing his reply the unfazed naked Lucy got out of the cab and walked around and stood in front of Officer Hardcock and whispered, 'Do you like?'

Officer Hardcock smiled as he took in the vision of the naked goddess that stood before him; as his eyes went from her ample charms downwards to her pussy, he suddenly gasped, 'Wow!'

He saw she had a shaven haven. Thus began a churning in his pants as his sleeping cock began to rise and his eyes never left her shaven haven as she slowly walked towards him and in an instance dropped to her knees and released his throbbing cock. Once released, she gasped, 'I know you're an officer of the law, but a truncheon in your pants too.'

She then wrapped her velvety lips around his rigid cock and began sucking.

'Oh my goodness,' gasped Officer Hardcock. He had never experienced suction on his hard cock like this before; it was magnificent. Then the sultry temptress Lucy took it to another level and began humming whilst she sucked.

'Where have you been all my life,' shouted the ecstatically happy officer Hardcock as wonderful tingling sensations ran down his rigid cock and began his milk balls churning, then came the final instalment of this sensational blow job, when Lucy stuck a finger up his ass and game over was seconds away. As her finger caressed his prostate gland, Officer Hardcock shouted, 'Oh my god!'

As his milk balls suddenly tightened and his milky-white fluids were on despatch up through his rigid cock and into her sucking mouth, taking the sultry temptress Lucy by surprise as she tried in vain to gulp those milky fluids down. But in turn began choking on those fluids and released his rigid cock from her mouth and got a face full of his milky-white fluids. In the spur of the moment, the flabbergasted officer Hardcock shouted, 'Marry me, please marry me, you horny temptress. That was one hell of blow job, honey.'

Lucy looked up at him and smiled, as his milky fluids dripped from her face and on to her ample charms and said, 'Marry you, I don't know about that. But I sure could do with your help this evening, Officer Hardcock.'

'What can I help you with, honey?' replied the curious officer Hardcock.

'Well, if you'd like to take me home, Officer Hardcock, we will discuss it after you've fucked me with that big cock of yours.'

'What about me?' shouted the jealous Sam, who was envious of the cop with a big cock; although his was big too, the cop was taking the lady home and that wouldn't do, so in desperation he picked up the strap-a-dick-to-me and said, 'Hey, missy, I thought you were going to fuck me in the ass later,' as he waved the strap-a-dick-to-me in the air.

'Oh yes, what about you? I know you can come too, and we can have a threesome, my favourite daydream.'

'Oh yes,' replied the intrigued officer Hardcock.

'Yes,' replied Lucy, 'I will have two big cocks to play with, and when it comes to fucking, one big cock thrusting in and out of my pussy whilst the other stays dormant up my butt is my ultimate daydream.'

The flabbergasted duo looked at each other and then down at their cocks that were rigid and staring back at them and wondered who this woman was that was sexually electrifying. *What wouldn't she do?* Wandered Sam and then shook his head as that wasn't on her criteria, as she was the sexually charged sultry temptress that electrified him in her sexual demeanour.

Lucy was off again, sucking intensely on Officer Hardcocks rigid cock; on seeing this, the sexually excited Sam got out of the cab and walked up behind her and dropped to his knees, at the same time lifting her ass to do her doggy style, while she sucked on Officer Hardcocks rigid cock. As he penetrated her shaven haven, Lucy began to hum, while she sucked on Officer Hardcocks rigid cock.

'Oh no,' murmured Hardcock as tingling sensations flooded his groin; thus, his milk balls began to churn, it wouldn't be long before his milky fluids were on despatch and it again would be game over for him. But for Sam, the cabbie man, he was sure enjoying the ride with his slow thrusting in and out of her shaven haven at the tempo of the tap that wouldn't stop dripping and decided to take it to another level by reaching around and massaging her magical button.

As his fingers massaged her magical button, those wonderful sensations flooded her body and her humming became more intense on Officer Hardcocks rigid cock. This was the final count down for Officer Hardcock as his balls suddenly tightened and his milky fluids were on dispatch into Lucy's sucking mouth, game over.

'Oh my goodness!' he cried, as he then wondered what he could do to enhance her sexual pleasure, and as his cock slipped from her mouth, he clicked his fingers and murmured, 'I know.'

As he then dropped to his knees and then crawled under Lucy and pushed Sam's hand away and began gently massaging Lucy's magical button himself with his hand free. Sam decided to take it to the next level. He placed his hand on her hip and increased his thrusting speed to the new tempo of the clock that wouldn't stop ticking, which began Lucy's murmurs.

'Yes, yes, harder, Sam. Let me feel it.'

On hearing her whims, Sam didn't know what to do and slowed his thrusting down to the tempo of the dripping tap and on every withdrawal stroke slapped her ass.

'Ouch-ouch,' screamed the excited Lucy to entice him to slap her harder, as she was fast approaching her destination, Climax City; here she comes, and she began saying, 'Yes, yes, yes, oh yes, I'm cumming.'

With her body shaking, she had arrived at Climax City at breakneck speed and was enjoying that wonderful orgasmic moment and yet the boys carried on with their own sexual chores; for Hardcock, he was gently massaging her magical button. While Sam the cabbie man and his piston-like slow thrusting cock was slowly thrusting his rigid cock in and out of her quivering pussy at the tempo of the tap that wouldn't stop dripping.

The sultry temptress was in her element; as those wonderful sensations flooded through her body, she was on her way to destination Climax City; here she comes. But she felt left out as she was the only one without a sexual chore to do and looked to her right and saw Hardcocks floppy cock and began coaxing it to life as the sound of sirens filled the air.

On hearing the sirens, Hardcock froze; he didn't know what to do, run and join his comrades or stay and continue his sexual fun with this voluptuous temptress, with his heart saying, 'Go, man, go,' and his dick saying 'Stay, man, stay. I want to fuck it.'

He was lost in turmoil, as he continually massaged her magical button with his gentle massaging fingers; his concentration was once again broken by the sound of a tooting horn and the sound of his sergeant's voice shouting, 'Hey, Hardcock, are you there stroking your rigid cock?'

On hearing this, the flabbergasted half-dressed Hardcock stood and shouted back, 'I'm over here, Sergeant. What's up?'

Seeing him standing, the sergeant stopped his rolling car and gasped, 'Fuck me, Hardcock. Have you been at it again?'

As he watched him doing up his pants, on hearing his remark, Lucy smiled and got off her knees and crept towards the cab to get her wonderful sex toy, the strap-a-dick-to-me, and strapped it on. Then she stood, turned, and slowly walked towards Officer Hardcock and then stopped, turned, and stared at the gawping sergeant and smiled, with just her voluptuous tits on show the gawping sergeant, gasped, 'Fuck me, would you look at that?' as he stared at her voluptuous breasts; on seeing him taking in her voluptuous curves, Lucy smiled and stepped out from behind the cab.

'Fuck me, she's got a dick,' shouted the astonished sergeant as he watched her slowly walk towards him, saying 'Yes, Sergeant, I would like to fuck you,' as she gently stroked that big rubber cock slowly walked towards him.

'Oh no,' murmured the flabbergasted sergeant as he sped off down the road, leaving the hysterically laughing Hardcock behind him; on hearing his laughter, Mistress Lucy spun around and said, 'I don't know what you're laughing about. Get them down as you're up next.'

As she pointed at his pants, silence was golden as he stared at her in disbelief, not knowing what to do, should he stay or should he go now, as he wasn't ready for any backdoor intruder of any kind entering his asshole.

'Come on, get them down', whispered Lucy, 'and get down on your knees in the doggy position and take it like a man.'

Hardcock began stuttering as he stared at that big rubber cock.

'But . . . but . . . it's . . . it's . . . so . . . so . . . big . . . big. It's . . . it's . . . never . . . never . . . going . . . going . . . to . . . to . . . fit . . . fit . . . in . . . in . . . my . . . my . . . ass . . . asshole . . . hole.'

On hearing this Lucy smiled and replied, 'Oh I know, but you keep saying fuck me, so I am willing to oblige if only you would drop your pants and get down on your knees and take it like a man.'

Hardcock stood there, staring at the voluptuous goddess that stood before him, and he began to sweat as he unbuttoned his pants and let them fall to his knees, Sam, the cabbie man, couldn't believe what he was seeing. When Officer Hardcock turned around and dropped to his knees and resumed the stance of a doggy, Lucy turned and looked at him and asked, 'Hey, Sam, are you ready for the invasion of this big rubber cock into your asshole too, as you too on numerous occasions have said fuck me? If you go over and drop your pants and resume the position next to Officer Hardcock, I will also do you. By the way, do either of you, Gentleman, have any oil?'

'Oil?' shrieked the panic-stricken Hardcock. 'What do you need oil for?'

'It's for you,' replied the smiling Lucy.

'Lubrication on your butt hole will ease penetration when I stick this big rubber cock up your butt.'

'Oh I've got some.' said Sam as he walked over to his cab and opened the boot and took out a small container of three-in-one oil and said, 'Will this do?'

He closed the boot and then turned and walked over to the voluptuous sex goddess with the big rubber dick, and as he handed it to her, he tenderly kissed her lips and then opened his pants and resumed his position next to the distraught officer Hardcock. Then came the lubrication as the smiling Lucy squirted the three-in-one oil over Hardcocks ass and began prodding his butt hole with her finger.

On insertion Officer Hardcocks eyes opened wide as her finger sank deeper into his butt.

'Oh my god,' he sighed as one finger quickly became two and hit his prostate gland; with his cock impersonating an iron bar and his milk balls churning, Hardcock was on the verge of an almighty climax. When suddenly Lucy withdrew her two probing fingers from his ass and then grabbed hold of that big rubber cock and placed it up against his asshole, Hardcock was gritting his teeth as he tried in vain to stop himself from farting, as he was literally shitting himself as he didn't know if it would be wind or shit coming out first.

He couldn't stand his built-up anxiety any longer and shouted, 'I can't stand it, honey. I'm out of here before I shit myself.'

With that he went to stand up with his ass just inches from her face; he blew her a kiss, but this was no ordinary kiss. It was one from his back door.

'Oh my goodness,' gasped Lucy as she tried to hold her breath, as she watched the stumbling officer Hardcock run away as he tried in vain to put his pants on, from holding her breath to laughter she went taking in the smell of that smelly fart. Oh what a smell it was. Her attention was drawn to the laughing cabbie Sam with the naked ass as she moved closer; she then oiled her fingers, getting them ready for lubricating of his asshole.

Suddenly Sam's eyes opened wide when he felt her two fingers run along the crack of his ass and stop and then slowly penetrate his asshole; as those two fingers sank deep into his ass Sam couldn't contain his excitement and whispered, 'Oh that feels so nice, darling. Are you going in with the big one soon?'

On hearing this, Lucy whispered, 'Are you sure?'

As she slowly withdrew her two fingers and placed that big rubber cock up against his asshole, and then, before penetration squirted the three-in-oil oil over it to ease penetration and then slowly thrust forward and in plunged the big rubber cock. As that big rubber cock sank deeper into his ass, Sam murmured 'Oh that feels so big!'

With no reservations coming from the calm mild-mannered Sam, Lucy smiled as she slowly began her thrusting at the tempo of the tap that wouldn't stop dripping. Sam remained silent, and the only expression on his face was shock cum joy, as that big rubber cock slowly thrust in and out of his asshole. This was something he had never visioned, being fucked in the ass by a voluptuous women, especially a goddess like Lucy.

An observer quietly watched whilst gently stroking on his rigid cock; it was Officer Hardcock, giving himself a treat, as he watched the voluptuous temptress fuck the cabbie man. He was sure glad it wasn't his ass being invaded by that big rubber cock. The eagle-eyed Lucy caught sight of a shadow on the wall; there seemed to be hand movement implying it was a man wanking. This intrigued her and she reached round and gently began stroking Sam's rigid cock.

When he felt her hand encase his rigid cock, Sam murmured, 'Wow!'

As her gentle fingers began stroking his rigid cock, with his balls churning, Sam tried in desperation to extinguish his burning loins, but it was of no use when Lucy saw the shadows hand moving faster; she herself increased her stroking speed to the tempo of the clock that wouldn't stop ticking. Sam murmured, 'Oh no,' as his milk balls suddenly tightened and the despatch of his milky fluids commenced; as Lucy felt his balls tighten she embedded the big rubber cock in his ass and whispered, 'Kiss me, Sam.'

On hearing this, Sam slowly lifted up and then looked around and was tenderly kissed by Lucy, as his milky fluids shot into the air and that was game over, or was it not as Lucy pushed him forward and again began her thrusting. The astonished Sam looked behind him and whispered, 'No more, please no more. That big cock of yours is hurting me.'

Lucy smiled and whispered, 'Okay, darling.'

With that she instantly stopped her thrusting and then slowly withdrew her big rubber cock to the relief of the grimacing Sam, who was thankful for the withdrawal of that big rubber cock from his burning ass. With the fun over, the laughter began when Sam stood and began hobbling around.

'What's wrong with you?' asked the giggling Lucy.

'Are you kidding me?' replied the astonished Sam whose asshole had been stretched to new limits; he shook his head in disbelief as he pulled up his pants and wondered if she was having a laugh as it felt like his asshole was on fire, from the stoking it had from her and her big rubber cock. Dressed, he slowly walked towards her saying, 'It's time I got you safely home, honey. I've had a wonderful time, and I don't want it to end. But I know I'm not on your agenda.'

'Agenda? What agenda?' replied the smiling Lucy.

'When you get me home, I'm going to bed. You're welcome to join me if you like. But I must warn you I'm going to sleep, but when I wake up and see you lying by my side, the day will start with a bang.'

With that she tenderly kissed his lips and then whispered, 'What do you say?' Sam smiled and whispered, 'Okay,' as he started the cab and drove off.

CHAPTER 20

A S THE SUNLIGHT filled the room, Lucy woke up, and through her sleepy eyes, she saw him sleeping there. Her heart began to beat faster as she wondered who he was, and then her sexual curiosity mind felt his groin and murmured, 'Fuck me, it's hard.'

On seeing her murmur didn't wake him, she went under the covers to begin her dawn patrol that was to suck his rigid cock as she encased his rigid cock in her mouth, Sam's eyes opened wide as he wondered where he was. Then he murmured, 'Oh.'

As she began sucking on his rigid cock, her lips were of velvet, and as her tender fingers caressed his ball bag, he silently sighed, 'Hmm, what a way to start the day!'

He closed his eyes to enjoy the moment, but the moment quickly passed when Lucy began intensely sucking on his rigid cock; it felt like he was getting head from the Deluxe Hoover or something. By gummy, it was unbelievable; her suction was out of this world, and then, she began to hum, sending tingling sensations down his rigid cock; thus began his milk balls churning.

On feeling this, his eyes opened wide as he tried in vain to stop himself from cumming, but it was of no use, and his milk balls exploded sending his milky-white fluids shooting into her sucking mouth and shouted, 'Oh my goodness, that was an unbelievable way to start the day!'

With her sucking duties over with, Lucy let his cock fall from her mouth and whispered, 'Would you like a cup of coffee, Sam?'

'Oh yes, please,' replied the smiling Sam.

'So do I,' replied Lucy.

'If you would like to go downstairs and make it, mine is milk, no sugar, thank you.'

With that she sat up and shuffled across the bed and picked up the phone, leaving the frowning Sam to his own devices as he got off the bed and headed for the open door, through the door and down the stairs he went and into the kitchen.

Lucy sat there frowning as she listened to the ringing tone; after several rings, the phone was answered and a woman said, 'Hello, who is it? Do you know what time it is?'

'No I don't know what time it is,' replied the delightful Lucy. 'But I must tell you, Mandy that I've had a big dick for breakfast, and now I must go shopping.'

'Who is it?' shrieked the sexually excited Mandy, intrigued by the conversation and who was calling her so early in the morning.

'It's me Lucy, Mandy. Do you fancy coming shopping with me?'

'Yes,' replied the excited Mandy, who was eager to be in the temptress Lucy's company and said, 'Where and when shall we meet, Lucy?'

'Meet?' replied Lucy. 'No I will pick you up in, say, an hour.'

'Okay,' whispered Mandy.

'I will see you in an hour's time, bye for now.'

She then hung up and shouted yippee as she stamped her feet on the bed, in anticipation of what was coming her way whilst in the company of the sultry temptress Lucy and then got up and headed for the shower.

It was 10.30 a.m. as the sound of a beeping horn filled the air, and Mandy rushed to the window to see who it was and smiled when she saw the gorgeous Lucy walking up towards her front door. She murmured 'Wow!'

She turned and opened the front door and was greeted by Lucy's smiling face, from a smile to a kiss went Lucy's voluptuous lips, as she stepped forward and tenderly kissed her lips and then grabbed her behind to turn the kiss into a smouldering kiss. The spellbound Mandy stood there motionless as the sultry temptress Lucy explored her open mouth with her probing tongue, whilst her hand went from caressing her ass up under her short skirt and began massaging her masked pussy.

On feeling those massaging fingers on her masked pussy, Mandy's eyes opened wide, what was she to do as she looked around for nosey neighbours, and instead of seeing neighbours, she saw the smiling waving Sam waiting in his cab. Then her eyes stared into Lucy's smiling eyes when she felt her fingers slip inside her panties and began massaging her magical button. Oh this was too much for her, so she stepped back inside and closed the door.

As the door closed the electrifying sexual moment was over; when the sound of the frustrated cabbies horn filled the air, Lucy came to her senses and withdrew her hand from Mandy's panties and then stepped back and whispered, 'Are you ready to go and have some fun, Mandy?'

'Where are we going?' asked the smiling Mandy.

'Clothes shopping,' whispered the smiling Lucy.

'Really?' whispered Mandy.

'Yes really,' replied Lucy.

'Clothes for me and you Mandy?'

'Who's paying?' whispered the curious Mandy.

'I am, silly,' replied Lucy. 'I am making lots of money in my new job, Mandy, and I would like to treat you to a fantastic shopping day, as a thank you.'

'Thank me? Thank me for what?' replied the confused Mandy.

'You know your adventure under the table the other day?'

'Oh,' whispered Mandy. 'Did you like it?'

'Did I like it?' replied Lucy. 'It was wonderful.'

She again embraced the smiling Mandy and then tenderly kissed her lips; the kiss was merely a peck as again the sound of the tooting horn filled the air.

'Who is that?' whispered Mandy.

'It's the man with the big dick I was telling you about, and he will be our chauffer for the day and we will reward him later.'

'Reward him? What do you mean reward him, Lucy?' replied the sexually curious Mandy.

'With our naked bodies, and you can sample his big dick, Mandy,' whispered the smiling Lucy, who then opened the door and took Mandy's hand and slowly led her towards pleasure land; as the smiling duo stepped outside, Mandy turned to close the door and she murmured, 'Keys,' and let go of Lucy's hand and ran back inside to get her purse; on seeing her desire of the day run inside, Lucy turned and slowly walked towards the cab. Sam smiled as he watched the sultry temptress walking towards his cab and wished he could see more of her hidden secrets. Suddenly a gush of wind blew her short dress up, thus exposing her hidden delights.

'Wow!' Sam murmured as he stared at her shaven haven and quickly released his sleeping cock and gently began stroking it, as to coax it to life as he watched the unconcerned Lucy suddenly stop and then turn around and bend over and touch her toes. This was too much for the gawping Sam as he quickly got out and ran up behind her; Lucy's eyes opened wide when his big rigid cock penetrated her pussy, and he began shagging her in the street.

'Oh Sam', she murmured, 'I heard somebody once sing dancing in the street, but shagging. Really, you are awful but I like you.'

With that she reached up and grabbed his balls and gently squeezed them; Sam's eyes opened wide as her fist clenched tighter and he whispered, 'Any tighter, honey, my eyeballs will pop out.'

On hearing this Lucy began to laugh and as she was about to speak, Mandy slapped his bare ass and said, 'Do you mind? You're in a public place, and we don't do that sort of a thing around here.'

'What? Have sex?' replied the smiling trying-not-to-laugh Sam.

'No no', screamed Mandy, 'yes we do have sex but not in public places.'

'Oh sorry about that,' whispered Sam.

'You see I had this raging hard-on and when I saw Lucy's naked delights and when she bent over, the raw animal instinct in me came to life and I stuck my rigid dick in her hole. Sorry or in the words of the dog woof-woof.'

Mandy smiled and replied, 'That's okay. You can do me later, woof-woof.'

With the conversation over with, Sam slowly withdrew his big rigid cock and placed it back in its hiding place and then softly spanked her butt before turning around and running back to his cab.

It was mid-day as the enthused Jim-bob walked around the clothes store, recalling his father's ceremony sermon to his flock of simple-minded believers on, how the world of sex was a sin; he held them spellbound by his words, 'You must not buy their dirty magazines and films.'

Suddenly his train of thought was broken by a sudden movement in the changing room and the glimpse of a woman removing her dress; his young hormones took centre stage as he rushed to get a clearer view. His eyes opened wide when he saw a woman on her knees in front of the other one and pulling her panties down, which began movement in his groin as his sleeping cock began to rise.

'Oh no', he murmured, 'what's going on down there?'

Jim-bob opened his pants to see what was going on, 'Oh no.'

He whimpered when he saw his rigid cock staring back at him. What was he to do? What could he do but run and find a hiding place and take it in hand as he watched; he couldn't believe what he was watching as he gently stroked his rigid cock. Lucy was muff diving Mandy; he had never seen anything like it before, and he got carried away with his wanking hand and murmured, 'Oh no,' as he felt his balls suddenly tighten and his milky-white fluids shoot into the air, and a young sales cashier shouted, 'Oh you dirty little pervert.'

The startled Jim-bob looked up to see the smiling cashier and murmured, 'Wow!'

She was a stunner, a five-foot-five blonde bombshell who replied, 'Oh what a shame! If you'd asked, I would have given you a blow job for ten bucks, but here, lick this for ten bucks.'

As she raised her skirt and showed him her neatly trimmed pussy, temptation was staring him in the face, and those haunting words of his father filled his mind.

Sex is a naughty thing son. Walk away.

But those youthful hormones were shouting out, 'Go on. What are you waiting for? Lick it.'

He held his breath as his face got closer and then stuck out his tongue and began probing her pussy, but this did nothing for her as he was merely a novice in the art of pussy licking, so she reached down and began massaging her magical button. But for Jim-bob, this was intoxicating and he was eager to explore more and slowly stood and began sucking on one of her nipples, whilst his finger slowly thrust in and out of her quivering pussy.

As those wonderful sensations rushed through her body, the sexy bombshell whispered, 'Hey, Jimmy, do you fancy a fuck?'

On hearing his name, the startled Jim-bob looked up at her smiling face and whispered, 'Oh yes please, honey, and I'm so thirsty to explore more of your naked charms.'

The young cashier smiled and took him by the hand to lead him to paradise; as she turned Jim-bob's finger slipped from her pussy and then, he quickly put it in his mouth as she slowly walked away and tasted her pussy's juices. Wow he was intoxicated on them as his eyes took in the vision of her swaying hips; he just couldn't believe he was going to lose his virginity at the tender age of sixteen, and those memories of his father were fast slipping away.

As it was time for him to be a man and step up enjoy the world of sex, as the young cashier led him into a storeroom and closed the door, she then whispered in his ear, 'Close your eyes. lover boy.'

On hearing this, Jim-bob closed his eyes as she removed her outer layers and bra too, and then she shouted, 'Surprise.'

On hearing this, the sexually excited Jim-bob spun around and stared open-mouthed at the naked voluptuous goddess that stood before him, from her smiling face his vision slowly travelled down her body and stopped, at her breasts as he quickly shed his clothes. With his cock slowly rising he walked towards her and embraced his naked charm; as his lips tenderly kissed hers, his hands gently caressed her ass. This wasn't on her agenda. She wanted to be fucked, not caressed and unlocked lips with him and whispered, 'Fuck me, Jimmy. I haven't got time to fool around, Jimmy. I should be working.'

Jim-bob looked at her and smiled and then whispered, 'How do you want to do it, honey?'

On hearing this, the young cashier smiled and quickly lay down on the floor and pointed to her pussy and said, 'Come on, Jimmy, get that rigid thing of yours in here.'

As she pointed at his rigid cock, Jim-bob smiled and was down on her like a shot; in seconds his rigid cock was penetrating her and then with one gentle thrust in plunged his rigid cock, going deep inside her to a place it had never gone before. His rigid cock felt like it had entered a furnace as it was so bloody hot in there and he began pulling faces, as he tried in vain to stop himself from cumming. But it was of no use; he had to get out of there before his milk balls exploded, and he shot his milky-white fluids deep inside her.

As he quickly withdrew his rigid cock, the young cashier frowned and asked, 'What do you think you are doing, Jimmy?'

On hearing this Jimmy smiled as he looked deep into her eyes, then came shock on her face as he placed his rigid cock up against her asshole and whispered, 'Do you take a back-door entry, Miss?'

The startled young cashier stared into his eyes and whispered, 'No I don't, but do you as I have something in my purse if you do.'

The bewildered Jim-bob didn't know what to say or what he was doing here anyway, he was told by his father that sex was a naughty thing and that he should only engage in such things when he was married, and yet, here he was indulging in his sexual cravings. The frustrated young cashier asked, 'Are you fucking me or what, as there will be no back-door entries on my body unless we do yours first?'

'Ouch,' replied Jim-bob as he had no intention of anything going up his ass either, what was he to do; he had already been inside her; he was lost in a wilderness of wonder when somebody whispered in his ear, 'Ask her to get up on her hands and knees, Jimmy, as you want to fuck her doggy style.'

On hearing, the woman's voice Jimmy froze, as he wondered who it was and then, a gasp from the young cashier brought him back to the moment when she whispered, 'Who are you?'

Lucy smiled and then whispered, 'Hello, my name's Lucy. I saw this young man masturbating, whilst I was helping my friend in removing her under garments, and when I saw you flash your pussy at him and he, in turn, sampled your delights, I got curious when you took him by the hand and brought him here, so I quickly dressed and followed you. Now if this young man's not up to it. I will gladly take his place.'

As she removed her jacket that was covering her waist revealing she was strapped and ready to go.

'What's that?' gasped the young cashier.

'It's my rubber cock', replied the smiling Lucy, 'and I will be using it to fuck you if the young master baiter doesn't perform.'

'I'm no lesbian,' gasped the young cashier.

'Neither am I,' replied Lucy. 'I'm only here to perform. If the master baiter doesn't get on with it, go on tell her to get up on her hands and knees as you want to do it doggy style.'

On hearing this, the young cashier quickly resumed the position and wondered who it would be. Would it be the young man or the voluptuous young lady who would be fucking her from behind? She held no reservations as she refused to look behind. Up stepped Jim-bob but Lucy wasn't having it and pushed him aside and took centre stage with rubber cock in hand and penetrated the young cashier's pussy.

The young cashier held her breath in anticipation wishing it was the young lady's cock and not young Jimmy's, as she knew the rubber cock had no shelf-life and the shagging would never end, whereas Jimmy's cock was human and if he came in a jiffy, she would have to go back to work. In plunged the rubber cock, taking the young cashiers breath away as it sank deep into her pussy; her wishes had been granted and the shagging began.

Lucy began her thrusting slow at the tempo of the tap that wouldn't stop dripping and whilst she slowly thrust in and out, she reached around and began massaging the young cashier's magical button.

'Wow!' murmured the young cashier as wonderful sensations rushed through her body and thus she began her journey, destination Climax City; here she comes. It would be a journey filled with wonderful sensations. The young cashier was in heaven as the sultry temptress Lucy slowly thrust her rubber cock in and out of her quivering pussy and began murmuring, 'Oh-ha.'

With every thrust, oh what a wonderful journey she was on when suddenly she thought I can suck cock and said, 'Hey, Jimmy, can you come and stand in front of me so that I can suck on your erect cock?'

On hearing this, the naked Jim-bob was in front of her; in seconds with his cock erect and staring up at the ceiling, the cashier smiled and began sucking on his cock's bald head as though it was her favourite lollipop.

'Oh my goodness, that feels so good,' murmured the excited Jim-bob as he tried in vain to think of something else to stop his milk balls churning as he was getting close to blowing his load, being a young man enjoying his first encounters in the world of sex. Oh it was wonderful. He wondered why he had taken so long to venture into the naughty side, and then, his father crossed his mind, him being a preacher and all, he remembered the time he saw his father masturbating in the vestry, as he watched the Norah Knockers show with her big buxom breasts whilst singing,

> I'm a secret master baiter, have a wank
> I've been trying to give it up but it's oh so hard, have a wank
> I just can't help believing, when I'm holding my cock in my hand and
> It feels, so big and hard and I wrap my fingers around it like a glove, have a wank
> This time she's really going to make me cum, have a wank
> Now I must get up and shoot my stuff over her buxom breasts, have a wank
> I'm a secret master baiter, have a wank have a wank
> I've been trying to give it up, but it's been one of those nights, have a wank

His vision suddenly ended as his milk balls suddenly tightened and his milky-white fluids were on dispatch; from his milk balls they went up through his rigid cock and into her sucking mouth and that was game over for him, Whereas Lucy was getting into the groove by upping the speed of her thrusting to the new tempo of the clock that wouldn't stop ticking; the young cashier began murmuring, 'Yes, yes, that's it. Finally I've found somebody special.'

'Special?' replied the smiling fast-thrusting Lucy.

'Yes, yes, oh yes,' screamed the ecstatic young cashier, who was experiencing that mind-blowing orgasmic moment, and her screams filled the storeroom and drifted out into the shop getting her boss's attention, the one and only Nick Nosey Parker, who quickly made his way to the store cupboard to see what was going on.

CHAPTER 21

AS HE OPENED the door, he stared flabbergasted at what he saw as there stood three naked people staring back at him, a young man and two young ladies, one of which was a member of his staff, and the other was wearing a rather large big rubber cock. He murmured those immortal words, 'Well fuck me would you look at the size of that?'

On hearing his words, Lucy smiled and then began slowly walking towards him, and again Nosey Parker murmured those immortal words, 'Fuck me.'

As his staring eyes were transfixed on that big rubber cock approaching him wishing it was up his ass, as he was having such a nice day and that would make his day complete, as he was a bisexual man who was always looking to enhance his sexual portfolio, and being fucked by a woman was top of his list. For Lucy she had ulterior motives as she stared at his bulging crotch and dropped to her knees and released his throbbing cock and then began sucking on its bald head.

'Oh my goodness,' murmured Nosey Parker as her velvety lips encased his erect cock, and then, she began sucking; Nosey Parker looked up as he tried in vain to stop himself from cumming before he had enjoyed that big rubber cock up his ass.

'Aren't you going to fuck me in the ass?' he murmured; on hearing this Lucy began to hum while she sucked, sending tingling sensations down his rigid cock. At the same time she stuck a finger up his ass; one finger quickly became two, and Nosey Parker didn't know what to do. He looked up, seeking for salvation, but there was no answer and then his body shook as Lucy caressed his prostate gland. Thus his milk balls exploded, sending his milky-white fluids into her sucking mouth, and that was game over for him or was it.

As Lucy let his cock fall from her mouth, she withdrew her two fingers from his asshole and slowly stood and then kissed him softly on the lips and then whispered in his ear, 'Get down on your knees, and get ready for something big going up your ass, man.'

Nosey Parker smiled and quickly closed the door and then walked a couple of steps and dropped to his knees and waited to be taken doggy style by the smiling Lucy, who in turn walked up behind him and then dropped to her knees and placed that big rubber cock up against his asshole. On feeling that big rubber cock, Nosey Parker closed his eyes and waited for that big rubber cock to penetrate his asshole.

As Lucy slowly thrust forward and in plunged that big rubber cock, Nosey Parker shouted, 'Fuck me, steady on back there, madam. That is hurting me.'

On hearing his words Lucy smiled and whispered back, 'Give me a chance. I've got it in there before I undertake the fucking stage of your asshole.'

Nosey Parker began pulling faces as that big rubber cock sank deeper into his ass and his whimpers of 'No more please no more' filled the air.

But Lucy didn't pay him no mind and slowly began pulsating that big rubber cock at the tempo of the tap that wouldn't stop dripping; Nosey Parker's face was a two-dimensional picture; one second it was horror, as that big rubber cock sank deep into his ass, and then relief as it slowly withdrew. He was lost in the pain cum relief scenario as a teardrop fell from his eye. He had waited a long time to be fucked this way, especially at the hands of a woman; never in his wildest dreams could he have dreamt that dream.

He loved the invasion of his asshole, and his cock slowly began to rise. What was he to do? Give him-self a wank while she slowly thrust or say, 'Excuse me, honey, I have something hard down here, and it needs a hand.' He decided on option 2.

On hearing this, Lucy reached around and smiled when she took hold of his rigid cock and whispered, 'Is that for me?'

As she gently began to stroke it, Nosey Parker closed his eyes and imagined he was her boyfriend, but that was merely a fantasy as she was every man's voluptuous dream girl. Oh why couldn't she be his? So he shouted, 'Marry me, please marry me, you buxom vixen.'

On hearing this Lucy smiled and wondered if he was insane or something; she was way out of his league you could say she was a pin-up girl, while he resembled no one at all. She didn't mind fucking him but that was all on her criteria. She suddenly upped the pace of her stroking his rigid cock to the new tempo of the clock that wouldn't stop ticking whilst leaving the big rubber cock fully embedded in his ass.

Nosey Parker's eyes opened wide as his milk balls began to churn.

'Oh no,' murmured Nosey Parker, as he tried in vain to think of something to extinguish his burning loins; he was lost in the moment and never wanted it to end as he wondered who this sultry temptress was. He had never experienced such versatility while being fucked in the ass, and his normal experiences were of him sucking their cocks, before they stuck their rigid cocks in his ass and fucking him profusely. This woman was something else; while she was fucking his ass, she was also stroking his rigid cock. Wow what an experience!

Suddenly his balls tightened, and his milky-white fluids were on despatch from his balls and then up through his rigid cock and then shot into the air. Oh what a cumming moment that was! Yet her big rubber cock remained buried deep in his ass. He wondered if it was over. No, it wasn't as Lucy then pushed his head forward and he dropped on to his hands and her thrusting began, but she didn't start slow as she was off at the pace of the ticking clock. This was too much for Nosey Parker, and he began shouting, 'Ooh-ha.'

With every thrust, this was enticing her to hurt him more, but he wasn't prepared for what was about to happen, when she began slapping his ass while she thrust at the tempo of the tap that wouldn't stop dripping and a teardrop fell from his eye. But these were not tears of pain but tears of joy as he loved it so much and he screamed out, 'Yes, yes, harder, you luscious temptress.'

On hearing this, the sultry temptress Lucy wondered what else she could do to enhance the pain on Mr Nosey Parker and then she clicked her fingers and instantly stopped her thrusting and then slowly withdrew her big rubber cock and Nosey Parker shouted out, 'No no, please carry on.'

Lucy smiled and then slapped his ass and then stood and walked away as the distraught Nosey Parker took in the sight of her luscious swaying ass; he couldn't stand it and got up and ran after her, as he had unfinished business with the sultry temptress and wrapped his arms around her. With his hands on her buxom breasts, Lucy whispered, 'Is there anything wrong, sir?'

On hearing this Nosey Parker kissed her neck and then whispered in her ear, 'Yes, there is. Please can I fuck you now?'

On hearing this Lucy smiled and stepped out of the strap-a-dick-to-me and then let it fall to the floor and then slowly turned around and caressed his floppy cock, while kissing his lips so the game began. Mr Nosey Parker's hands were caressing her ass, but this wasn't enough for him, so he slowly lowered her to the floor, and when her back hit the floor, their kissing stopped as he went on manoeuvres to taste her pussy.

From her lips to her neck he went with tender kisses and then on downwards to her ample charms, where he sucked on her nipples coaxing them to life, where they stood like bullets, and then onward he went down her body with tender kisses towards her Holy Grail that was her shaven haven. As he arrived at her shaven haven, he began probing her inner labia with his flickering tongue, while his fingers gently massaged her magical button, and Lucy, in turn, waved Jim-bob over with his rigid cock to give him some head.

On seeing her waving hand, Jim-bob rushed over and dropped to his knees and put his rigid cock up to her mouth, which Lucy quickly engulfed in her mouth and began sucking.

'Oh no,' whimpered Jim-bob as her velvety lips encased his rigid cock and then began sucking; her sucking was electrifying and Jim-bob looked up and murmured, 'Oh help me, Lord.'

But his words were not answered, as he had entered the valley of sin and the man upstairs wasn't listening. Suddenly her sucking turned to humming; thus, Jim-bob began praying as his milk balls began churning and he murmured, 'Oh no.'

As his milk balls suddenly exploded sending his milky-white fluids on despatch; from his exploding balls, they went through his rigid cock and into Lucy's sucking mouth, and that was game over for him. As Jim-bob's cock fell from her mouth, Lucy smiled as she watched him walk away, and then her vision took in the sight of the young cashier, who had joined the Master Bates society as she stood there massaging her magical button.

On seeing this Lucy said, 'Hey, darling, come over here and sit on my face.'

On hearing this the young cashier smiled and took away her massaging fingers and quickly skipped towards her; in seconds she straddled Lucy's face and was slowly dropping to her knees with her pussy just inches from her face. Lucy began her muff diving mission with her probing tongue while her two fingers gently massaged the young cashier's magical button; as the sensations flooded her body, the young cashier closed her eyes and began dreaming.

But these were not dreams of men. No they were not; they were dreams of the one and only Lucy, the sultry temptress, and her desire to be her lover. She had never dreamt of a woman before, but Lucy was someone special, a goddess that wore no panties and big bosoms too. She had given her a wonderful orgasmic moment earlier, the likes of which she had never experienced before, as her normal lovers were men and they were the wham bam thank you Maim merchants.

Lucy wanted more durability in her muff diving mission and whispered, 'Hey, Nosey Parker, get lost.'

On hearing this Nosey Parker looked up and said, 'Excuse me?'

'Why what have you done?' replied Lucy.

'Farted?'

It began the young cashier laughing as Lucy pushed her buttocks upwards to get her pussy off her face and shouted, as she stared down at the puzzled looking Nosey Parker.

'Listen, little man, take your clumsy fingers and un-projectile tongue and go away, as I have to take this young lady on a journey of unimaginable pleasure that ends with a pussy explosion where her built-up fluids will spray into the air, so if you want to stay go over there and watch so you are out of the way.'

On hearing this, the young cashier's eyes opened wide. What did Lucy mean by pussy explosion? She had never heard of that before or encountered it with former lovers, so what was a pussy explosion? Lucy then said, 'Excuse me, honey; please can you lie down on the floor so I can begin my muff diving mission?'

On hearing this, the excited young cashier quickly stood up and looked around for something to lie on, and she saw a pile of reject coats and quickly skipped towards them and in seconds she was lying in comfort. Lucy was on her in seconds, and as her flickering tongue probed her pussy, she gently massaged the young cashier's magical button with two fingers.

The young cashier closed her eyes and enjoyed the sensations, as they flooded her body, and still she was mystified by those words pussy explosion. The answer came quickly when Lucy stopped her probing tongue on her pussy and started at her magical button instead. While her tongue probed and flickered over the young cashier's magical button, she then entered a finger into her quivering pussy; one finger quickly became two, as she went searching for her G spot.

On locating it the young cashier's eyes opened wide as she murmured, 'Oh.'

As Lucy slowly began her thrusting fingers at the tempo of the tap that wouldn't stop dripping and with every inward thrust caressing her G spot, which sent shock waves through the young cashier's body, and she began murmuring, 'Oh my goodness, yes, yes, yes.'

On hearing this, the slow hand wanking Nosey Parker was intrigued and then moved closer to see what was going on, as Lucy then upped the speed of her thrusting fingers to the new tempo of the clock that wouldn't stop ticking and with every inward thrust caressed her G spot. The young cashier was on her way to destination Climax City; here she comes, a journey filled with electrifying sensations that were blowing her mind.

But Lucy was still thinking of what to do to enhance her pleasure even more and then decided to massage her magical button while her piston-like fingers thrust in and out of the shaking young cashier's pussy. This was unbelievable for the young cashier; she had sensations coming from her magical button and those two fast-thrusting fingers too as she was fast approaching Climax City at breakneck speed and began shouting, 'Yes, yes, I'm cumming.'

On hearing this Lucy smiled and then slowly withdrew her fingers, thus releasing the young cashier's built-up fluids, which went spraying into the air and fell on the staring Nosey Parkers face. Never before had he seen such a wonderful sight and, in turn, began stroking his rigid cock faster and murmured, 'Oh no.'

As his milk balls suddenly tightened and his milky-white fluids were on despatch, flying through the air and falling on to the young cashier's naked body and that was game over for him, but not for the ecstatic young cashier who was still shaking from the mind-blowing orgasmic moment; never before had she experienced such a thing. This sultry temptress had taken her to a place she had never visited before and was eager to visit again; little did she know her wish was going to be fulfilled.

As Lucy once again inserted two fingers into her moist wet pussy and slowly began finger fucking her, the flabbergasted young cashier whispered, 'No no, please no more, you delightful temptress.'

On hearing this, Lucy smiled and then leaned forward and kissed her lips, but this was no ordinary kiss. No this was hot and smouldering and never ending, as neither wanted to part as they were lost in desire for one another, especially the young cashier. She was in heaven; she had found her angel, an angel she was falling for who had introduced her to the joys of sex where the orgasms flow often and, on occasions, are earth-shattering.

As they kissed the jealous agitated Nosey Parker suddenly shouted, 'Come on, Mary, it's time you got back to work.'

On hearing this reluctantly Mary pulled away from her smouldering kiss, as a teardrop rolled down her face and then stood and slowly walked away. On seeing her voluptuous swivelling ass Lucy got up and ran after her latest desire. Taking her in her arms as her fingers tenderly caressed her ass; their lips locked together in a kiss that neither wanted to stop so to end this scenario. Nosey Parker got up and slapped Lucy's ass hard.

But Lucy didn't pay him no mind and continued her smouldering kiss with Mary; Nosey Parker then went to pull them apart and then entered Dominatrix Lucy and kneed him in the groin, down went Nosey Parker with teardrops in his eyes, and there would be no more intervention from him. Lucy then whispered in Mary's ear, 'What are you doing tomorrow, honey bunch?'

'Nothing, nothing at all,' replied the smiling Mary.

'That's good,' whispered Lucy.

'Can you give me your address? You will be picked up at ten by my driver Sam, and you will be spending the day with me.'

'Really?' whispered Mary.

'Yes really,' replied Lucy. 'You will be spending the day naked in my bedroom, where I will introduce you to many more sensations in your sexual tutoring course where my imagination will take you on a journey filled with wonderful sensations that will be coming from here, there, and everywhere'

As she touched her pussy and bottom too and then bent down and sucked a nipple, the astonished Mary murmured, 'Tits, ass, and pussy too and more. Oh my goodness, my mind will be exploding.'

Lucy smiled and then tenderly kissed her lips and whispered, 'Goodbye, my love.'

Then Lucy turned and walked away, picking up her sex toy, the strap-a-dick-me, and coat too, which she quickly put it on and walked out the door, leaving the dumbfounded Nosey Parker with his blue balls staring at her swaying behind, who wished he could fuck this sultry temptress for ever more, as he had finally found the woman he'd been looking for naked in a storeroom, wearing a big rubber cock and smiling as she slowly walked towards her prey.

On seeing his staring eyes glued on the disappearing Lucy, Mary quickly dressed; with her body dressed, she slowly walked towards Nosey Parker, who was tenderly nursing his floppy cock and blue balls.

'Are your balls painful?' asked the smiling Mary.

'Yes they are,' replied Nosey Parker. 'Do you want to see?'

As he took hold of his floppy cock and lifted it up revealing his blue and purple balls, Mary whispered, 'Oh that looks nasty,' and she knelt and tenderly grabbed his blue balls.

'What are you doing?' whispered Nosey Parker who was literally shitting himself that she was going to squeeze; Mary smiled and then leaned forward and tenderly kissed his lips, as her hand slowly squeezed his balls. Nosey Parker's eyes opened wide as her hand squeezed tighter.

'Oh my goodness, let go, Mary,' screamed Nosey Parker as his eyes began to water; there would soon be teardrops rolling down his face. On seeing this, Mary smiled and whispered in his ear, 'That will teach you not to interfere with my business, Mr Nosey Parker. Lucy took me to a place I seldom visit, Climax City, where I had a monstrous orgasmic moment, where I watched my pussy explode spraying my built-p fluids into the air, which took my breath away.'

Nosey Parker smiled and whispered, 'Was it good for you, because it was sure good for me when she stuck that big rubber cock in my ass.'

Mary smiled and tenderly kissed his lips, as she released his blue balls from her clenched hand and then slowly stood turned and walked away.

As Lucy walked towards the changing cubicles, she was wondering where Mandy was, as all the curtains were drawn standing in front of the three cubicles.

She murmured, 'Eany, meany miney mo,' and un-drew the middle curtain and gasped, 'Oh no!' when she saw a young man in his boxers standing there. He looked in the mirror and saw the smiling Lucy staring down, so he slowly turned around, revealing a rather big bulge in his boxers, so Lucy stepped inside and drew the curtains and then dropped to her knees and pulled his boxers down, thus releasing his big floppy cock.

'Oh my goodness, that's a big one you've got there,' she murmured; on hearing this, the young man looked down and smiled, when he saw the young lady encase his cock in her mouth and closed his eyes. Her lips were of velvet and her sucking so gentle; suddenly his eyes opened wide when his cock began to rise and her fingers gently caressed his balls over his sighs. Lucy then took it to another level as he softly moaned and his eyes opened even wider, when she stuck a finger up his ass; one finger quickly became two as she sank them deep into his ass.

'Oh my goodness,' he suddenly cried out, as she suddenly hit his prostate gland and his milk balls began churning; he was at bursting point and he tried in vain to stop himself from cumming, and Lucy suddenly stopped her sucking and took his rigid cock in hand and vigorously began to stroke it. This was the final straw for him as his milk balls suddenly tightened and his words of 'Oh no' filled the changing cubicle.

'What was that?' shouted a voice as the curtain was un-drawn, and there stood Nosey Parker staring down, wishing he was on his knees, but he wouldn't be stroking that big cock. Oh no, he would be sucking it. Wow what a size! But that was merely a fantasy. That's when his train of thought was brought back to the presence. When the young man's milk balls exploded and then up through his big rigid cock and shot into the air, hitting Nosey Parker in his gawping face, and that was game over for the young man.

As Lucy withdrew her two fingers from his asshole, the young man bent and pulled up his boxers and then pulled up his pants and picked up his garments and said, 'Please can you excuse me, honey?'

On hearing this Lucy smiled and then quickly stood up and leaned towards him and tenderly kissed his lips, then turned and walked away, leaving the young man staring at her voluptuous swaying ass. As Nosey Parker wiped the dripping fluids from his face, the young man quickly drew the curtain and smiled. 'Wow, what a shot!' he whispered as he turned and placed his stuff on the hook and then began dressing, leaving the gob-smacked Nose Parker staring at the curtain, not knowing what to do. Suddenly his train of thought was broken by the sound of a woman's voice, so he looked to his right, and there stood the smiling Mary.

'Yes, what is wrong?' he inquisitively asked.

'I need your assistance with a customer,' replied Mary.

So he turned and followed her to the counter and stopped as there stood the stunning Lucy and said, 'Good afternoon, young lady, how may I help?'

'Oh hello, Parker,' replied Lucy. 'Oh sorry, I forgot your first name. Nosey, that's it? Mr Nosey Parker, that's right? Oh what an awful name that is?'

'My names Nicholas,' replied Parker. 'That's Nicholas Parker at your service. How may I help you today?'

'I need to leave my purchases here until three if that's okay with you,' asked the smiling Lucy.

'That's fine, see you at three.'

With that he picked the bags up, then turned and walked away, impersonating someone who had been shot in the ass, to the amusement of the laughing ladies.

CHAPTER 22

As THE LAUGHING Lucy and Mandy walked hand in hand around the shopping centre, they had many watching eyes observing their every move and curious if they were lovers, on seeing those staring eyes on her. The sultry temptress took centre stage and turned and kissed Mandy's lips, but this was no ordinary kiss. No this was hot and passionate, and while their lips were locked together, her hands caressed Mandy's bottom.

This was a hot and steamy erotic show in the middle of a shopping centre, and all the hot horny men stopped and stared, at the disgust of their wives and partners, it was too much for one lady, when she shouted do you two mind will you please get a room or something. On hearing this, the sultry temptress Lucy clenched her fist and stuck a middle finger up at her then parted lips with Mandy and turned and said, 'Why don't you sit on that?' and then gasped when she saw the size of the women standing there and murmured, 'no, that won't do.'

With that she clenched her fist and said, 'Try that for size that should fit thunder thighs.'

On hearing this, the enraged thunder thighs went to punch Lucy; on seeing this, Lucy pushed Mandy aside and caught thunder thighs arm and then turned and threw thunder thighs over her shoulder to the amazement of those watching men. Then came the laughter when the watching crowd saw thunder thighs bloomers on show, as they were enormous and the blushing thunder thighs quickly covered them up, then stood and ran away to the sound of the laughing crowd, as they watched her fat ass wobble off into the distance.

Lucy then once again took Mandy by the hand and walked towards the escalator; in minutes they were on it and going upward and then came those immortal words, 'Fuck me, would you look at that? Somebody's smiling at me,' as he pointed a finger at Lucy's naked ass; on hearing this Lucy turned around and with her left foot took a half step to the side and then lifted her short skirt, thus exposing her shaven haven for all to see, as she was the sultry temptress and she didn't have a care in the world. Then came those wolf whistles when she sucked a finger and then inserted into her pussy and began thrusting it in and out, caressing her G spot and in a short time shouted, 'Look out,' to the man below her, when she withdrew her finger, thus releasing her built-up fluids spraying into the air and falling on the staring man's face, then Lucy began singing.

Rain drops keep falling on your head.

Then she blew him a little kiss and then turned around and stepped off the escalator and took hold of Mandy's hand and then walked towards the jewellery shop to Mandy's amazement; she looked at Lucy and asked, 'Where are we going, Lucy?'

'To buy a necklace,' replied Lucy.

With that they walked into the store and headed towards the sales clerk who said, 'Good afternoon ladies, how may I help you today?'

'Can I see your diamond necklaces please?' asked the smiling Lucy.

On hearing this, the sales clerk turned and went and got a tray of diamond necklaces and quickly brought them back and placed them down in front of Lucy; on seeing the prices starting from $5,000, Mandy's eyes opened wide, when Lucy asked to look at the $25,000 one and said, 'Would you help me try it on, Mandy?'

'This one is much too expensive,' whispered Mandy.

'Please place it around my neck and do it up,' replied Lucy; on hearing this, Mandy tut-tutted and took the necklace from her and then placed it around her neck and fastened it. Lucy then twirled around and stopped and looked in the mirror with her neck alive with diamonds. She then said, 'Excuse me, young man, what do you think?'

The young clerk's eyes were not on the necklace, but her ample charms, which were hidden under her jacket. Lucy smiled and always the temptress whispered, 'Close your eyes, young man; I have a surprise for you. But no peeking until I say, "Open them."'

The young man closed his eyes, and Lucy pointed to Mandy's hands and then the young man's eyes and she quickly covered hers, indicating to Mandy what she wanted her to do the same; on seeing this Mandy smiled and then quickly walked around behind the counter and stood behind the young sales clerk and put her hands over his eyes. Lucy then removed her jacket and then her cameo too; bare-breasted she stood there smiling and shouted, 'Surprise.'

On hearing this, Mandy removed her hands from his eyes and looked around and smiled when she saw the bare-breasted Lucy standing there.

'What do you think? Does this diamond necklace look good on me, young man?' asked the smiling Lucy. With his eyes transfixed on her massive tits, he did not reply and went to slip his hand in his pants pocket; on seeing this, Mandy got there first and slipped her hand in his pocket and began feeling around for his sleeping cock. But it was no longer sleeping; it was coming to life and getting firmer by the second. Mandy smiled and withdrew her hand from his pocket and then opened his pants.

As they dropped to his knees, she pulled his shorts down, thus releasing his rigid cock and then wrapped her fingers around it and gently began to stroke it. The young man was in heaven, a woman wanking him off, whilst the other Lucy showed him her naked delights, as she was now sitting on a chair, massaging her magical button.

'Oh no,' murmured the young man as his balls tightened and game over was nigh, as his milk balls exploded and his milky-white fluids were on despatch, up through his rigid cock and into the air and came splashing down on Lucy's massive tits.

'Oh', sighed Lucy, 'so your cock doesn't want any action in there,' as she pointed at her shaven haven. On hearing this, the flabbergasted young man quickly pulled up his shorts and pants too and hopped over the counter, walked a couple of steps, dropped to his knees, and whispered 'Oh yes please.'

He sank his tongue into her shaven haven and tasted her womanly delights; this was heaven, and his floppy cock once again began to rise. With his cock rigid he withdrew his tongue from her shaven pussy and raised up and tenderly kissed Lucy's lips. As he then guided his rigid cock towards her simmering pussy, Lucy's eyes opened wide as his rigid cock penetrated her pussy and gasped, 'Fuck me hard already.'

'Give me a chance,' replied the smiling sales clerk; with that he was off thrusting slow at the tempo of the tap that wouldn't stop dripping, and as he slowly thrust, he began tenderly kissing her lips, but it felt as though he got an electric shock as her lips were so soft. He had no choice and instantly stopped the kissing before he blew his load; it was time for him to be the driver on a leisurely Sunday drive, as he slowly plunged in and out of her pussy.

'What's wrong with the kissing?' asked the bewildered Lucy.

'There hot sizzling hot,' replied the smiling sales clerk, who was still slowly thrusting in and out of pussy at the tempo of the tap that wouldn't stop dripping; on seeing this Mandy shook her head in disbelief as she wanted to be fucked too. So she quickly skipped round the counter, sucking two fingers, and then dropped to her knees behind the slow thrusting sales clerk and looked at his naked bare ass and smiled; it was hairless.

Then she cautiously put her wet finger up to his ass; on feeling the finger penetrate his butt hole, the young sales clerk looked around and whispered, 'What the fuck?'

That was a big mistake as Mandy pushed the finger home straight up his ass, and his eyes opened wide when she hit his prostate gland, that was it his time was up as his milk balls began churning and he began pulling faces as he tried in vain to stop himself from cumming. But that was of no use as his milk balls exploded and that was game over for him, as those milky-white fluids went on despatch up through his rigid cock and shot deep into Lucy's quivering pussy.

That would be his first and only entry into Lucy's pussy, as in walked the shop floor manager shouting, 'What's going on here then?'

'Oh, oh,' murmured the young sales clerk, as he quickly withdrew his deflating cock from Lucy's pussy and then stood and quickly pulled up his shorts and pants too and said, 'Good afternoon, sir, did you have a nice lunch?'

Belch went the manager quickly followed by a loud fart, which was the final straw for Lucy. Still bare-breasted she stood and slowly walked towards him; Dominatrix Lucy shouted, 'Manners, fat boy?'

On hearing this, the manger smiled as he watched the voluptuous woman walk towards him; again he belched and smiled and then let rip louder than before. On hearing this Mandy was on the move, crawling; cautiously she made her way up behind him. Seeing this Lucy smiled and then whispered, 'I told you, fat boy, manners. If you do it again, you're in trouble.'

With that Mandy lit her lighter and held up close to his ass and looked away, enter the flame thrower when he let rip and a treacherous flame shot into air; his eyes opened wide when he saw the reflection of the glass.

'Oh my goodness,' he cried, with the flame gone, and Mandy back in position Lucy shouted, 'I told you not to do it.'

With that she pushed him hard in the chest, making him resemble a *Russian* doll, as he tried in vain to keep his balance. Seeing this Lucy smiled and pushed him again; down went fat boy and knocked himself out. On seeing this, Lucy began to laugh and then dropped to her knees and opened his pants and then pulled them off, thus releasing his fat belly, then off came his shorts and she began to laugh when she saw his small cock.

How on earth did he find it when he wanted to pee? She wondered, and then she smiled as she gently coaxed it to life; his little cock began to grow and became firm in her hand, resembling a German sausage. She then began sucking it, and Mandy began to laugh and whispered, 'what are you doing, Lucy? He is fat and ugly, and you are a goddess, so can we buy something and get out of here before he wakes up?'

With her mouth full of cock, Lucy couldn't speak and began to hum instead; fat boy's eyes opened wide as tingling sensations shot down his rigid cock.

'What's going on?' he murmured as he looked down and saw Lucy's head about his mid-drift and then closed his eyes when Lucy began to suck as it had been a long time since a woman had sucked on his cock; it felt wonderful and then disaster struck. He farted and that was not all, a second followed, this was too much for Lucy. She had warned him about manners and now he was farting, while she was down there sucking his cock.

The end was nigh for fatty boy now, as the sucking stopped and her teeth slowly sank into his rigid cock and he began shouting, 'Stop that, stop that, now.'

As he was at panic stations, wondering if she was going to bite it off, and while she bit, she was crushing his balls; as the teardrops fell from his eyes, he began sobbing, 'If you stop that now, I will give you anything in the shop to the value of $50,000.'

On hearing this Lucy's teeth sank no deeper and she released his blue balls from her clenched fist and looked at him and said, 'A small diamond bracelet for my friend, so the total is $55,000.'

On hearing this fatty boy nodded his okay, as he wasn't prepared to argue with her, as he didn't know what she would do next. Lucy smiled as she slowly stood and began admiring the necklace she was wearing, as this would be the one she would be wearing tonight, when she attended the dinner party at Mr Haskins's house with Officer Hardcock in her arm. Tonight was going to be the night she would introduce the prudish Mrs Haskins to the world of sex where she would experience multiple orgasms at the hands of the sultry temptress and end with a pussy explosion that would take her breath away.

But first she had to get inside her panties, and the only way to do that was while Officer Hardcock held her in deep conversation, she would get under the table and crawl towards frigid draws open thighs, and her mission would begin. Lucy smiled and then began dressing her half naked body and whispered, 'Mandy, please can you pick a necklace so we can get out of here? Don't worry about the money as I will pay the difference.'

On hearing this Mandy smiled and then walked over and looked at the diamond necklaces still on display on the counter with the young sales clerk standing behind them, still with a rigid cock in his pants that he was gently stroking. As he watched the sultry temptress Lucy dressing, wow she was voluptuous, he was lost in the haze of a sexual daydream when Mandy whispered, 'Young man, please can I look at that necklace?'

On hearing this, the still topless Lucy walked over to see what Mandy had chosen; the young sales clerk opened the display cabinet and took out a diamond necklace that was priced at $40,000 and handed it to Mandy, as his eyes were not on Mandy's pointing finger but on Lucy's voluptuous tits. Mandy smiled as she took the necklace from him, as it sparkled under the shop lights.

'This is the one,' she murmured as she tried it on and then looked in the mirror and gasped, 'Oh my,'

'You look stunning,' whispered Lucy as she kissed her neck and then moved up and tenderly kissed her lips. Mandy instantly responded and wrapped her arms around her; the young sales clerk looked up and murmured, 'They're driving me crazy.'

He then released his rigid cock from its entrapment and gently began to stroke it, as he watched these two beauties kissing. Wow what a sight! With his hand stroking his rigid cock, he walked around and stood behind Lucy and then let go of his rigid cock and in turn reached round and unbuttoned her short skirt and then slowly pulled it down as it came off her hip it then fell, to the floor, the young sales clerk took his rigid cock in hand and pushed it up against her asshole.

Un-lubricated he tried to push his cock in, but it was of no use as it was such a tiny hole. Lucy then pulled away from the kiss and whispered, 'Mandy, can you please bend down and spit on his cock so that he can perform a back-door entry on my behind?'

Mandy smiled and bent down and dribbled over his rigid cock and then spread Lucy's ass cheeks and repeatedly spat on her asshole; with his rigid cock lubricated and Mandy out the way, he placed his rigid cock up against her butt hole and slowly thrust forward. It was a tight squeeze, but his rigid cock slowly entered. With his cock half-entered, he began to slowly thrust in and out at the tempo of the tap that wouldn't stop dripping.

His rigid cock was slowly going deeper into her ass with every thrust. Lucy loved this sort of sex and craved this sort of sex and shouted, 'Go on, and fuck me harder. Let me really feel it.'

On hearing this, the young sales clerk began slam dunking her ass, and Lucy began shouting, 'Yes, yes, oh that feels so good. Harder.'

'Harder?' murmured the sales clerk as he didn't know what to do as he couldn't go any harder and so instead slowed it down to the tempo of the tap that wouldn't stop dripping and on, every withdrawal thrust slapped her ass.

'Ouch, ouch,' screamed the ecstatically happy Lucy who loved the slapping on her ass, as it bought more sensations to the fucking game; the fat manager was finally up on his feet, walking towards his slow thrusting sales clerk, still whistling a tune through his asshole. On hearing the farting, the young sales clerk stopped, and with his rigid cock embedded in Lucy's ass, he slowly looked around and saw his fat manager standing there and smiled.

'What are you doing, boy?' asked the trumpeting farting fat manager who couldn't stop farting, to the amusement of the giggling laughing lady's, who were wondering what on earth he'd been eating to fart so much; it seemed as though he was whistling a tune but not through his mouth but his ass instead. The fat manager then said, 'Don't you have any work to do, boy?'

On hearing this, the young sales clerk slowly withdrew his rigid cock from Lucy's asshole and bent and then pulled up his shorts and pants too and then quickly stepped away, leaving the fat manger staring at Lucy's voluptuous ass. He couldn't stand it and dropped to his knees and bit Lucy's ass cheek; that was a big mistake. Lucy smiled and let go of loudest fart he ever heard and he began choking as it was smelly too. Lucy smiled and let rip again.

'Oh come on,' shouted the fat manager on his knees, who was choking on the smell and said, 'What on earth have you been eating. It smells like a sewer down here?'

'What have I been eating?' replied Lucy. 'What have you been eating? You've got more gas than a hot air balloon, and I know your ass is big, but come on, you're not a human rocket.'

With that she slowly turned around and pointed at her shaven pussy and said, 'Lick it, fat boy.'

The manager smiled and then leaned forward and probed her shaven pussy with his flickering tongue; it seemed as though he was impersonating a cat licking the cream, as that was all he was doing. Licking her pussy he had no imagination. The frustrated Lucy then pointed at her magical button and said, 'Lick my clitoris, fat boy.'

The fat manager then looked up at Lucy, as if to say what the fuck, and that was a big mistake on his part, because the woman with the split personalities instantly turned into Dominatrix Lucy and slapped his face and shouted, 'Just do it, fat boy. Lick my clitoris or my friend and I are gone.'

With a red face the fat manager began probing her clitoris with his flickering tongue, and that was all he was doing, as he didn't have any sexual imagination like sticking a finger into her pussy while his tongue flickered over her clitoris. Lucy couldn't stand it any longer and shouted, 'For fuck sake, can't you do anything? I had been fucked in the ass by the young sales clerk geezer, until you jealously came along and sent him away. Look I'm looking for hanky panky, and if you're not up to it, I'm out of here.'

'What do you want me to do?' asked the fat manager, who was so mixed up; he didn't know what to do, fuck her, but he wondered if his rigid cock would ever enter her pussy, if he was on top as his very fat belly would be the obstacle he would have to overcome. Being deep in thought he was unaware that Lucy and Mandy quietly crept away, with Lucy paying $35,000, the outstanding balance of the $40,000 price tag; before leaving the shop they tenderly kissed the sales clerk and took one last grope of his rigid cock.

CHAPTER 23

HAND IN HAND they walked with necks a glow in dazzling diamonds; Mandy felt she was Cinderella and she was going to the ball, hoping her wonderful diamond necklace would attract her Prince Charming and he would ravish her and fuck her hard. But this was merely a fantasy as her real love stood by her side; the temptress Lucy was always on her mind. She had always dreamed of spending one night with her and to wake up and see her smiling face lying close beside her.

That's when Lucy suddenly whispered in her ear, 'Mandy, do you fancy staying in bed naked tomorrow with me and another one?'

'Another one?' whispered Mandy. 'Who do you have in mind, Lucy?'

'Young, Mary, the sales woman from the clothes store. We were in earlier and will be going back later to pick up our clothes we purchased.' replied the smiling Lucy, who was still wondering what dress to buy to wear tonight as they stood outside a shop, staring at those dazzling dresses.

'Let's go in here,' whispered Lucy.

'No, it's to expensive,' replied Mandy. 'We don't have that much amount of money to spend on dresses like that. They're thousands of dollars each.'

Lucy didn't pay any attention to her whims and walked into the shop, closely followed by the figure hugging Mandy who just wouldn't let go. Lucy walked over to the dazzling dresses and then stopped and turned and stared at Mandy and said, 'Look, Mandy, I have a diner party tonight at my former boss Mr Haskins's house.'

On hearing this, Mandy whimpered in a high-pitched voice, 'What do you mean by former boss, Lucy? Have you left?'

Lucy smiled and replied, 'Yes, but let's not get into that. Help me pick a dress and then let's go back to your place and get naked and have some fun together until six.'

On hearing this, the excited Mandy wrapped her arms around her and kissed her full on the lips in front of the staring open-mouthed staff, who couldn't believe what they were watching in their store. Lucy pulled away from the kiss and said, 'Are you going to help me, Mandy?'

'Yes I am,' replied Mandy as she began sifting through the dresses; after she had collected a few dresses, she looked at Lucy and said, 'Let's try these.'

With that she walked over to the changing room, closely followed by Lucy, who in turn walked by her and walked into the cubicle and stripped off her clothes and then turned and looked at Mandy; the staff shook their heads in disbelief full nudity in their shop. Mandy stared at her voluptuous body while handing her a dress, leaving the curtain open; Lucy tried it on, and as it got closer to her hips the tighter it got.

So with regret she let it fall and stepped out of it and hung it on a hook, to the disapproval of the watching staff, especially the supervisor Kathy Jenkins, who couldn't stand it any longer and rushed over to the naked Lucy to see if she could help. She stopped not six feet from her and stared at her voluptuous naked curves. God, she was intoxicated by Lucy's naked curves; her heart began to race as her panties became wet on the dirty thoughts she was having. As she wanted to get down on her knees and lick Lucy's bald pussy.

Suddenly she was brought back to reality when Mandy asked, 'Is there something wrong?'

'No nothings wrong,' replied Kathy. 'I could see this young lady was struggling to get into the last dress, so I came over to see if she needed a helping hand.'

With that she turned and looked at the naked voluptuous Lucy and smiled, as her eyes captured her full frontal delights and then she whispered, 'Wow!' as she walked towards Lucy with her tape measure in hand and said, 'Hello my name's Kathy. Please can I measure your voluptuous body so I can get an idea of your size and I can then find you the dress that enhances your every move?'

'Please do so,' replied the smiling Lucy, who was aching to be touched by the straight-faced shop girl, who seemed to be ogling her every move, since she had removed all of her clothes and stood there naked trying there expensive dresses on. Lucy took a deep breath as Kathy wrapped the tape measure around her and measured her big breasts, and then Kathy waited until Lucy breathed out, before measuring her breasts, and then squatted and measured her hips.

As she squatted there with her face just inches from Lucy's shaven pussy, she took a deep breath of air and her eyes opened wide, as the air was filled with the essence of Lucy's pussy. Wow what a delightful smell! Her hands began to shake as she wrapped that tape measure around Lucy's hips, with her hands shaking as she held the tape measure against Lucy's skin; on feeling her trembling hands, Lucy looked down and smiled and she saw the squatting Kathy's panties on show. They were elegant and literally see through.

The sultry temptress Lucy instantly dropped to her knees and whispered, in Kathy's ear, 'Nice.'

Her fingers went up her skirt and then pulled her panties to the side, thus allowing Lucy to begin her finger fucking patrol with her right hand. Kathy's eyes opened wide when she felt Lucy's finger slip inside her pussy and even wider when one finger became two. As those two fingers began to slowly thrust in and out of her pussy, she looked at Lucy and whispered, 'What are you doing to me?'

That was a big mistake on her part as her lips were there for the taking; on seeing this Lucy was on them in an instant. This was not a tender kiss. No it was a kiss of passion where their tongues intertwined. Kathy was lost in haze of wonderland where her mind was saying, 'Touch her shaven pussy.' Never before had she had the desire to touch another woman's pussy, but Lucy was the special one, whose voluptuous naked body cried out to be touched.

With her hand shaking, she placed it up against Lucy's magical button and gently began to massage. Lucy's eyes opened wide as wonderful sensations flooded her pussy; this was getting too much for the observing shocked staff, who were all mystified by the actions by their supervisor Kathy Jenkins. Never before had they seen anything like this in their shop, especially with their supervisor being involved in such an erotic show.

What were they to do? What could they do as Kathy was in charge not them? Suzy Smith had seen enough and began clapping her hands, as she slowly approached her kissing supervisor Kathy Jenkins; on hearing the clapping, Kathy came to her senses and pulled away from the kissing and looked up and smiled. She quickly became the supervisor and took her hand away from Lucy's pussy and then stood up and straightened her attire and went in search of a dress for Lucy.

Returning quickly with a stunning red dress Kathy said, 'Miss, will you please try this one on?'

Lucy smiled as she stepped into the dress, and then Kathy slowly pulled it up encasing her boobies before zipping it up. Wow it fitted her body like a glove, and Lucy twirled around like a ballerina on a musical box. She looked stunning with her neck glowing in diamonds and her body bathed in red.

'This is the one,' she said as she stared in the mirror and again twirled around on her tiptoe; she looked drop dead gorgeous and every ogling man's dream girl and she knew it. She then skipped over to Kathy Jenkins and kissed her cheek and whispered, 'Thank you, Kathy. This looks wonderful. I'll take it and what's more I will be wearing it.'

Kathy smiled and then cut the sales ticket off the dress followed by the security tag and then walked over to the till and rung it up, closely followed by the dazzling Lucy, who was eager to pay and be on her way. Kathy asked, 'How will you be paying, honey?'

'Cash,' replied the smiling Lucy, who was now sucking on her two fingers that had been inside Kathy's pussy; on seeing this Kathy smiled and whispered, 'Do you like the taste of my juices, honey?'

Did this lady know who she was talking to? Lucy was the sultry temptress, a woman who would have her stripped off her clothes and tasting her naked delights in minimal seconds.

Lucy smiled and then whispered, 'Oh Kathy dear, please can I have a quite word with you in the storeroom?'

And then she turned and whispered in Mandy's ear, for her to go and clean the strap-a-dick-to-me and bring it to her in the storeroom and then took the confused Kathy by the hand and then quickly led her to her interrogation room, where she would strip her off her clothes and begin her interrogation on her naked body. The smiling happy Kathy quickly walked alongside the horny temptress, with many thoughts going over in her mind.

Kathy was lost in a haze of wonderland, as they entered the storeroom and then, shock as Lucy embraced her and began tenderly kissing her lips; the shock instantly became desire as Kathy responded by caressing Lucy's butt. The kissing became smouldering hot as they shed their clothes, each yearning to taste the other's honey pot. In seconds they were on the floor locked in the sixty-nine position, tasting each other's delights.

As the amateur Kathy tenderly licked Lucy's shaven haven, Lucy was already in the groove and finger fucking her, not with one finger but two and then came the full on attack on Kathy's magical button.

'Oh my god,' gasped Kathy. This was getting to much for her; never before had anybody brought her magical button to life. This was electrifying, and she was on her way next stop Climax City; here she comes. With Kathy lost in the haze of the moment, as those wonderful sensations rushed through her body up to her exploding mind, Mandy quietly entered and quickly shed her clothes and then quickly fitted the strap-a-dick-to-me.

Strapped and ready for action, she quietly moved closer and dropped to her knees behind Kathy, then took hold of that big rubber cock and gently penetrated Kathy's honey pot.

'Oh my god, what is that?' gasped the shocked Kathy, as Mandy slowly thrust forward and in plunged that big rubber cock. Lucy whispered, 'Oh Sam, your cock is so big.'

On hearing this, Kathy froze. Was there really a man with a big cock about to shag her? Was he wearing protection on that cock of his? She was lost in wonderland as the full attack began on her pussy. There were the magical fingers of Lucy massaging her magical button and now, this big cock pulsating in and out of her pussy at the tempo of the tap that wouldn't stop dripping.

Suddenly Lucy increased the tempo of her massaging fingers, and Kathy began screaming, 'Oh my god, yes, yes, I'm cumming.'

Her body began to shake as she arrived at Climax City at breakneck speed, and yet, the slow pulsating big cock and Lucy's massaging fingers carried on. *What was going on?* wandered Kathy as she began her multiple orgasms scenario. Never before had she experienced sensations like this; her mind was exploding from the onslaught of sensations, as orgasm after orgasm flooded her body.

'No more, please no more,' screamed the ecstatically shaking Kathy.

'What's that?' replied the smiling Lucy, as she continued frantically massaging Kathy's magical button.

'No more,' screamed Kathy, 'please no more, Lucy.'

On hearing her pleas, Lucy smiled; her job was done and it was time for her to go now and plan her action for tonight's evening meal, with the delightful Mr Haskins and getting his frigid wife's panties down. Tonight was the night that Mrs Haskins would taste eroticism of the third kind at the hands of the sultry temptress and her two chaperones Officer Hardcock and Sam, her driver.

They would both be in uniform, enhancing their action man figures to the full; they would be her decoys to charm Mrs Haskins whilst she got ready to pounce.

The shaky Kathy stood staring at the smiling Lucy, unable to believe the sexual encounter she'd just encountered at the hands of this stunning temptress. Who was this stunner? What did she do and where did she learn how to enlighten her sexual charms? Never before had she had the desire for someone that she had for Lucy now; she wanted to touch her, kiss her, and taste her naked charms all night long.

Dressed they embraced each other, but this wasn't enough for the sultry temptress, and her tender lips once more kissed Kathy's, as her hand went on manoeuvres under Kathy's skirt and then upwards towards her masked sacred haven. Kathy responded by caressing her butt. Would this ever end? The answer came quickly. No. Lucy dropped to her knees and pulled Kathy's panties down and then off with the skirt and hello honey pot here she comes.

Kathy gasped, 'Oh.'

As Lucy sank her tongue deep into her honey pot, as her fingers gently massaged her magical button,

'Oh my goodness,' murmured Kathy as wonderful sensations flooded her body. Oh those sensations had Kathy staggering on her feet.

'Lie down', whispered Mandy, 'before you fall down.'

'Yes good idea,' whispered Kathy as she slowly lowered herself to the floor; little did she know she was right where Lucy wanted her on her back in position for a full attack on her pussy, from her probing flickering tongue and massaging fingers that would take her breath away. Kathy gasped, 'Oh.'

As Lucy inserted a finger into her sacred haven, one finger quickly became two. As she went in search of her G spot, again Kathy gasped, 'Oh yes, that's it.'

As Lucy's slow thrusting fingers gently caressed her G spot, Kathy began murmuring, 'Oh-ha.'

On every thrust she was on her way to a destination she'd never visited before, where she would see her honey pot explode as her built-up fluids sprayed into the air. Feeling left out Mandy moved closer and began kissing Kathy's succulent lips. Kathy was lost in turmoil. She didn't want to kiss; she wanted to scream, as Lucy had increased her thrusting fingers to the tempo of the clock that wouldn't stop ticking, and the sensations were electrifying.

Kathy began screaming, 'Oh my god, yes, yes, I'm cumming. Yes, I'm cumming.'

On hearing this Lucy withdrew her two fingers, and Kathy's honey pot exploded spraying her built-up fluids into the air. Kathy stared in disbelief as she watched; never before had she seen anything like it. With the sensational finger fucking over with Lucy on top of Kathy and locked in a smouldering kiss, which neither wanted to pull away from; for Kathy she was falling in love with Lucy.

This day would live long in her memory, and for Lucy, she definitely had to see her again; a sudden shriek of 'Oh gosh, Miss Jenkins, what are you doing?'

It was the shocked Suzy Smith staring down on her naked canoodling supervisor; she couldn't believe what she was seeing and disgustedly turned and walked away, as the stunned Kathy stared at her tiny swaying hips. It was time for her to go now as she was in shock at being caught with her panties down, whilst in the act of sexual pleasure with the voluptuous Lucy. She had to stop Suzy.

She shouted, 'Please stop, Suzy. I can explain.'

On hearing this Suzy stopped where she was and slowly turned around to see the naked Kathy walking towards her; she was stunned when Kathy embraced her and whispered in her ear, 'Please don't tell anyone, Suzy.'

Suzy smiled and curiously fingered Kathy's pussy that was saturated in her juices.

'What's been going on here?' she whispered. 'Why are you so wet?'

'Are you kidding me?' replied Kathy. 'I've just had an orgasm you wouldn't believe.'

'Why? What happened?' whispered Suzy, as one finger became two and then she slowly began finger fucking Kathy; stunned by Suzy's actions Kathy then responded by kissing her lips and caressing her butt. This was what Suzy yearned for as she secretly lusted after her supervisor. Every time she looked at her, she imagined her naked. Oh what was she doing? She had her fingers in her honey pot; she had to taste it from a kiss. She dropped to her knees and tasted her desire.

As her tongue probed and flickered over her juicy pussy, Mandy and Lucy quietly left the room and quickly made their way out of the store.

CHAPTER 24

OUTSIDE LUCY STOPPED and stared, as there stood the smiling officer Hardcock. She walked up to him and tenderly kissed his lips and then whispered in his ear, 'Hello, are you doing anything tonight, Officer?'

'Call me Richard,' replied Officer Hardcock. On hearing this, Lucy smiled as she tried in vain to stop herself from laughing, as there in front of her stood one Dick Hardcock. What was going on?

Was his dick hard? If so, he was certainly born into the right family Hardcock indeed; curiosity got the better of her. She had to know, so she leaned forward and began passionately kissing Officer Hardcock, and while they kissed, she slipped her hand inside his pants. Her eyes opened wide when she found his floppy cock, but wait a minute something was happening. It was coming to life in her hand and getting firmer by the second.

She had to have it, suck it, lick it, and have it inside of her moist wet pussy, where as the dumbfounded officer Hardcocks mind as on uneasy street. Yes he wanted to fuck her, but here he was a copper locked in a smouldering kiss with the sultry temptress in the mall, who was gently stroking his rigid cock whilst they kissed. What was he to do? What could he do? He had to get out of there, so reluctantly he pulled away from the stimulating kiss.

With their lips apart he whispered, 'I need to see you somewhere quiet, honey.'

'What for?' whispered the smiling Lucy.

'To take down your particulars,' replied Officer Hardcock.

'What particulars?' whispered the puzzled looking Lucy?

'Your panties, in particular,' whispered Hardcock. 'As I have a throbbing rigid cock in my pants, and that needs to see some pussy action now.'

'Oh I know,' whispered Lucy as she vigorously began stroking his rigid cock.

'Oh-oh,' murmured Hardcock.

'What are you doing to me, honey?' whispered the frantically staring Hardcock. Was someone watching him? If so, were they saying to their partners, 'Hey, darling, look over there, that officer's been vigorously wanked off by that voluptuous lady. Oh he is such a lucky man'?

Hardcock couldn't stand it; this was to public a place, to be doing this sort of thing and with his milk balls churning had he left it too late

'Oh-oh,' he softly murmured as his balls suddenly tightened and his milky-white fluids were on despatch, up through his rigid cock and oozing out into his pants.

'Oh, you mucky thing,' whispered the smiling Lucy as she withdrew her hand and tasted his juices. Then she took his hand and led him to Mary's store where she intended to buy him a suit and Sam too. As they entered, Nosey Parker quickly walked towards the temptress that was Lucy and asked, 'Have you returned for your purchases, madam?'

'Yes and no,' replied Lucy. 'First I would like to buy my friend Officer Hardcock a suit.'

'Oh I see,' murmured Nosey Parker as he measured Officer Hardcock inside leg, wishing for a hard cock centre stage; as the tape measure got closer to his groin, Lucy began kissing Hardcock. As her lips kissed his, Officer Hardcocks eyes opened wide. There was something rising in his midriff, and it certainly wasn't his temperature. No it was his rising cock, now portraying a bulge in his pants.

Then came contact as the tape measure hit centre stage and Nosey Parker's eyes opened wide, as he murmured, 'What's going on in there?' As he opened Hardcocks pants and released his throbbing cock, temptation stood erect before him; he had to taste it, and as his lips encased that rigid cock, Officer Hardcock shrieked. 'What's going on down there, boy?' Lucy smiled. this wasn't a time for shouting it was a time for kissing and began kissing the distraught officer Hardcocks lips, Hardcock was lost in the moment and pulled up Lucy's dress and began finger fucking her shaven haven. The in the groove sucking Nosey Parker decided to take it a step further and stuck a finger up Officer Hardcocks asshole.

'How e,' shrieked the nervously shaking Hardcock. 'Get that effing finger out of my ass.'

On hearing this Nosey Parker looked up and decided to try and stick a second finger up his ass too, and that was the final straw for Officer Hardcock. What was he to do, punch him or arrest him? He decided on option two. Reluctantly he withdrew his fingers from Lucy's shaven pussy and quickly tasted her juices before he took his handcuffs from his belt and said, 'I'm arresting you.'

'What for?' whimpered the panic Nosey Parker.

'For your act of indecency on another, especially the other being the same sex in a public place,' replied the straight-faced officer Hardcock.

'Oh don't be so silly, Dick. You were enjoying it,' whispered Lucy as she tenderly kissed his lips.

'No I wasn't,' whispered the red-faced officer Hardcock.

'Never mind,' said the laughing Lucy and then looked down at the frightened Nosey Parker and said, 'Do you have a suit for this, gentlemen, Nick.'

Nick smiled and replied, 'What colour do you have in mind, honey?'

'White,' said the gorgeous Lucy. Nosey Parker stood and went off to get the suit, as Lucy led Officer Hardcock to the changing room and said, 'Please remove your clothes, Dick.' As she then turned around and went and got him a shirt, returning at the same time as the smiling Nosey Parker carrying a white suit, she handed Dick the red shirt to put on.

'Oh I say, honey, that will go very nicely with this suit,' said Parker as he handed her the suit and turned and went and got a tie and red handkerchief to complete the suit; on his return he found Dick Hardcock suited and said, 'No, they won't do,' as he pointed down at his work shoes.

'Oh yes', gasped Lucy, 'they won't do at all.' On hearing this Nosey Parker quickly went and got some cowboy boots; on his return officer Hardcock shook his head in disbelief.

'Red or white,' he murmured.

'What happened to good old black?' Lucy smiled and said, 'Will take the white ones, Nick.'

'White ones?' shrieked Officer Hardcock.

'Yes, the whites,' replied the giggling Lucy.

'As tonight, Dick, you and Sam will be dressed the same, you will be my virginal soldiers.'

'Virginal, soldiers? I don't think so,' whispered Hardcock.

'Oh yes, you are,' replied the smiling Lucy as she then tenderly kissed his lips.

'Where are we going?' asked the inquisitive officer Hardcock.

'To a dinner party,' replied the smiling Lucy.

'Dinner party what dinner party?' asked the nervously shaking Hardcock, who was always shaking like that leaf on a swaying tree whilst in the company of this sultry temptress, as he never knew what she would do next. All he knew was that it would be sexual and it scared him to death. Lucy smiled as she looked at the nervously shaking officer Hardcock and wondered why he was so nervous.

'What's wrong, Dickie?' she asked.

'Nothing's wrong,' replied the shaky officer Hardcock. Lucy smiled as she looked at his shaky leg and whispered in his ear, 'Sing us a song. Dickie. It's like your trying to impersonate Elvis Presley with that shaky leg.'

'I can't sing,' shrieked Hardcock. With that Nosey Parker began singing; Lucy smiled and moved closer to him and opened his pants and gently began stroking his growing cock.

'Wow!' murmured Nosey Parker as his cock became rigid in her hand; he didn't want this now. He wanted another poking in his asshole from that big rubber cock she wore around her waist, the ten inch strap-a-dick-to-me. The kissing had to stop as Lucy was passionately kissing him, whilst she stroked his rigid cock; he just couldn't stand it. He had to ask, so he pulled away from the kiss and said, 'Honey, will you fuck me in the ass before you go?' On hearing this Lucy smiled and led him by the cock, closely followed by Mandy to the storeroom, where she would once again fuck him. As they entered, Lucy took off her diamond necklace and then handed it to Officer Hardcock, who took it gracefully and stared dumbfounded as the dress came off. He burst into song.

Holy smokes and tits alive, I never saw a pair that big before.

On hearing this, the naked Lucy began twirling around as though she was a ballerina on a musical box; this was getting too much for Hardcock, whose rigid cock was crying out.

'Let me out, you fool. I want to fuck it.' On hearing his cock's whims, he quickly opened his pants and took his rigid cock in hand and began portraying Master Bates, as he watched.

'Bugger me,' shrieked the flabbergasted Nosey Parker.

'Give me half a chance,' replied the smiling Lucy as she took the strap-a-dick-to-me from Mandy and strapped it on, as she stared open-mouthed at the masturbating officer Hardcock, wishing she could fuck him in the ass as well; but that would remain a daydream for now. She then whispered in Mandy's ear, 'Take good care of our masturbating policeman, dear.'

Mandy smiled and then tenderly kissed her on the lips before turning around and dropping to her knees in front of Officer Hardcock and gently began caressing his balls; suddenly Hardcock eyes opened wide, when she began to gently squeeze his balls.

'What's up, Doc?' shrieked the panic-stricken officer Hardcock. On hearing that sarcastic remark, Mandy squeezed harder; with that the panic Hardcock began to cough and in doing so made Mandy laugh, so she released his balls from her clenching hand and said, 'Look here, Hardcock, let go of your rigid cock.'

On hearing her command Hardcock let go of his rigid cock and in doing so quietly began to pray.

'Oh my goodness,' he gasped as her lips encased his rigid cock and she began to suck. Wow this was sensational! He didn't know what to do, as his milk balls had begun churning; he began murmuring, 'Oh yes that feels so good.' On hearing this, Mandy began to hum while she sucked.

'Oh my god, hold on there, boy,' sighed Hardcock as tingling sensations rushed down his rigid cock, towards his churning balls; this was to much for him, and he couldn't hold on any more and shouted, 'Fuck me, here I come.' On hearing this Lucy withdrew that rubber cock from Nosey Parker's ass and got up and was behind Hardcock in an instant and then grabbed hold of that rubber cock and slowly ran it up and down between the cheeks of Hardcocks ass.

'What are you doing back there?' shrieked the panic Hardcock.

Lucy smiled and then whispered in his ear, 'I am going to fuck you, as you keep saying fuck me while you are in my company, so I am going to fulfil your request.' With that she slowly thrust forward and in plunged that big rubber cock; Hardcocks eyes opened wide as he shouted, 'Fuck me, get that thing out of there.'

Lucy smiled and then replied, 'Don't be so silly. How can I fuck you if I take it out of there?'

'Get it out, get it out of there,' shrieked Hardcock. 'It's hurting me. Get it out of there, you bitch.'

Oh what had he done? He had a big one thrusting in and out of his asshole, and now, he was calling the sultry temptress a bitch. Was he insane or something? Hardcock shook his head in disbelief as he wondered if he had angered the temptress and then came retribution from Lucy when she shouted, 'Bitch? You're calling me a bitch, Officer?'

'Oh-oh,' murmured Hardcock as he was literally shitting himself, as he didn't know what she was going to do, then came shock as she stopped her thrusting and began slapping his ass, while the head of the big rubber cock just penetrated his asshole and he began screaming, 'I'm sorry. I didn't mean to say that nasty word, honey.'

'Honey?' shrieked Lucy. 'First bitch and then, honey what's next? Will you marry me and have my babies, honey?'

'No no,' replied the panic Hardcock as he didn't know what to say, as if he said the wrong thing, what would happen to him. The frustrated Lucy had heard enough and decided she would bring tears to his eyes; she then stopped her slapping on his pink-coloured butt and then grabbed hold of his waist with both hands and shouted, 'Are you ready?'

'Ready for what?' replied the panic Hardcock, who wanted to run but couldn't move as the head of that big rubber cock was stuck in his asshole and any sudden movement by him would bring pain or maybe bleeding to his asshole. His eyes suddenly opened wide as Lucy began her thrusting and then came those tears as her thrusting was at the tempo of the ticking clock.

'Oh my god,' shrieked the tearful Hardcock; as the teardrops began to roll down his face, he began shouting, 'Stop, stop. My asshole's on fire.' As that big rubber cock at piston-like speed thrust in and out of his inflamed asshole, it felt like it was burning as it was so sore yet, the big rubber cock thrust on. He couldn't stand it and shouted, 'Fuck it. I can not stand it any more. You must stop, or I will arrest you. And you won't be attending the dinner party tonight as you will be in jail instead.'

'Huh,' murmured Lucy. This man was insane; on numerous occasions, he had said fuck me whilst in her presence and yet here she was honouring his wishes and he wanted to stop. She didn't; she was the sultry temptress, a woman who revelled in sexual pleasure. Whether it was straight, kinky, or fantasy she didn't care, she was the good time girl, any time, any place, anywhere and she'd be there.

Suddenly she was woken from her daydream by the shouting Hardcock, 'Get it out. Get it out. You're hurting me.'

'What was that?' replied the fast-thrusting Lucy. 'Get it out? Look, Dick all I am doing is complying too your wishes.'

'What wishes?' shrieked Hardcock.

'Fucking you,' whispered Lucy.

'But why?' again shrieked Hardcock.

'You keep saying fuck me and this is what I am doing to you, so shut up or else . . .'

Hardcock thought long and hard and remained silent, whereas Nosey Parker was jumping up and down, shouting 'What about me? I like it. Fuck me. Fuck me now.'

On hearing this, Hardcock breathed a sigh of relief, as Lucy had stopped her thrusting and was slowly withdrawing that big rubber cock from his burning asshole and moving on to pastures new, the on all fours Nosey Parker, with his legs spread displaying the hole that needed fucking. As the big rubber cock left his asshole, Hardcock shouted, 'Alleluia, thank heavens for that. I'm free.' With that he quickly put his shorts on and became that man on the run, leaving the room in seconds; just in case Lucy changed her mind and that, would be his last encounter of a backdoor entry on his body, as it hurt like hell and he wasn't a cry baby. No he was a policeman; he stood for law and order. Wow, did his asshole ache? Would he ever be able to sit down again as his butt was so sore.

He dressed quickly and headed back to the storeroom to see if Lucy was ready to go. As he approached the storeroom, he heard Nosey Parker shouting, 'Harder, harder, Mistress Lucy. Oh that feels so good!'

On hearing this, Hardcock cautiously entered and smiled, as he looked on Lucy's fast-thrusting hips. Wow her body was voluptuous! She was every man's dream woman; from her beautiful face down to her tender swaying hips, she was a sex goddess. There was a stirring in his pants as his floppy cock began to rise; he then opened his pants and took his rigid cock in hand and began portraying Master Bates as he watched.

On seeing this Lucy whispered, 'Hey. Mandy, Officer Hardcock is wanking over there. Please go over and give him a hand.'

On seeing the sexy Mandy walk towards him, Hardcock heard his cock shout, 'Look at that pussy, man. I need to get in there. Let go of me and get me in there, Hardcock.'

On hearing this, Hardcock took Mandy in his arms and began kissing her; as he slowly lowered her to the floor in just seconds, they were in the missionary position, with his rigid cock kissing her pussy lips. Again he heard his rigid cock say, 'There's no time for kissing. Get me in there. I want to fuck it.'

With that Hardcock thrust forward and in plunged his rigid cock, and he was off, very slow at first at the tempo of the tap that wouldn't stop dripping. Mandy responded by hungrily kissing him as her hands caressed his butt.

'Oh, oh,' murmured Hardcock as her hand slowly moved down towards his asshole. He couldn't stand it; there would be no more entries in there tonight as it was so sore. He then pulled away from the kiss and whispered, 'Shall we try the doggy style?' As he slowly withdrew his rigid cock from her simmering pussy, Mandy whispered, 'Yippee,' As she rolled over and got up on to her hands and knees and spread her legs, whether it be asshole or pussy she didn't care, she just wanted to be fucked by Officer Hardcock and his big rigid cock. As he penetrated Mandy's pussy from behind, Lucy shouted, 'Well, that's game over for me.' As she slowly withdrew that big rubber cock from Nosey Parkers burning asshole, he said, 'Thank you, my mistress. That was wonderful.' As he fell to the floor smiling as he recalled the shagging he had just enjoyed, Hardcock smiled as he watched the voluptuous Lucy stand and remove that big rubber cock from her waist and said, 'It's nearly time for us to go, as I don't want to be late.'

'Late for what?' asked the inquisitive Mandy.

'My dinner party with the Haskins silly,' replied the smiling Lucy; as she dressed, no more was said on the matter. Dressed, Lucy said, 'I will see you later. Enjoy.' With that, she quietly left the room.

CHAPTER 25

IT WAS SEVEN twenty as Haskins nervously paced up and down; as he awaited the arrival of his temptress secretary Lucy, his heart was racing. What had he done inviting Lucy to his home? She was a voluptuous temptress who held no boundaries to fun. What would his young wife's reaction be when she saw the voluptuous goddess that was Lucy? Oh my god, what would she be wearing?

This was getting too much and anxiety was setting in; he opened his pill box and took a couple of pills to calm him down. Suddenly the den door opened and in walked his young wife wearing nothing special.

'Oh my god,' he gasped.

'Are you wearing that? We've got guests coming to dinner in five minutes.'

'Oh so we have,' replied the sarcastic Sandy. 'If you had given me more notice of the dinner, I would have got a dress to wear.'

Haskins couldn't stand it, his heart was break dancing in his chest. Would this be a cardiac arrest? He had to calm down, so he sat down and popped another couple of pills.

'What are you taking them for?' asked the intrigued Sandy.

'To calm me down,' whispered Haskins.

'You look like a tramp.'

The door bell rang.

'Oh no, she's here,' shrieked the panic Haskins.

'Who's she?' asked the inquisitive Sandy.

'My secretary.' replied Haskins. 'Are you going to go and put something nice on?'

On hearing this Sandy shrieked, 'Who do you think I am?'

'My wife,' whispered Haskins; his heart was racing, as he couldn't calm down. He was so agitated by his estranged wife. Oh what could he do?

The confrontation ended abruptly as in walked the stunning voluptuous Lucy, wearing her figure-hugging red dress and dazzling diamond necklace. Haskins stared open-mouthed at the beauty that stood before him. On seeing this, Sandy looked to her left and gasped, 'Fuck me.' Hearing those two words, Lucy smiled and then turned and walked a couple of steps and tenderly kissed the startled Sandy's lips. The shocked Sandy responded to the dismay of Haskins's staring eyes. He just couldn't believe there were two lovely ladies kissing in front of him, and one was his frigid wife. It was unbelievable; the kissing abruptly stopped when she saw two muscular men in white suites standing there.

'Who are you?' she gasped, as her wandering eyes took in the sight of their masculine bodies, and her imagination wondered how big their cocks were. Lucy quickly answered as she introduced Sandy to her men.

'This is Sam, my driver.'

'How do you do, madam?' said Sam as he walked up and tenderly kissed the back of Sandy's hand; then Lucy paused as she wondered how on earth she was going to introduce Officer Hardcock.

'Don't laugh,' she said. 'Here is my personal body guard, Officer Hardcock.'

'Really?' replied the smiling Sandy.

'You're telling me his surname is Hardcock, or is it really Jones and he has a hard cock in his pants, which is looking for some pussy action?' With that she walked up to Officer Hardcock and grabbed his groin, to the dismay of the staring Mr Haskins.

'Nope,' she said. 'But hang on a minute. Something's growing in there.' As she stared at the growing bulge in his pants, seeing Sandy's vision was pre-occupied with the growing bulge, in officer Hardcock pants, Lucy quietly left the room and went in search of the dining room to prepare for tonight's mission on the frigid Mrs Haskins. *Was she frigid?* thought Lucy and then she shook her head, as if to say, 'No.' Their kiss was soft and tender and Lucy sensed she wanted more and tonight she would get more at the hands of the sultry temptress and her three accomplices, her two virile men, Sam and Officer Hardcock, not to mention old Mr Haskins and her up all night wonder toy, that was her strap-a-dick-to-me.

Oh she couldn't wait and quickly stepped out of her dress and took that wonder toy from her purse and strapped it on and then phoned Sam and said, 'Hi, Sam, would you and Officer Hardcock like to join me in the dining room and bring the old fart and his young wife too?' The call ended to the dismay of the puzzled Sam.

'What is wrong, son?' asked the inquisitive Mr Haskins.

'Lucy wants us to join her in the dining room,' replied the bewildered Sam.

'Oh yippee,' shrieked the sexually excited Sandy. There were two young cocks in the house, as well as the old fart who couldn't get it up, her husband. She walked arm in arm between Sam and Officer Hardcock, as though she was Dorothy on the way to see the wizard {Wizard of Oz}; little did she know she was going to the sultry temptress's lair, which would lead her into sexual encounters of the third kind, the likes of which she'd never experienced before. They entered the dining room.

'Where's Lucy?' shrieked the excited Sandy, as she stared around the candle-lit room.

'Shell we get seated?' whispered her husband.

'Good idea,' replied Sandy as she sat between Sam and Hardcock, hoping she would feel a hard cock tonight; as Sam poured the wine, Sandy whispered in Hardcocks ear, 'Open your pants, Officer, and release your cock from its entrapment so I can play with it and get it hard, darling.' With that she tenderly kissed his cheek, as her intrigued husband looked on, wondering what was going on over there. Officer Hardcock smiled and quickly released his floppy cock from its entrapment and then placed his hand on her thigh, as Sandy gently began stroking his floppy cock that seemed to be changing identity.

It seemed to resemble a rocket destined for her pussy; she suddenly gasped, 'Oh,' as Sam placed his hand on her right thigh and gently squeezed. She looked to her right and smiled at him and curiously looked down at his groin and murmured, 'Well, fuck me. Would you look at the size of that?' She took it in hand and gently began to stroke it, as her mind was filled with dirty thoughts. Then a shocked expression crossed her face at the thought of two rigid cocks and only one pussy.

Oh maybe tonight, for the very first time, a back-door entry on her sensual body from one of those rigid cocks.

'Oh my goodness,' she suddenly gasped at the thought of a rigid cock going up her butt. Where was Lucy?

Sandy's eyes opened wide as she felt her panties being pulled to the side and even wider when someone began massaging her magical button. She closed her eyes as wonderful sensations flooded her body and then increased her wanking speed on those two rigid cocks. The startled Sam and Hardcock looked at her. They had to stop her now; their milk balls were churning and neither wanted to cum.

Then Sandy slowed those two vigorously stroking hands on their rigid cocks as a finger slipped into her pussy; one finger quickly became two as they went in search of her G spot at the tempo of the tap that wouldn't stop dripping.

Sandy wanted to shout but couldn't make a sound as her engrossed husband looked on and what was he doing with his right hand, under the table. It couldn't be wanking as he had told her his cock would be missing in action when it came to sex. He couldn't get it up. 'Thank heavens for that,' she always said, him being a wrinkly old man of seventy-five. She married him only for his money.

Her eyes opened wide when those two slow pulsating fingers increased in speed; she couldn't remain silent any longer and screamed out, 'Oh my god, I'm cumming.' She approached Climax City at breakneck speed to the astonishment of her slowly masturbating husband; he had never seen her sexual face before and always wondered why he had married her.

Sandy was on the brink of an almighty orgasm, and her cries of 'Oh yes, yes, yes' filled the room and then the finally 'Oh my god, yes, yes, here I cum.' On hearing this Lucy slowly withdrew her two fingers, and the honey pot explosion commenced, washing her face with spraying liquids.

'That was amazing!' screamed the ecstatically shaking Sandy; never before had she experienced anything like that and lifted the table cloth to see who was hiding under the table and said, 'Hello,' when she saw Lucy's smiling face, and whispered, 'Thank you, honey.'

Lucy smiled and whispered back 'Did you like that, madam? There's more if you would like to carry on.'

Sandy smiled and said, 'Just a minute. I've got some cock to suck.' She then turned to her left, bent down, and began sucking Officer Hardcocks rigid cock, to the amazement of her husbands staring eyes. On seeing this he said, 'Hey, Sam, aren't you going to fuck her?'

'Okay,' shrieked the excited Sam as he stood up and lifted Sandy's hips. In doing so she quickly got into position, and he lifted her skirt and pulled her panties down. With her pussy unmasked, invasion was merely seconds away. As Sam took his rigid cock in hand and dropped to his knees and guided it towards the Holy Grail that was her pussy. The insertion was short and sweet as she was still dripping from the honey pot explosion.

As his rigid cock slowly began to thrust in and out of her pussy at the tempo of the tap that wouldn't stop dripping, Sandy began to hum sending tingling sensations down Officer Hardcocks rigid cock; it had been a long time and it felt good having a cock deep inside her pussy. Hardcock looked up as his milk balls began to churn. He tried in vain to think of something else to stop himself from cumming.

He just couldn't stand it; he was about to explode and whispered, 'Hey, Sam, do you mind if we change positions?'

'Okay,' replied the smiling Sam; he looked around for his temptress, but there was no sign of her. Was she still under the table? She was his ultimate prize; he didn't want a blow job, but he wanted her and her sexual ways. He then withdrew his rigid cock from Sandy's simmering honey pot and looked under the table. There was no sign of her, but there was a solid shape by Haskins. He looked up and sees Haskins's smiling face and murmured, 'Lucky so and so, he's getting good head, and I'm left with the amateur.'

On hearing this, Sandy asked, 'Who is getting good head, Sam?'

Sam looked at her and smiled; he didn't know what to say as there was only two other males in the room, her husband and Hardcock, who was now shagging her. He shrugged his shoulders and said, 'I don't know, honey.'

Coming to her senses, Sandy looked at her husband and smiled with the look of ecstasy on his face. She knew Lucy was still under the table, and if her mouth was anything like her fingers, he was having a wonderful time. Sam suddenly sucked a finger and put it up against Sandy's asshole and said, 'Have you had anything go in there, honey?'

'Oh my god, no, it is such a tiny hole,' shrieked the very excited Sandy, who so wanted to try this suggestion, but she didn't care if it would it hurt. She had been a lonesome pussy, walking in the wilderness, since she had met Haskins. She needed to be truly fucked as there was absence of cock whilst in his presence, especially a rigid one. She looked around to say okay but please be gentle, but instead gasped, 'Oh.'

There stood the voluptuous Lucy, wearing nothing but a smile; from her smile Sandy's eyes travelled downwards, taking in the sight of Lucy's naked charms and gasped out loud, 'Fuck me. Would you look at the size of that?'

She stared at that big ten-inch rubber cock.

'Oh that is a big one you've got there,' shrieked the flabbergasted Sandy. 'That will never go up my ass. It is too big.'

'Let us have a try,' replied the smiling Lucy, as she began lubricating her asshole.

'What is that?' shrieked the excited Sandy, as she was about to be fucked in ass for the first time.

'K Y jelly, silly' replied the smiling Lucy. 'It eases penetration.'

With that, she took hold of the rubber cock and placed it up against her asshole and then held on to her hips and slowly thrust forward and in plunged that big rubber cock,

'Goodness, gracious me,' shrieked Sandy. 'That's hurting me.'

On hearing her cries of pain, Haskins began to laugh as he watched his wife being fucked in the ass by the voluptuous Lucy, his temptress extraordinaire. This woman excited him like no other woman ever did. She dressed like a temptress, walked like a temptress, talked like a temptress, and above all teased like a temptress; whilst in his presence and while she took dictation, she regularly flashed her unmasked pussy as she was a panties-free lady.

She never knew how to stop her titillation show; as if she was hot, she would take all her clothes off and masturbate in front of him by sitting on a chair and massaging her magical button. He would sit transfixed by the sight of her massaging fingers, wishing he had a rigid cock to fuck her with and not a cock missing in action, as his was.

Sandy was in sexual heaven; she had that big rubber cock fucking her asshole, whilst she sucked on two rigid cocks at the same time. Oh what a mouthful that was! Suddenly Lucy upped her thrusting speed to the new tempo of the clock that wouldn't stop ticking. Sandy's eyes opened wide and let the cocks fall from her mouth and shouted, 'Fuck me. Steady on there, Lucy. You are hurting me.'

'She's in the wrong hole to be fucking you,' said the laughing, wanking Haskins, who was having a good time wanking his hard cock as he watched the voluptuous

Lucy. He wanted her more now than he ever did before; and it was time for his wife to go, but how? That would be a debate. He would have his lawyer, first thing, Tuesday morning and above all change his will, leaving the house to his wife and an annual income of one million dollars and the rest of his estate {Fortune} to Lucy, his voluptuous temptress.

On hearing his sarcastic comment, Sandy shouted, 'Oh my god, old man, when are you going to die?'

On hearing this Haskins smiled and said, 'Wouldn't you like to know?'

'Yes, I would,' snapped Sandy.

'I want you in the ground, even better cremated, so I know you won't be coming back.'

The startled Haskins said no more, as he digested in her words, a death wish from his wife. What would be next, him becoming a stuntman and falling down the stairs, at the thought of been tripped by her booby trap rope, set across the top step of the staircase falling to his death, as he rolled down the stairs. That thought sent a shiver down his spine; he had to get out of there. He wasted no time, stood and re-housed his rigid cock, and quietly left the room.

The observant Hardcock smiled as he watched the old man leave; as Lucy slowed her thrusting and reached around and began massaging Sandy's magical button, as Sandy said, 'Oh.' Hardcock startled the open-mouthed Sandy by sticking his cock back in her mouth, to her dismay. Sandy tried to suck, but how could she when those wonderful sensations coming from her magical button and asshole too rushed through her body up to her exploding mind? As she sucked she hummed, sending tingling sensations down his cock, as her hand gently caressed his balls and it was Hardcocks turn to say, 'Oh-oh.' His milk balls began to churn and he too had to get out of there, her mouth that is, so he shouted, 'Let us change position, please, Lucy.'

'Okay,' whispered Lucy as she stopped her massaging fingers on Sandy's magical button and slowly withdrew that big rubber cock from Sandy's asshole and said, 'Are you going in here, Officer Hardcock?' as she patted Sandy's butt.

'Yes, I am,' replied the intrigued officer Hardcock, knowing damn well she had something in mind to take Sandy's breathe away. Then came shock and horror on Sandy's face, when Lucy asked, 'Front or back door, Dick?'

'Front . . . front, or . . . or, back . . . back door . . . door' shrieked the stuttering Sandy.

On hearing her stuttering, Lucy smiled and said, 'One in your pussy, silly, that pulsates in and out of your pussy while the one in your butt, remaining dormant.'

'A rigid cock up my ass while the second one shags my pussy. Oh how lovely! How do you want me, Lucy?' replied the excited Sandy, who would do anything to feel a stiff cock shagging her all night long. As up until now, her young pussy had been absent in the joy's of sex, when she had married her husband and his absent cock in the field of sex, not that she had any intention of having sex with him anyway, all she wanted was his personal fortune estimated at one billion dollars.

Lucy smiled and suggested that she would lie down on the table with her legs dangling over the side and Sandy to sit down on her lap so that the big rubber cock would be inserted into her asshole and remain dormant, giving Officer Hardcock full access to her pussy.

'Okay,' said Officer Hardcock as he gently stroked his rigid cock.

'What about me?' said the dumbfounded missing in action Sam, who was aching for some pussy action to.

'You can take it in turns,' whispered Sandy as she slowly lowered her butt towards that big rubber cock; her eyes opened wide as it penetrated her asshole and even wider as it sank deep into her butt, as she sat down on Lucy's lap. Officer Hardcock moved closer, guiding his rigid cock towards her pussy, but was pushed out of the way by the agitated Sam, who so wanted to get in there first.

Sandy began laughing as she looked at the dumbfounded Hardcock, who was mystified by why he was pushed aside when he was eager to shag some pussy too. On hearing the laughter Lucy asked, 'What's going on up there, Sandy? Why are you laughing?'

'I got pushed out of the way by Sam, the fucking man,' replied Hardcock, as he watched Sam fucking Sandy and her cries of 'Oh-ha' filled the air. With every pulsating thrust, this was the first time for this sort of fucking, and she was enjoying every second. Oh those sensations were wonderful.

It was 9 p.m., and Haskins had left the building in search of solitude and a drink. He had many thoughts and a new will to write.

CHAPTER 26

I T WAS EIGHT thirty in the morning and the sound of music filled the air, waking the sleeping Mary who smiled when she heard a male voice sing,

Nothing's quite as pretty as Mary in the morning
When through the sleepy haze I see her lying there
Soft as the rain that falls on summer flowers
Warm as the sunlight shinning on her golden hair
When I wake and see her there so close beside me
I want to take her in my arms
The ache is there so deep inside me

As she listened, she gently began massaging her magical button as she reminisce yesterday in the clothes shop with the sultry temptress Lucy and her wonderful sex toy, the strap-a-dick-to-me, and her wonderful imagination too. She couldn't wait to take her in her arms and kiss her softly, as she had ignited a flame inside her that ached to touch and feel another woman's body lying close beside her.

She jumped out of her skin with shock when someone softly kissed her lips. She opened her eyes and was relieved to see Candy, last night's latest flame, a conquest in her search of love. She smiled at her and then started tenderly kissing her lips as her two fingers gently massaged her magical button.

'Oh what a way to start the day,' sighed Candy as Mary began her manoeuvres; from her lips to her neck she went with tender kisses, then onward towards her ample charms and her erect nipples. Candy loved her sensual touch. She was lost in a haze of wonderful sensations, as they travelled through her body up to her exploding mind. From her nipples went Mary downward towards her Holy Grail, which was Candy's neatly trimmed pussy, where her tongue probed and flickered over her magical button. Next stop was Climax City; here she comes.

'Oh yes, that's it,' murmured Candy, as Mary's probing tongue flickered over her magical button and a finger was inserted into her moist honey pot. One finger quickly became two as she went in search of her mythical G spot, a spot that had never been reached before.

'Oh my god,' shrieked Candy as Mary hit that spot and her honey pot was flooded with wonderful sensations, as Mary's two fingers slowly thrust in and out caressing her G spot at the tempo of the tap that wouldn't stop dripping. Mary hadn't finished, and as her slowly thrusting fingers caressed her G spot, her probing tongue continually flickered over her magical button.

Candy lay there transfixed as those sensations exploded her mind; next came act two. She seemed to change, she acted strange, and began shouting, 'Yes, oh my god, yes,' as Mary, in the morning, increased her thrusting fingers to the new tempo of the ticking clock.

Candy began to shake as she approached Climax City at breakneck speed, and her screams were getting louder.

'Yes, yes, I'm cumming,' screamed the ecstatic Candy.

On hearing this, Mary withdrew her two fingers, to the amazement of the staring Candy, as she watched her honey pot explode for the first time, spraying her built-up watery fluids into the air, hitting the open-mouthed Mary full in the face, as the sound of a ringing phone filled the air.

'Who's that?' asked the inquisitive Candy.

'How do I know?' replied the shrugging Mary, who picked up the phone and said, 'Hello.'

'Hello,' replied a woman's voice.

'Is that you, Mary?' asked the puzzled-looking Lucy, as she stared at Officer Hardcock and his big rigid cock, which he was gently stroking, as he stared at her voluptuous naked charms. Where had she been hiding? He had dreamt of such a woman with the body of a Greek goddess and the face of an angel with the sexual prowess of that devil in disguise. Oh yes, she was. Officer Hardcock murmured, 'Oh no,' as he shot his load into the air that fell on his astonished-looking face.

'Fuck me,' shrieked the laughing Lucy.

'Why? What's happened?' asked the excited Mary.

'Officer Hardcock has just shot himself in the face.'

'Oh no, he hasn't.' replied Mary. 'I didn't hear a bang.'

'Don't be so silly,' whispered the laughing Lucy. 'With his dick and not his gun?'

'His dick?' replied the astonished Mary.

'Yes, his dick,' said the laughing Lucy.

'He woke up with a very hard cock and saw me massaging my magical button while I was talking to you, so he decided to give himself a treat too and took his big cock in hand and gently began to wank it, but unfortunately for him he got too excited and shot himself in the face.'

'What with?' asked the naive Mary?

'Oh with his cum, silly. You know his milky-white fluids his rigid cock shoots into your pussy when he cum's.'

'Oh,' sighed Mary.

'It looks like the milky bars are on him then.'

With that both ladies began to laugh as Lucy moved closer and licked the dripping cum from Hardcocks dripping chin.

'What are you doing, Lucy?' asked the horny Mary, who couldn't wait to be in the sultry temptress's company to have fun,

'Mary, Mary, are you there?' said the inquisitive Lucy.

'Yes, I'm here,' replied Mary. 'Where are you? I can't wait to play with you.'

'Are you sure you want to play with me, Mary, as I hold no reservations in my sexual play?' replied Lucy.

'Oh I know,' whispered Mary.

'No, you don't know, Mary,' replied Lucy. 'As did you know, when I turn up at eleven, I will be accompanied.'

On hearing this, Mary gasped, 'Oh, who will be accompanying you?'

'Two men with big dicks,' replied Lucy, 'and be ready to take it in the ass and pussy too as you are sucking cock.'

'Wow!' said the confused Mary, who asked, 'Didn't you tell me, Lucy, two men with big dicks would be accompanying you, but didn't you say I would be fucked in the asshole at the same time as my pussy, whilst sucking cock? How's that going to happen when there are only two cocks on parade and where is the third one coming from?'

'That would be me,' replied Lucy. 'I will be wearing it, my favourite sex toy.'

'No way. Not your big ten-inch strap-a-dick-to-me,' shrieked the ecstatic Mary. 'How am I going to cope with that? I will be saying, "Look, three big cocks ahoy, let me out of here."'

They began to laugh; the laughter suddenly ended for Lucy when she gasped, 'Fuck me, he's off.'

'Who is off?' asked the intrigued Mary.

'Sam, Sam is,' whispered Lucy as his big rigid cock sank deep into her pussy.

'Oh that feels so good. Got to go now Mary. See you at eleven. Bye for now.' Lucy then hung up to the amazement of the dumbfounded Mary, as she wanted to be fucked too.

She put the phone down and opened the bedside cabinet draw and then took out her rabbit vibrator to the amazement of Candy, who wanted to play too, and quickly took it from her and slowly inserted it into her juicy wet pussy.

'Oh yes, that's it,' murmured Mary, when Candy turned it on and the ears began massaging her magical button.

'Oh, that feels so good,' whispered Mary as wonderful sensations flooded her pussy and then came act two when Candy bent and began sucking on her sleeping nipples; in just minutes, they stood proud as Candy's tongue simultaneously flickered over both of them. Next stop was Climax City; here she comes. But Mary was on act three as those wonderful sensations travelled through her body up to her exploding mind, as her thoughts were of Lucy being shagged by that big cock of Sam.

She couldn't wait till eleven to step into Lucy's world, where she would enjoy a sexual encounter like no other at the hands of her friend Lucy, the sultry temptress, and her imaginary imagination. Then the thought of three big rigid cocks crossed her mind.

'Oh my god,' she sighed; as her body began to shake, she had arrived at Climax City and was experiencing that magical orgasmic moment,

'Yes, yes, oh yes,' she screamed as the wonderful sensations carried on, thus starting her multiple orgasmic scenario, where the orgasms flew so freely.

The jealous Candy suddenly stopped sucking her nipples and whispered, 'It's my turn,' to the relief of the orgasmic shaking Mary, who said, 'Thank heaven for that.'

As Candy turned the vibrating rabbit off, she slowly pulled it from her simmering pussy and sucked it as though it was a melting Popsicle-tasting Mary's yummy juices.

Then she went to insert it into her abandoned pussy but was quickly snatched by the smiling Mary, who said, 'It's my turn, Candy. Lie down and enjoy.'

Candy quickly got into position and spread her legs as she waited the insertion of that vibrating wonder toy and its magical ears. But the insertion was not swift to the disappointment of Candy as Mary began muff diving her instead.

'No no,' she screamed, 'get that thing in there. My pussy is aching to feel the vibration of that big rubber tool, especially those ears on my magical button. I can't wait get it in there before it's too late and I have to go.'

'Why? Where are you going?' asked the intrigued Mary.

'Oh come on,' snapped Candy, 'your friend will be here soon with three big cocks. I heard you say.'

'Oh yes. That is right. Three big cocks are coming, No, that's not right. I will be coming.'

'Yes you certainly will,' whispered the jealous Candy as she sat up and tenderly kissed her lips.

Mary smiled and whispered, 'I know. Why don't you stay and play too?'

'Really?' shrieked the excited Candy, as she then passionately began kissing Mary. It had been just one night with her and she was falling in love. Lost in the sexually passionate embrace, Candy whispered, 'I love you, honey.'

'Do what?' replied the stunned Mary.

'I love you, I love you,' whispered the smiling Candy as she again began tenderly kissing Mary's lips. The stunned Mary didn't know what to say. Mary then responded by passionately kissing Candy. Yes, she craved this sexual lust of a woman but loves this, was too soon for such nonsense. She had only met her last night.********************

But Candy didn't care; she loved this moment and craved this moment. A woman's body was all she craved for, their kisses were tender and succulent, and they certainly knew how to get her off. Then came shock as Mary said, 'Shall we play a trick on the men?'

'Trick? What trick?' asked the naive Candy.

Seeing the puzzled look on her face, Mary smiled, then opened the draw and took out a white box, opened it, and took out the Viagra tablets and said, 'With these,' as she waved the pills in front of Candy's eyes.

Candy smiled and said, 'What's that then?'

'Viagra,' replied the laughing Mary.

'I'm going to crush them in some juice, and their two dicks will go hard, very hard.'

'Two dicks,' shrieked Candy.

'What do you mean by that, they have two dicks and they call them, Cyberdick, as they fuck you in the ass at the same time as they fuck your pussy, oh what a man.'

'No no,' replied the laughing Mary.

'There are two men, each with a very big dick, and when they drink my special juice, their dicks will be hard all afternoon, and to their dismay, they will cum again and again and we three ladies will milk their balls dry.'

'Really?' whispered Candy.

CHAPTER 27

WITH HER MIXED fruit punch made, Mary crushed a 100 mg Viagra tablet and then sprinkled it over the ice in a glass and then poured the juice over the ice and stirred. With her first magical concoction made, she quickly made a second one and put them in the fridge. Then she took the luscious Candy by hand to dress their naked bodies; as Mary looked through her dresses for a frilly one to wear, the mesmerised Candy stared at her peachy ass.

With temptation before her, Candy couldn't resist and walked a couple of steps, dropped to her knees, and delicately bit Mary's peach of a butt.

'Ouch, ouch,' cried the excited Mary. Candy then spread her butt cheeks and began licking her crevice. Mary smiled when Candy inserted a finger into her honey pot; one finger quickly became two, but this wasn't a time for playing. No, it was a time for dressing as Lucy and her two male companions with their big dicks would be there soon.

Reluctantly Mary said, 'Please can you stop that Candy? We should be dressing, not playing. Lucy will be here soon. But if you stay again tonight, we can play all night long and it is your turn to experience those wonderful sensations that come from the vibrator with the big ears.'

'Oh yes please,' shrieked the excited Candy, thrilled at the thought of spending another night with Mary, her dream girl and soon to be her lover. She reluctantly withdrew her two fingers from Mary's honey pot, tasting Mary's juices by sucking those two fingers. Then she wrapped her arms around her and gently squeezed as she began tenderly kissing her neck; she then whispered sweet nothings in her ear.

To the amazement of Candy, the lost in the moment Mary whispered, 'Be my girlfriend, Candy. I love licking your honey pot. Your juices taste divine.'

'Yes, oh yes,' whispered the infatuated loving Candy. She had got her dream girl and she didn't even have to ask. She had been overwhelmed last night by Mary's sexual prowess as she discreetly stared at her from across the bar. Little did she know Mary desired her too, after seeing her entering the club and losing her dignity, when her skirt had blown up revealing her unmasked pussy, as she was a panties-free lady?

Mary had gone to this female-only club, looking for lust, after her breath encounter with the sultry temptress Lucy and her wonderful sex toy, the strap-a-dick-to-me, a rubber cock with no defaults. As its rival, a man as when a man's rigid cock shoots its milky-white fluids deep inside a woman's pussy, it slowly loses is sexual powers and deflates back to a floppy cock, whereas the strap-a-dick-to-me will carry on.

She slowly turned around and faced Candy and smiled as she gently caressed her butt cheeks and then began tenderly kissing her lips. Candy wanted more and gently began massaging Mary's magical button. Coming to her senses, Mary smiled and slowly stepped back and whispered, 'Later, Lucy will be here soon. Let's dress and have a drink while we wait.'

Candy smiled and began sucking on her fingers, whilst Mary flickered through dresses and stopped and then took a short white one off the rail and handed it to Candy and said, 'Try that one on, darling.'

On hearing the word 'darling', the smitten Candy took it from her and quickly tried it on. It fitted her body like a glove; it looked smashing. She then twirled around and up went the dress, displaying her unmasked pussy to the smiling Mary, who said, 'Wow, that's the one, Candy.' She took her hand and twirled around together, to the delight of the smiling Candy.

Suddenly the twirling stopped as the sound of banging filled the air.

'They're here,' shrieked the excited Mary. 'Go, open the door, Candy. I will be there in a minute.'

Candy smiled and went to open the door. On opening it, she was greeted by Lucy's smiling face, who stepped forward and tenderly kissed her lips and then walked on by, closely followed by Sam, who in turn kissed the stunned Candy's lips as he followed the voluptuous Lucy. Candy gasped, 'Who are you?' at the approaching Hardcock, who intended to kiss her lips too, but Candy stepped aside and closed the door, leaving the dumbfounded stumbling Hardcock heading towards the stationery Sam and Lucy to Candy's amusement.

'Look . . . look . . . out . . . out, Sam . . . Sam,' he stuttered as he tried in vain to stop himself, but it was of no use as Sam turned around, Officer Hardcock pushed him over to the amusement of the laughing ladies.

'Steady on there, Officer Hardcock,' whispered the laughing Lucy.

'What's his name?' shrieked the hysterically laughing Candy.

'Officer Hardcock,' replied the tearful laughing Lucy.

'I don't believe it,' shrieked Candy.

On hearing this, Officer Hardcock stood up and opened his pants and released his big cock; he then took his cock in hand and gently began to stroke it. As he slowly turned around to face Candy, now facing one another, Candy gasped, 'Well, fuck me gently. Officer Hardcock has a hard cock, a really big hard cock actually.' With that she started cock patrol as she quickly walked towards officer Hardcock and his big rigid cock and whispered, 'Please let go of your cock, officer big cock.' As she dropped to her knees, Hardcock smiled and released his cock, but Candy began sucking on one of his balls instead. It had been a long time since she encountered such an act. She didn't like this sort of thing, as she had stepped to the other side.

She was a pussy-licking lady; but on seeing the size of Officer Hardcocks erect cock, curiosity had intrigued her, and she wanted to know if she could deep throat that big cock of his and took it in hand as she continued sucking on one of his balls. Mary couldn't believe what she was seeing as she entered the room; there was her latest fling sucking cock. What was she doing that for? She was a lesbian and cocks were not what they yearned for, but pussy.

As she stared dumbfounded by the sight, Lucy was by her side in an instant and tenderly began kissing her neck. The stunned Mary turned, and in the blink of an eye lid, Lucy's lips were on hers, but this was not a tender kiss. No, it was a kiss of passion. Locked in a smouldering kiss, Mary was there for the taking; the naked Sam crept up behind her and lifted her short dress, revealing the bare cheeks of her naked butt.

With his rigid cock in hand, he moved closer and slowly ran it upwards between the cheeks of her butt to the startled Mary's delight, whereas Candy was sucking on Hardcocks big cock, literally choking as she tried to deep throat it. But it was of no use and decided to go for a different angle, so she stopped sucking and looked up and said, 'Would you mind lying down on the floor, Mr Hardcock?' On hearing her request, Hardcock quickly obliged her and lay down on the floor and said, 'Can we try the sixty-nine, honey, so I can play too?'

On hearing this, Candy cringed as her honey pot was out of bounds; to all male admirers it was for the ladies pleasure only. What could she say, as she was about to suck his cock? She had no other alternative but to sit down on his face. As she then leaned forward and began sucking on his big rigid cock, Hardcock began probing her honey pot with his flickering tongue.

'Oh no,' murmured Candy as she blew a kiss out of her ass at him, but this was no ordinary kiss. No, it was the smelliest fart you ever did smell; the laughing trio of Lucy, Mary, and Sam began applauding when they heard him shout, 'By gum, Candy, where were you born? In the sewer?'

'No,' replied Candy as she blew off again, but this time she followed through, to the disbelief of the screaming officer Hardcock; as he stared at the big long piece of shit on his nose, he didn't know what to do, as the stench was unbearable, so he went to clench his nose, but instead spread the shit all over his face. This was unbelievable to the shock come horror expression on, officer Hardcocks face as he stared in disbelief at his shitty fingers, as he tried in vain to hold his breath.

But he just couldn't do it; he then got up and stared at the trio, now laughing hysterically at him. He began to move as though he was a lost soldier; this was too much for the laughing Sam, who said, 'Look, he's camouflaged his face. He's impersonating a soldier.' On hearing this, the ladies could hardly breathe, as their chuckle muscles ached too much from all the laughing. Officer Hardcock stopped and stared at him and shouted, 'It's not camouflage, you silly man. It's shit out of her ass.' He turned and pointed at the laughing Candy and said, 'If you don't believe me, tell her to stand up and bend over and show you her dirty ass.'

Then came more laughter when Candy stood up bent over and spread her butt cheeks and said, 'Oh no, it isn't.'

Officer Hardcock looked around and rubbed his eyes, as he stared open-mouthed at her white clean ass and shouted, 'I don't believe it.' He turned back around and stared at the laughing trio and said, 'I know the song says smoke gets in your eyes. But look I got shit in mine. Where's the shower?'

The laughing trio couldn't speak as their bellies ached from all the laughter, then came the fin-nah-lee. If it had been a stage show, it would have brought the house down when Candy picked up the microphone and held it up to her butt and then switched it on and blew a kiss out of her butt. But this was no ordinary kiss; no, it was the loudest longest fart you ever did hear and it was in stereo too.

This was too much for the laughing Lucy and Mary, who were now wetting themselves, as the sound of the stereo fart echoed around the room.

'Oh come on,' shrieked the dumbfounded choking officer Hardcock, 'where's the shower, as this stuff stinks on my face?'

On hearing this Candy smiled and put the microphone down and then stood upright and turned around and slowly walked towards Officer Hardcock and stopped and pinched her nose and said, 'Phew you smell.'

Hardcock replied, 'I know I do. What have you been eating?' On hearing this Candy smiled and whispered, 'Wouldn't you like to know?'

'No not really,' replied officer Hardcock. 'I just want a shower.'

Candy looked at him and then her eyes looked at his floppy cock and said, 'Really your name is Hardcock?' She pointed down at his floppy cock.

'Yes, that's right,' whispered Hardcock.

'That's Officer Hardcock to you, young lady.'

Candy smiled and then whispered, as she pointed down at his groin, 'You don't meet the right credentials to be called Hardcock as it seems to me you are an impostor, Officer Hardcock, as here you stand with a floppy cock down there.'

As she slowly turned around to the applause of the laughing trio, Sam shouted out, 'I don't believe it. Officer Hardcock is being interrogated.'

On hearing this, Officer Hardcock frowned, as he watched the sexy Candy slowly walk away with his eyes capturing her peach of a butt and swaying hips. His eyes suddenly opened wide when he felt something rising. He then looked down and smiled when he saw his rigid cock standing to attention and smiling at him; he then said, 'Excuse me, honey, but didn't you say I was an impostor? Yet true to my name, here I stand with a hard cock.'

On hearing this Candy stopped and then spun around and said, 'fuck me. Yes you do have a hard cock, and you certainly are not an impostor, Officer Hardcock.'

She then smiled as she stared at his face, and then a naughty thought crossed her mind delay-delay. She stared at his dirty brown face and murmured, 'Shit, he isn't going anywhere.'

With that she skipped over to Officer Hardcock and then dropped to her knees and began sucking Officer Hardcocks big rigid cock, as the trio began their fore play, while the two ladies passionately kissed, Sam got down on one knee and began probing Mary's pussy with his flickering tongue. Mary loved this moment and craved this moment; her only wish was for it to be Candy probing her pussy and not Sam as she kissed the voluptuous Lucy.

The sultry temptress Lucy wasn't here for kissing. No, she was here to induct Mary into her world of exotic sex; suddenly Mary decided she wanted to finger her pussy, but there was an obstacle in the way.

'What is that?' whispered Mary.

As she took hold of that big rubber cock and shrieked, 'Fuck me, Lucy, what are you going to do with that?'

Lucy smiled.

'Oh oh,' said Mary as she looked at the smiling Lucy, who said, 'Do you have any K Y jelly, Mary?'

'Yes, I do.' replied Mary.

'What will you be needing that for?' 'To lubricate your butt hole, silly?' whispered Lucy.

'Oh,' replied Mary, 'but it's such a tiny hole, especially for that thing you are wearing. It's huge.'

Lucy smiled and whispered, 'Oh I know its ten inches of rubber delight, with no shelf life.'

'Fuck me,' shrieked the ecstatic Mary.

'If you like,' whispered Lucy.

'We can do the butt thing later. Please get out of the way Sam as it is time for me to fuck her.'

On hearing this, Sam instantly stopped his muff diving mission and moved over, letting Mary lie down on the floor; in the blink of an eye lid, Lucy was on top of her with the big rubber cock in hand, guiding it towards her sacred haven. Mary's eyes opened wide as that big rubber cock penetrated her pussy and even wider when it began to slowly thrust at the tempo of the tap that wouldn't stop dripping.

'Oh my god,' cried Mary.

It had only been yesterday since she last enjoyed this big rubber cock at the hands and imagination of the sultry temptress Lucy. She had never dreamt of enjoying sex more with a woman than she did a man. As their touch was gentle and their kisses tender, the sex was never ending if you were in the hands of a nymphomaniac, especially the sultry temptress Lucy.

She loved Lucy, but she knew that was merely a fantasy, as after today that would become just a mere memory of a wonderful weekend she once had. But now the end was near, as she approached Climax City at breakneck speed and began saying, 'Yeah, yes, oh yes.'

But she was with the sultry temptress Lucy, who then decided to reach around and began massaging her magical button.

'Oh my goodness,' said the trembling Mary as wonderful sensations rushed through her body up to her exploding mind.

'Who are you?' screamed the shaky Mary.

'She's Lucy,' said Sam as he put his big rigid cock in her open mouth.

'Hmm,' screamed Mary, sending tingling sensations down Sam's big rigid cock.

'Oh oh,' murmured Sam as his milk balls began to churn; he had to get out of there, so reluctantly he withdrew his big rigid cock from her mouth and said, 'Is there any chance of fucking someone's pussy today?'

'Oh yes, there is,' said the smiling Lucy.

'Where is that K Y jelly, Mary? We need it to try the double whammy.'

'Double whammy,' gasped Mary.

'What is a double whammy, Lucy?'

'You know,' whispered the coy Lucy as she tenderly kissed her neck.

'No, I don't know,' replied the confused-looking Mary. 'If I did know, I wouldn't be asking, would I?'

Lucy smiled and whispered in her ear, 'the jelly is to make it easy for penetration into you butt.'

'My butt?' gasped the horrified Mary.

'Yes your butt,' whispered Lucy.

'Where is the jelly, Mary?'

'In the draw,' said the flabbergasted Mary as she pointed at the draw.

Sam saw where her finger was pointing at and went over and opened the draw as Lucy slowly withdrew her big rubber cock from Mary's pussy and then stood up and then went and sat down on the sofa. Sam quickly walked over to Lucy, waving the K Y jelly in the air saying, 'I've got it.'

'Good,' said Lucy.

'Please can you come over here Mary so we can have some fun?'

On hearing this, the frightened Mary stood and slowly walked towards Lucy, wondering if it would be rubber or the real thing going up her butt. She frowned when she looked at both cocks; they were huge. She wanted to run but couldn't move as she watched Lucy lubricating that big rubber cock of hers; then came those horrid words from Lucy when she said, 'Mary darling, please can you come and sit down on my lap.'

Mary's eyes opened wide and she shrieked, 'What? On that?' as she pointed at the big rubber cock with a shaky finger.

'You are only going to feel a small prick,' said the smiling Lucy.

'Small prick? My ass,' shrieked the open-mouthed staring Mary.

'Yes, that is right. I do want your ass,' said the smiling Lucy as she gently patted her thigh. 'So get over it and sit down on it.'

Reluctantly Mary slowly walked towards her, wishing her asshole was the size of a golf ball to ease penetration. As she slowly lowered her butt towards that big rubber cock, Lucy smiled and then squirted jelly on her fingers and lubricated her butt hole. Mary's eyes opened wide when a finger was pushed up her butt, even wider when one finger became two.

'Fuck me, what are you doing that for?' shrieked Mary.

'You will see,' whispered Lucy as she slowly withdrew her fingers and took hold of the big rubber cock and penetrated her butt.

'Oh my goodness, that is so big,' gasped Mary.

'Take it easy. Slowly lower yourself into my lap,' whispered Lucy as Mary slowly sat down on it and in plunged that big rubber cock, expanding her butt hole to new limits as it sank deeper. Mary's face was a picture of horror as Sam slowly walked towards her, gently stroking his big rigid cock. Her eyes opened wide when he penetrated her pussy and slowly pushed it in, taking Mary's breathe away.

And then came act two. Lucy reached around and began massaging her magical button; this was too much for the flabbergasted Mary. She had sensations coming from here, there, and everywhere, and yet Lucy carried on. By reaching around and tweaking her left nipple to life,

'Oh my god, Lucy,' shrieked the stunned Mary, 'what are you trying to do to me?'

Lucy smiled and whispered, 'Take you on a journey, honey, to the promise land, where the orgasms flow so free.'

On hearing this, Mary shook her head in disbelief as those wonderful sensations rushed through her body to her exploding mind where she entered the orgasmic zone, a zone she would become a frequent visitor too all afternoon long at the hands of the sultry temptress.

It was four in the afternoon when finally the shattered Mary took Candy's hand and quietly crept off to her bedroom, leaving the sultry temptress Lucy fucking the distraught officer Hardcocks butt.

'Oh what a day!' sighed Mary as she stared into Candy's eyes. They lay there motionless; neither wanted to move. Their pussies were of the colour of pink candy floss; they had been truly fucked by the sultry temptress and her two matadors, with their very hard cocks unknowingly induced, by the fruit cocktails they had drunk laced with Viagra.

Candy's eyes lit up when Mary whispered, 'I do like you, honey. Will you please be my girlfriend?'

'Yes, yes, oh yes,' screamed the ecstatic Candy, getting Lucy's attention in the other room, who quickly stood and went to see what all the commotion was about. She stared open-mouthed at the passionately kissing young ladies and never said a word. It was time for her to go now, so she slowly turned and walked away.

CHAPTER 28

I T WAS EIGHT in the morning as Lucy lay there, wondering what to do.

Should she go into work and flirt with her boss, the old Mr Haskins, but wait a minute, he was no longer her boss. He was soon to become her fuck buddy and sleeping partner too; her only wish was, he wouldn't die on the job, him been a man of seventy-five. With a malfunctioning dick that didn't work without taking that wonder pill Viagra, her only concern being he needed 2 × 100 mg to get it up.

Anyway she wanted to play today, as she was stripping tonight, as the star light girl, at the In Your Vision nightclub.

A thought suddenly crossed her mind.

'Mrs Haskins,' she murmured. 'I wonder what Sandy's doing today.' With that she threw the bed covers aside and sat up, picked up the phone, and dialled Mr Haskins's personal number and waited; after only two rings, a male voice said, 'Hello.'

'Good morning,' replied Lucy. 'May I speak to Mr Floppy Cock please?' On hearing this Haskins frowned and said, 'There's no floppy cock here, this is Mr Haskins speaking. How may I help you?'

On hearing the word floppy cock, Sandy began to giggle and whispered, 'Who is it, darling?'

Haskins looked at her and shrugged his shoulders and whispered, 'I don't know, honey.'

On hearing this, Lucy smiled and said, 'Ah Mr Floppy Cock, may I speak to your wife please.'

On hearing the word floppy cock, Haskins couldn't contain his outrage and shouted, 'Mr Floppy Cock doesn't live here, Miss.'

'Oh yes, he does,' replied Lucy.

'Oh no, he doesn't,' shrieked the agitated Haskins.

'Yes, he does,' replied the smiling Lucy.

'No, he doesn't,' said the astounded Haskins.

'Okay,' whispered Lucy, 'please tell me, are you or are you not sitting there with a floppy cock?'

'Oh,' sighed Haskins.

'Oh what?' replied Lucy. 'Tell me, are you sitting there with a floppy cock or a hard-on, Mr Floppy Cock.'

'Wouldn't you like to know?' whispered the smiling Mr Haskins.

'No, not really,' replied the stern Lucy. 'I do know who I am talking to, Mr Floppy cock. May I speak to your wife?'

'Who is calling please?' replied the bemused Haskins.

'It is your former secretary Lucy speaking.'

'Former?' shrieked Haskins. 'What do you mean former secretary Lucy? You are my secretary, Lucy.'

'Oh no, I am not,' replied Lucy. 'I quit last week. Please can I speak to Sandy?'

Haskins hesitated before handing the phone to his wife, saying, 'my secretary Lucy wants to speak to you, darling'

On hearing this, Sandy quickly took the phone from him and said, 'Hello, Lucy, if you are not doing anything today, would you like to accompany me to my health spa?'

'Health Spa?' shrieked Haskins. 'She's not going to any health Spa; she is working with me today.'

'Oh no, I'm not. Tell him I don't work there any more, and if he says no more on the matter, I have a treat for you both tonight.'

On hearing this, the intrigued Sandy said know more to her husband only frowned and said,

'I will pick you up at eleven, bye for now.'

With that she hung up and went to take a shower as the dumbfounded Haskins stared at her back and then looked down at her swaying hips and murmured, 'Wow!'

Then he looked down at his groin. Something was happing; his sleeping cock was stirring.

'What is going on down there?' He then opened his robe and stared open-mouthed at his erect cock and murmured, 'I don't believe it, this has never happened before.'

On hearing this, Sandy stopped and then turned around and said, 'What's never happened before?'

Haskins looked at her and then stood pointing down at his groin and said, 'This.' He then opened his robe, revealing his erect cock.

'Fuck me,' said the astonished Sandy. 'I have never seen that before.'

Haskins smiled and replied. 'Do you really want me to fuck you, honey?'

On hearing this, Sandy stared open-mouthed at him, not knowing what to say and then unknowingly undid her robe and let it fall to the floor, revealing her naked charms as the inner demon inside her cried out for sex.

Haskins stared open-mouthed at the sight of his naked wife, standing there before him. This was ignition fluid for his inner demon to take her in his arms and kiss her, but Sandy was repulsed by this and pushed him away saying, 'I don't want kissing, I want fucking,' as she quickly lay down on the floor pointing to her pussy. Seeing this Haskins went down on her with his rigid cock in hand and penetrated her pussy and then with one gentle thrust in plunged his rigid cock. Sandy just couldn't believe her husband was fucking her for the first time. 'Why was she mental?' she kept asking herself, as he slowly thrust in and out of her pussy at the tempo of the dripping tap.

Why wasn't he dead yet? She hadn't married him for this sort of thing; she only wanted his money, yet here he was fucking her with a rigid cock. Where was Mr Floppy?

'Oh my god, fuck me hard, not slowly,' cried Sandy.

On hearing this, Haskins frowned and began slam dunking her pussy.

'Yes, that's it, harder,' screamed the ecstatic Sandy. She wanted it fast and furious and aching for him to cum, so she could be on her way and shower, dress, go and get Lucy, and have their day of relaxation at the health spa. Was she mad? It would be like stepping into a hornet's nest, whilst in the company of the sultry temptress, a woman with sexual cravings like a hungry bear, who would tease you and tantalise you in anyway for her sexual play.

Haskins was at the point of no return as his milk balls tightened, and end of game was seconds away as his milky-white juices flooded her pussy and Sandy said, 'Thank heavens for that, dear. It was lovely, but it's time for me to go now.'

Haskins frowned and slowly withdrew his deflating cock and then stood and went to take a shower, leaving the self-satisfied Sandy lying on the floor smiling. She had finally got his juices inside her; with any luck she would become pregnant. That would be a guarantee income on his estate if anything ever happened to him and he had left her nothing.

It was eleven as the sound of a car horn filled the air; on hearing this, Lucy smiled when she saw Sandy waving. She opened the door and went outside closing the door behind her, then down the steps, then onward towards the car she went. As the smiling Sandy looked on; in just seconds, she opened the car door and then got in, leaned across and tenderly kissed the shocked Sandy's lips, and said 'Hello.'

'Hi,' said the smiling Sandy, as she slowly drove off and then murmured, 'Oh,' when Lucy put her hand on her bare thigh and slowly moved it upwards towards her masked pussy. Then shock crossed Sandy's face when Lucy slipped her hand inside her panties and then gently began massaging her magical button.

'Oh my goodness,' murmured Sandy as those wonderful sensations flooded her pussy. How could she drive as those sensations rushed through her body? This was too much for the naive Sandy as she had never encountered a situation like this before whilst driving. She couldn't stand it any longer and pulled over and parked the car and then reclined her seat and lay back and enjoyed the moment.

On seeing this, Lucy whispered, 'Please lift your butt, Sandy.'

As she did, Lucy pulled her panties down to gain easier access to her pussy, as it was finger-fucking time. Sandy closed her eyes when Lucy slipped a finger into her pussy; one finger quickly became two, and then the slow thrusting began at the tempo of the tap that wouldn't stop dripping, on every inward thrust caressing her G spot.

'Oh my goodness,' murmured Sandy as new sensations flooded her honey pot, but Lucy hadn't finished and began massaging her magical button too. Suddenly Sandy's eyes opened wide as another set of sensations travelled through her body up to her exploding mind.

She was on her way next stop Climax City; here she comes. Sandy looked at her smiling face and whispered, 'Are you enjoying yourself, dear?' That was a silly thing to do; she was in the hands of the sultry temptress. Anything could happen and it did; Lucy upped the speed of her thrusting fingers to the new tempo of the clock that wouldn't stop ticking.

'Oh my god,' said the devastated Sandy as she approached Climax City at breakneck speed and began saying, 'yes, yes, oh yes, I'm cumming.'

Lucy smiled and stopped her thrusting fingers and quickly withdrew them, releasing the dumbfounded Sandy's built-up fluids spraying into the air and splashing on the windscreen. Then the tapping on the window startled the pair, and they looked up to see the smiling face of Officer Hardcock staring in. The horrified Sandy smiled and rapidly waved at him as she brought the seat straight.

Then she quickly masked her on-show pussy by pulling up her panties and pushing her skirt down to cover them.

'Did you see that, Dickie?' said the smiling Lucy as the auto-window lowered.

'Yes, I did,' said the smiling Dickie.

'It was amazing, Lucy, but I must warn you that you are in a public place, Sandy, and you must move on.'

On hearing her name, the horrified Sandy said, 'It wasn't me, Officer.'

'Oh, it was me then,' said the smiling Lucy. 'They call me Miss Sexual Fingers Amore.'

On hearing this, Dickie began to laugh; Lucy smiled and said, 'If you and Sam aren't doing anything tonight, Dickie, why don't you come along and watch me dance at In Your Vision at, say, nine thirty. I go on at ten, Dickie.'

'But that's a strip club,' replied the smiling Dickie.

Lucy smiled and said, 'Oh I know, and I go all the way and so much more, Dickie.'

'Fuck me.'

'A stripper?' shrieked the flabbergasted Sandy. Was this woman insane? Did she know who she was with? Lucy was the sultry temptress and anything said in jest would be stored in Lucy's mind and used on her later, whilst she was relaxing at the health spa. Would she be ready for what soon would be happening to her, as Lucy held no inhibitions on sexual fun, any time, any place, anywhere and she'd be ready for sexy fun?

It was midday when the sultry temptress and Sandy entered the health spa; while Sandy got ready for her pampering, Lucy quickly skipped off to the restroom and strapped the strap-a-dick-to-me-on and returned quickly. On her return, she smiled when she saw the half-naked Sandy bent over and removing her panties, and in an instant, she was up behind her with the big rubber cock in hand, guiding it between the cheeks of Sandy's butt.

'Fuck me, who's that?' murmured the shocked come excited Sandy. Then her eyes opened wide when the big rubber cock penetrated her pussy and even wider when it slowly plunged in.

'Oh my god, that's huge,' said the flabbergasted Sandy, and then she froze when she saw the open-mouthed staring masseur, who shouted, 'What's going on here?'

On hearing this, Lucy smiled and replied, 'What is going on? You can see what is going on any how; you can get your clothes off, as it's your turn next.'

With that she slowly withdrew that big rubber cock from Sandy's pussy and then stood up and stared at the open-mouthed masseur and said, 'What are you waiting for, missy? Get your clothes off, and get over here now.'

The young masseur couldn't speak as she stared at that big rubber cock, while she quickly removed her clothes and then skipped over to the smiling Lucy and said, 'What do you want me to do, honey?'

Lucy smiled and replied, 'Get down on your knees, missy, I want to shag you doggy style.'

On hearing this, missy turned around and resumed the position, as requested by dropping to her hands and knees, and then spread her legs and looked around and said, 'Ready, honey.' Lucy smiled and then walked up behind her and took that big rubber cock in hand and dropped to her knees and guided that big cock between the cheeks of her butt and penetrated her pussy. Missy's eyes opened wide as that big cock sank deep into her pussy and began to thrust in and out at the tempo of the tap that wouldn't stop dripping.

'Oh my god,' cried missy as that big rubber cock slowly thrust in and out of her pussy. She had never had someone so big before, but little did she know that she was in the company of the sultry temptress and this was merely an appetiser for what was yet to come. Feeling left out, the newly sexually re-energised Sandy lay down on the floor and crawled under young missy and began massaging her magical button.

'Oh my goodness,' sighed missy, as those wonderful sensations flooded her honey pot, and then onward they went to young missy's exploding mind and she began her journey, destination Climax City; here she comes. Oh what a journey it would be, filled with wonderful sensations from her magical button and that slow thrusting big rubber cock too; a sudden slap on her ass from Lucy took it to another level.

As a new set of sensations flooded her body, but these were not wonderful sensations. No, they were stinging sensations.

'Ouch, ouch,' shouted the stunned but excited missy. Oh what a wonderful day she was having at the hands of the sultry temptress! It continued all afternoon long.

CHAPTER 29

I T WAS 9 p.m. as the excited Sandy and her ancient husband Mr Haskins entered the In Your Vision nightclub, and the sound of the cheering punters filled the room, as they watched the dancing girls loose their clothes. The intrigued Sandy sat down and watched while her husband got their drinks; she sat there mesmerized by the naked dancing girls, and she couldn't believe that her new friend, the voluptuous Lucy, would be up there dancing too.

She couldn't wait to see her and wondered what her stage presence would be like; then she smiled and murmured, 'Titillating.'

As the smiling Haskins placed the drinks on the table, Sandy gasped, 'What have you got in there?' as she stared at the prominent bulge in his pants. He had got an erection as he stared at the raw gyrating pussy on the stage and replied, 'Nothing at all, darling,' as he sat down.

'Yes, there is,' whispered Sandy as she cupped his bulge in her hand and gently squeezed and said, 'You have got a hard cock in there, let me see it.'

'What do you mean you want to see it?' replied the startled Haskins, as he frowned at her.

Now imitating her friend Lucy, the sultry temptress, she leaned over and whispered in his ear, 'Oh come on, darling, please stand up and get it out. I want to see it and what's more, I want to suck it.'

'Suck it?' whispered the shocked Haskins. He just couldn't believe his once-frigid wife wanted to suck him off in a public place. What had Lucy done to loosen her sexual inhibitions?

'Yes come on, get up, and get it out,' said the smiling Sandy. What was he waiting for? He quickly stood up and released his throbbing cock from its entrapment and smiled when Sandy began sucking on it. He just couldn't believe it; he wanted to laugh as he looked around him at those disbelieving staring faces, all jealous of his good fortune, wondering how an old fart like him was being sucked off by a beauty queen.

It didn't matter who she was. After all they were in a strip club; suddenly the lights faded and the naked girls left the stage. There was a sudden silence as the Master Bates society of hand wanker's gently coaxed their floppy cocks to life as they waited the arrival of the star light girl. The stage was lit by flashing lights, and the music began to play and Elvis began to sing,

I've got a woman

Then out came the delight they'd all been waiting for, the stunning, voluptuous, sultry temptress to the cheers of the applauding audience.

The sound of the cheers got Mr and Mrs Haskins' attention; they looked up to see the voluptuous Lucy skipping across the stage towards the microphone; Lucy then stopped and took the microphone off the stand and said, 'Good evening, gentlemen, are there any wanker's in the house?' as she stared at the Master Bates society of hand wanker's, who all had their erect cocks out and were gently choking them, as they waited to see the stage show.

'Yes,' they roared.

On hearing their cheers, Lucy smiled and said, 'Tonight, gentleman, I will be performing in aid of raising much-needed funds for the blind, so, gentleman, it's peak a boo time and it is going to cost you to see my bits and pieces.'

'Oh come on,' shrieked the frustrated standing Haskins.

'I want to see some pussy, so if you take it all off now, I will give you twenty thousand dollars and twenty more if you come home with me and my wife.'

On hearing this, Lucy smiled as the audience jeered, 'Boo.' This was too much for one of the members of the Master Bates society of hand wanker's, who stood up and re-housed his big erect cock before marching over and confronting old Mr Haskins about his suggestion. But much to his annoyance, he had been beaten by a group of angrily shouting men, who were outraged by his presence and his suggestion of leaving, especially their star performer.

As one man went to hit old Mr Haskins, the startled Lucy shouted into the microphone, 'Stop, look, and listen, gentleman, it was a very nice offer, but I am here to entertain you, so if you would all like to look at the stage now, the first one's on me.'

On hearing this, the young man who was about to hit Haskins spun around and stared open-mouthed at the voluptuous topless Lucy and whispered, 'Wow!' and then from a smile to a frown, he turned around and looked at the nervously shaking Mr Haskins and said, 'Look, old man, this young lady'–he pointed at the stage–'Because of you, she has a short fall on her donation, which I want you to make up with a donation of ten thousand dollars or else . . .'

'Okay,' replied the frowning Haskins as he sat down next to his wife and then turned and tenderly kissed her lips, to the astonishment of the staring young man, who shook his head as he wondered how an old man could get a young lady like her. Then he looked around and saw Lucy standing there; she then smiled at him as she stepped closer and to his astonishment tenderly kissed his lips.

She had gotten off the stage to stop any harm to her former boss the old Mr Haskins and soon to be fuck buddy; suddenly her eyes opened wide as the young man had slipped his hand inside her panties and was massaging her magical button while they kissed. This was intoxicating for him as he was kissing the star light girl and massaging her magical button too. This was too much for his throbbing cock, which was crying out, 'Let me out of here as it's time for me to fuck some pussy.'

But the sultry temptress was already one step ahead of him, as she stopped the kissing and then dropped to her knees and released his erect cock from its entrapment and to his amazement wrapped her lips around it and began sucking.

'Wow!' he murmured as her velvety lips encased his erect cock and then she began to suck.

'Oh my god,' he murmured. Her suction was sensational, and his milk balls began to churn. This was electrifying as he looked around him and saw many a smiling face, whilst others stared at him through jealous eyes, envious of his good fortune of having their dream girl sucking his cock. His eyes suddenly opened wide when Lucy began to hum, sending tingling sensations down his erect cock towards his churning balls.

This was sensational and he tried in vain to stop himself from cumming, but it was of no use as he was so excited at being the main attraction and game over was eminent when his milk balls suddenly tightened and dispatched his milky-white fluids into Lucy's sucking mouth. As Lucy swallowed his fluids down, she looked at Sandy, who seemed to be in a trance as she stared at her sucking cock in public.

As the slowly deflating cock slipped from her mouth, she looked over at the gazing Sandy and smiled; when she saw no response, she stood and walked over and tenderly kissed her lips, as the startled Haskins looked on as did all the horny regulars. Then came the chant of 'More, more.'

On hearing this, Lucy took hold of Sandy's hand and whispered, 'Come up on the stage with me, and let us two plays naked together.'

'Naked?' gasped the shocked Sandy, who was hornier than she ever had been before, and she ached for this excitement, so she quickly stood and whispered in old Haskins ear, 'Don't be shocked, darling, I am going up on the stage with Lucy.' Haskins smiled before shock crossed his face, when Lucy whispered in his other ear, 'That is naked, old man, and what's more I have a surprise for you?' Hearing this, the shocked Haskins grabbed hold of his heart with shock.

'Fuck me,' he murmured.

'That was nearly seventy-five and out,' as he watched his young joyous wife, skip off hand in hand with Lucy to the loud cheers of the regular patrons, up on to the stage they went as the patrons roared, 'Off, off, off.'

On hearing this, the pair began dancing, and to the royal cheering patrons Lucy began removing Sandy's clothes, to the disbelief of her staring husband old Mr Haskins. He couldn't believe he was watching his frigid wife, up on the stage, being stripped by his horny secretary Lucy. He once again released his throbbing cock from its entrapment and took it in hand and gently began to stroke it as he watched.

The cheers got louder when Lucy removed Sandy's bra and then knelt and pulled her skirt down; then she stood and began tenderly kissing Sandy's lips, then on to a full hot smouldering kiss they went to the cheers of roaring patrons. Little did they know they were falling in love with each another? As the smouldering kiss lingered on, they both began caressing each other's ass as they slowly gyrated to the music and the cries of 'More, more' filled the air, but neither was interested in their cries and the kiss lingered on.

Five minutes passed as Haskins stared spellbound by the erotic stage show involving his wife; he just couldn't believe his once shy and frigid country girl wife was up on the stage topless and about to have her panties removed by the voluptuous Lucy. Then the live pussy show began as Lucy slowly pulled her panties down, exposing her dark hairy pussy for all to see. With her pussy unmasked, it was pussy-licking time.

Haskins gasped, 'Fuck me,' when he saw Lucy probe his wife's pussy with her tongue. That was the end of his slowly wanking expedition. His milk balls tightened and that was the end of the wank for him, as his milky-white fluids shot through the air and hit the bald-headed man in front of him, who then stood up and shouted, 'What the fuck was that?' as he felt his head and frowned when he found that gooey mess; he then rubbed his fingers together and they became sticky.

'What is it?' he shouted as he smelled his fingers and then curiosity got the better of him and he tasted them, and then horror crossed his face as he murmured, 'Spunk.' He then spun around and stared at the open-mouthed Haskins, who himself was staring up at the stage, not believing what he was seeing; his wife was locked in the sixty-nine position, munching on Lucy's pussy, and he was oblivious to Mr Spunky Fingers cries of 'Was that you who hit me in the head, with your cum shot old man?' When Haskins didn't answer him, he stormed over and tapped him on the shoulder saying, 'did you hit me in the head with your cum shot, old man?' Again Haskins was oblivious to his words, making Mr Spunky Fingers very angry. He began shouting, 'Look, old man, answer me, or I'm going to hit you with this clenched fist of mine,' as he held his fist in-front of Haskins staring eyes. On seeing this Lucy picked up the ten-inch strap-a-dick-to-me and got up and then walked a couple of steps and jumped off the stage and was standing behind the bald man in seconds. The bald man's eyes opened wide when Lucy rammed that big rubber cock up against his ass and then whispered in his ear, 'Do you have a problem, curly?'

On hearing this, Haskins looked at the man's head. It was bald and shining and he began to laugh, making the bald man angrier. Seeing this Lucy decided to defuse the situation and knelt and opened the bald man's pants. The bald-headed man gasped, 'Fuck me,' when Lucy began sucking his floppy cock and he looked around at those faces staring at him, envious of his good fortune. On seeing this, the bald headed man shouted, 'Yeah I'm the king of all you losers.' That was a big mistake on his part. Little did he know he was in the presence of the sultry temptress; his eyes opened wide when Lucy stuck a finger up his ass and even wider when one finger quickly became two. He looked down and said, 'what are you doing down there missy-y-y?' Lucy had hit the spot and was caressing his prostate; his cock now resembled an iron bar in her mouth whilst his milk balls churned.

'Oh no,' he whimpered as his balls tightened and his milky-white fluids got despatched into Lucy's sucking mouth; as she swallowed his fluids, she withdrew her two fingers from his asshole and then stood. Mr bald head was all smiles as she glared into his eyes, before saying, 'Are you ready?'

'Ready for what?' replied the puzzled looking bald-headed man.

'Fucking,' whispered Lucy as she bent and picked up the big rubber cock and strapped it on.

'Fucking? Guck what, Miss?' replied the intrigued bald-headed man.

'You,' whispered the smiling Lucy.

'Fuck me, fuck off,' shrieked the petrified bald-headed man as he stared down at that big rubber cock. Disaster was eminent when he turned around to run away and was brought down by his pants that were around his ankles. Seeing his bare ass smiling at her, Lucy took hold of the big rubber cock and was on him like a dog on heat, and the petrified bald-headed man's eyes and mouth opened wide; it looked like he'd been electrocuted, when actually he'd been penetrated by that big rubber cock.

'Fuck me,' he shrieked as that big rubber cock sank deep into his ass; he couldn't stand it as that big rubber cock slowly began to thrust in and out of his asshole at the tempo of the tap that wouldn't stop dripping, and he began shouting, 'Get it out, get it out of there now, you're hurting me.'

On hearing his painful cries, Haskins began to laugh, as he watched Lucy's slowly thrusting hips; she wouldn't stop as she was hurting a man that had intended to hit her former boss Mr Haskins. The bald-headed man was getting abrupt now and screaming, 'for fuck's sake, you cow, get that thing out of my ass, or I am going to hurt you.' Was this man insane? Did he know what he was saying? He was threatening the sultry temptress, who was fucking his asshole with that big rubber cock.

On hearing his insult, the enraged Lucy shouted, 'Cow, what you mean by that, baldy?' Baldy didn't reply. Not replying to the sultry temptress question angered her even more; she took hold of his hips and upped the pace of her thrusting to the new tempo of the clock that wouldn't stop ticking. Sandy was laughing intensely as she stared at baldy changing expressions on his face; one second it was horror the next relief as that big rubber cock thrust in and out of his asshole at the hands of fast-thrusting Lucy.

She was infatuated by Lucy as she excited her like no one ever had before; you never knew what to expect when you were in her presence. She ached for this excitement being married to an old man with a flaccid dick. She had to have her today, tomorrow, and forever, but she wondered how she could entice someone as wonderful as Lucy into her life when she was the wife of old Mr Haskins.

Three months had passed as the naked Sandy lay there smiling as she looked at the sleeping Lucy and thanked her lucky stars her husband was rich, as it had cost them ten million dollars for her twenty four seven company in their household. Old man Haskins had become a recluse, a recluse like no other he had given up work and spent the last three months in harmony with his two naked angels, his wife Sandy and the voluptuous sexy Lucy.

Their house had become a naturist zone where they wore no clothes and he had spent numerous hours, watching the sultry temptress Lucy fucking his wife with that big rubber cock while he gently stroked his, re-energised with a Viagra pill. It was better than watching any pornographic film as he could take part in the live show he was watching when one of the ladies wanted a rest. He would be called upon to fuck the other while the resting lady watched.

He was living a dream, a wonderful dream where he fucked angels, but these were not angels from heaven. No, these were two angels from the earth, one of which had a body of a Greek goddess with ample charms and shaven haven too. She was his heart's desire, the one and only sultry temptress Lucy, a woman he adored and above all loved like no other as he was intoxicated by her voluptuous body, especially when naked.

He loved her temptress ways, the way she walked, talked, and above all teased him, while she took dictation in his office, by displaying her unmasked pussy to him, but that was merely a memory of his past. As today she was with him 24/7, and he loved every second of every day; he had found harmony at last and his only wish was to be able to stick around and enjoy the ride, for as many months and years he had left.

Little did he know his wife was expecting their first child due late August, after conceiving after their first and only fuck, just before their adventure at Lucy's place of work, In Your Vision, where she was stripped for the very first time on stage by the sultry temptress Lucy to the cheers of those cheering patrons. She had loved that excitement and craved this sexual excitement. She was in love with the sultry temptress and she loved fucking her with the strap-a-dick-to-me, as she also loved to be fucked by that wonderful sex toy too, especially at the hands of Lucy.

It was Friday, 23 August, as the joyful Haskins watched his heavily pregnant wife Sandy being fucked by the voluptuous Lucy; any day now they were expecting the birth of their son Jonathon, his soul heir to his fortune. On hearing the news he was to be a father six months ago, he had changed his will for the final time, leaving everything to his son, after his final bequeaths to his wife Sandy and the voluptuous Lucy.

Suddenly the fucking stopped as the feeling of warmth touched Lucy's thighs, Sandy's waters had broken and it was time to go to the Hospital. Dear Jonathan was born the next day at 10.50 a.m. to the delight of the watching Mr Haskins. A father at last at the tender age of seventy-five, a man who had one foot in the grave, with a new lease of life now that he was a father.

The next couple of years passed fast for old man Haskins, as he watched young Johnny grew from crawling to footsteps. As the trio familiarised their ways with parenthood, Sandy was pregnant again with their second child. But this was one child Haskins wouldn't see as his passing came midterm, to the joy of his wife Sandy and her lover Lucy, who had been looking for a way out to rediscover her sultry temptress ways.

She was missing the excitement of stripping in front of a live audience, she missed their cheers and money was a craving to much for her. On Haskins passing she had visited the In Your Vision strip club and went looking for the owner Sally. On seeing the voluptuous Lucy in her club, Sally took her by the hand and led her to her office, unknowingly closely followed by the jealous Sandy, who had followed her lover Lucy to the club.

Any day now she was expecting their second child, she couldn't bear to be apart from the voluptuous Lucy, and she was packing heat. As the door closed she impatiently waited outside, holding the gun in her shaky hand. The minutes passed and the anxious Sandy couldn't stand it and slowly opened the door and gasped, 'Oh no,' as there stood her bare-breasted lover Lucy, smooching with the half-naked Sally and finger fucking her as well; this was too much. She walked in pointing the gun at them and shouted, 'Stop that, Lucy'

On hearing her lover's voice, the startled Lucy pulled away from the kiss and looked at Sandy and said, 'my god, what are you going to do with that gun, Sandy?'

On hearing her concerns, Sandy pointed the gun at Sally saying, 'you . . . you horrible person, you were fooling around with my woman.'

With tears rolling down her face, Sandy pulled the trigger, at the same time as Lucy stepped in front of Sally, taking the bullet full in her chest to the dismay of the sobbing Sandy. This was the demise of the sultry temptress. This was the death of a sex goddess at the hands of her lover Sandy, to the dismay of her former boss, the sobbing Sally, who cradled the sultry temptress's head in her lap as she stared at the distraught Sandy and screamed, 'Oh what have you done to my good time girl?' 'What have I done to your good time girl,' replied the sobbing Sandy. 'I have just killed my girlfriend, my lover, my life long partner.'

She just couldn't stand it; she wanted to die and held the gun to her head. 'Oh, what are you doing?' asked the intrigued Sally.

'I'm going to kill myself,' sobbed the distraught Sandy.

'Don't you dare do that' murmured a woman's voice.

On hearing this Sandy looked at Sally and said, 'What did you say?'

'Say? I didn't anything,' replied the puzzled looking Sally, as she looked around as though someone was there. But no one was there other than the three of them, the supposedly dead Lucy and her two concerned-looking girlfriends looking around for a ghost or something and again the voice whispered, 'Why did you do that Sandy?'

On hearing this, both ladies simultaneously farted as they were literally shitting themselves. Was there a ghost in the house? On hearing their farting Lucy began to giggle.

'You're alive,' shrieked the happy Sandy as she rushed over to her lover, who was locked in a passionate kiss with Sally. On seeing this, Sandy stopped and rang for an ambulance. I was rushed to the Hospital and the bullet removed. I live with my lover Sandy and my lady boss Sally. Thank you for reading my memoirs.

Lucy. The Sultry Temptress.